Diane Gaston

The Vanishing Viscountess
"*The Vanishing Viscountess* is an unforgettable
romance expertly spiced with adventure
and passion."
—*Chicago Tribune*

The Mysterious Miss M
"A real emotional roller-coaster ride…you simply
cannot put [it] down – absolutely mesmerising!"
—*Historical Romance Writer*

Deb Marlowe

An Improper Aristocrat
"Marlowe unfurls a treasure hunt for gold, jewels,
missing persons and love in this fast-paced read."
—*Romantic Times BOOKreviews*

Scandalous Lord, Rebellious Miss
"…engaging characters and a mix of
heartwarming emotions and sensuality…"
—*Romantic Times BOOKreviews*

Amanda McCabe

A Notorious Woman
"a lushly sensual, exquisitely written love story."
—*Chicago Tribune*

A Sinful Alliance
"Court intrigue, danger, passion and love war with
loyalty and duty to produce this unforgettable
novel. Historical romance at its best…"
— *Cataromance*

Diane Gaston, as a psychiatric social worker, spent years helping others create real-life happy endings. Now Diane crafts fictional ones, writing the kind of historical romance she's always loved to read. The youngest of three daughters of a US Army colonel, Diane moved frequently during her childhood, even living for a year in Japan. It continues to amaze her that her own son and daughter grew up in one house in Northern Virginia. Diane still lives in that house, with her husband and three very ordinary house cats. Visit Diane's website at http://www.dianegaston.com

Deb Marlowe grew up in Pennsylvania with her nose in a book. Luckily, she'd read enough romances to recognise the true modern hero she met at a college Halloween party – even though he wore a tuxedo T-shirt instead of breeches and tall boots. They married, settled in North Carolina, and produced two handsome, intelligent and genuinely amusing boys. Though she now spends much of her time with her nose in her laptop, for the sake of her family she does occasionally abandon her inner world for the domestic adventure of laundry, dinner and car pool. Despite her sacrifice, not one of the men in her family is yet willing to don breeches or tall boots. She's working on it. Deb would love to hear from readers! You can contact her at debmarlowe@debmarlowe.com

Amanda McCabe wrote her first romance at the age of sixteen – a vast epic, starring all her friends as the characters, written secretly during algebra class. She's never since used algebra, but her books have been nominated for many awards, including the RITA®, *Romantic Times* Reviewers' Choice Award, the Booksellers Best, the National Readers' Choice Award, and the Holt Medallion. She lives in Oklahoma, with a menagerie of two cats, a pug and a bossy miniature poodle, and loves dance classes, collecting cheesy travel souvenirs, and watching the Food Network – even though she doesn't cook. Visit her at http://ammandamccabe.tripod.com and http://www.riskyregencies.blogspot.com

Regency
SUMMER
SCANDALS

Diane Gaston,
Deb Marlowe & Amanda McCabe

*M&B™ and M&B™ with the Rose Device
are trademarks of the publisher.
Harlequin Mills & Boon Limited, Eton House,
18-24 Paradise Road, Richmond, Surrey TW9 1SR*

REGENCY SUMMER SCANDALS
© Harlequin Books S.A. 2009

The publisher acknowledges the copyright holders of the
individual works as follows:

Justine and the Noble Viscount © Diane Perkins 2009
Annalise and the Scandalous Rake © Deb Marlowe 2009
Charlotte and the Wicked Lord © Ammanda McCabe 2009

ISBN: 978 0 263 87542 3

010-0709

*Printed and bound in Spain
by Litografia Rosés S.A., Barcelona*

CONTENTS

Justine and the
Noble Viscount
by
Diane Gaston

Dear Reader,

Regency Summer Scandals is such a special anthology for me because Amanda McCabe, Deb Marlowe and I were all friends before we became Harlequin Historical authors. Amanda and I became friends years ago, right after she'd sold her first Regency and I was still an aspiring writer. In 2003 we befriended Deb while on a tour of England, designed for lovers of the Regency. Together, Amanda, Deb and I devoured all the Regency sites of London, Bath, and Brighton. We even danced in Regency costume in the Assembly Room in Bath. I'd just sold my first book to Mills & Boon, and Amanda was with me when I visited their UK offices.

I was thrilled when my books were released by Mills & Boon® Historical and doubly thrilled when Amanda joined me as one of Mills & Boon's authors. So when Deb became a Mills & Boon author and the three of us were invited to do an anthology together, it was utterly fantastic. Three friends who came together in "Regency England" are together again in this Regency anthology.

Diane

Chapter One

The Family is the Country of the heart—
                                        Giuseppe Mazzini

Summer 1818

'This is a hellish errand,' Gerald Brenner muttered to himself as the hackney coach he'd been forced to engage rumbled away. He stood alone before the Palladian villa gleaming in the afternoon sun. He could almost laugh at the irony of its name.

Welbourne Manor.

Brenner's vision had been fixed on the house's white façade for the past half-hour. His first glimpse had come from the other side of the Thames.

Surrounded by verdant land where sheep grazed, it made a beautiful vista, but its land was cultivated, not for crops, but for pleasure. There was no industry of any kind, merely beautiful gardens lush with flowers and shrubbery, paths for walking, perhaps even a summerhouse to provide a shady resting place.

Or so Brenner imagined. He'd never set foot on this property and wished his connection with it had not brought him here this day.

He hesitated at the arched doorway, glancing up at windows rising four storeys. From one of those windows came the sound of loud voices and laughter.

The voices must belong to the progeny of the Duke and Duchess of Manning. Of course, the Duchess had only been the Duchess for about four months, having married the Duke after the proper grieving period was over for his first wife. She'd been the Duke's lover for the last twenty years, however.

Their illegitimate children were known to the world as the Fitzmanning Miscellany. Brenner now knew their given names. Leo Fitzmanning, the oldest at age nineteen. Miss Annalise Fitzmanning, aged eighteen. And Miss Charlotte, the youngest at sixteen.

'A spirited group of young people,' others had described them. Undisciplined, Brenner's father always declared.

Brenner took a quick breath and sounded the door's knocker, pounding hard to be heard over the revelry from above.

A footman in pale blue livery opened the door.

Brenner crossed the threshold and immediately caught the scent of flowers.

The footman gestured towards a carved mahogany staircase. 'The party is above stairs, sir.'

Brenner's brows rose. 'Party?'

'The house party.' The footman's forehead wrinkled. 'You have not come for the house party?'

Brenner handed the man his card. 'I have business with the Duke's children.'

'Which one of them?' the footman asked.

'All of them,' Brenner said sharply. He was unaccustomed to being questioned by a footman.

The footman walked away, leaving Brenner standing in the entrance hall like a tradesman still holding his hat and gloves.

Brenner frowned. His card had clearly read *Viscount Brenner*. Why had he not been shown to a room where he might wait in comfort?

Perhaps the servants in this household were not up to London standards. This was, after all, the house in which the Duke and his lover had settled after leaving their respective spouses. Even if such scandal had not entirely damaged the Duke's popularity among the *ton*, servants were often more particular for whom they worked.

He glanced at the vase of flowers on a narrow table against the wall and had a flash of memory. He was a child again walking through a garden. A woman's voice said, 'And these are roses. And these are jasmine…'

Pink roses, white jasmine, purple lavender. He could recognise the flowers even now.

He quickly turned away and crossed the foyer to peek through a doorway that opened to a formal hall. The room was large and square with windows looking out on the Thames. An arched door that was a mirror to the street entrance lay open to the summer breezes. One hundred years ago guests would have arrived in river barges and would have entered through that door.

The hall looked as if it had been transported from ancient Greece, with its four Ionic columns, sculpted friezes and patterned marble floor. Interspersed among statuary that appeared as if it had, indeed, been gathered from the ancient world, were gilded chairs and marble-top tables upon which more vases of flowers made a colourful and fragrant display.

From an upper floor came the muffled sound of a pianoforte and voices raised in song. The house party in full cry, no doubt.

Brenner's brows knitted. Who was chaperoning these young people?

At that moment a young man burst into the hall, waving a paper and shouting, 'A love poem! I've found a love poem!'

Two yapping pug dogs, one a mere puppy, nipped at the fellow's heels. A girl pursued him, her dark hair coming unpinned as she ran.

'Give it back,' she cried. 'Give it back.'

Brenner jumped aside as they shot past him, into

the foyer and up the staircase, the girl still shrieking, the young man laughing, the dogs yapping. Were they Fitzmannings or guests? Brenner did not know.

'Lord Brenner?'

He swung around.

A grey-haired man seemed to have materialised behind him. Thin as a whippet and dressed in plain black, the man was obviously the butler. He looked completely unruffled by the rowdy escapade he must have just witnessed.

He gave Brenner a quizzical look. 'You wished to see the Duke's children?'

Brenner returned a curt nod. 'I have news of the Duke and Duchess.'

The man's eyes widened. 'Indeed?' He quickly bowed. 'Come this way, m'lord.' He led Brenner through the hall to a small parlour whose windows faced the river. 'Please be seated, m'lord.' He bowed again and left.

Brenner had no wish to sit. He paced the perimeter of the room decorated in the chinoiserie style made fashionable by the Prince Regent.

The Duke's décor was of no consequence, however, given Brenner's errand. Making him the messenger must be a joke at his expense, a cruelty to him and to the Duke's children. He would carry it out none the less. The duty had been thrust upon him, and Brenner was not a man to shirk duty.

He'd dispose of this business as quickly as

possible and return to his life as it had been before the Duke's solicitor had summoned him early that morning.

Brenner's curiosity got the better of him. He leaned forward to examine a small blue-and-white vase that held pink roses, white jasmine and purple lavender. The piece looked authentically Chinese and very old.

'Gerald?'

Brenner straightened at the sound of a young woman's soft voice. A stunningly beautiful woman walked towards him, tall and graceful.

His breath caught in his throat.

Her eyes were a riveting light grey-blue, her hair, a glorious chestnut. She appeared to be in the full bloom of womanhood.

Too old to be one of the Fitzmanning Miscellany.

Her full pink lips glistened as if she'd just moistened them. 'You have news for us, Gerald?'

'I am called *Brenner*.' He hated his given name. He never allowed anyone to use it. How did she even know it? 'Forgive me, but I do not know who you are.'

She lowered her gaze and a tinge of colour stained her cheeks. 'Of course you do not.' She lifted her gaze again and met his. 'I am Justine Savard.'

Her name meant nothing. 'I still do not know who you are.'

A wan smile flashed across her face. 'I am the Duke's daughter, the eldest of his children here.'

Brenner must have continued to look perplexed, because she waved her hand in impatience. 'I have a different mother. She was a French émigrée. I have lived here most of my life.' She touched his arm. 'But, please, you have come with news.'

Her fingers seemed to shoot sensation through his body. 'My news is for the Fitzmannings.'

She nodded and her hand slipped away.

The Duke's solicitor had not told Brenner of Justine Savard. Even his father, who seemed to make it his business to know everything about this household, had never mentioned her.

Again those lovely eyes touched his. 'I fear I know why you have come. She told me, you see.'

'Told you?' he breathed.

'The others do not know,' she added. 'But she told me what she would ask you to do.' Her gaze seemed to sear into him. 'And why.'

'She?' He knew what her answer would be, but, even so, he could not help asking.

'The Duchess,' she responded. 'Your mother.'

Justine struggled to maintain her composure. 'I am so very sorry, Brenner.'

Before the Duchess had left on her wedding trip, she'd told Justine what she and the Duke had chosen Brenner to do.

Justine and her siblings knew the Duchess had another son, a legitimate one by her first husband, the Earl of Linwall. Many times the Duchess had told them she'd not seen her son—Gerry, she called him—since he'd been ten years old. After the Earl had divorced her, which must have created a very public scandal indeed, she'd stopped asking to visit him.

'There was no use,' she'd once confided to Justine.

Now looking upon Gerry—Brenner, she should say—Justine could only surmise that this task thrust upon him was not a welcome one.

She observed the emotion flicker in his eyes, green eyes that looked so much like his mother's she would have known him even if Halton had not shown her his card. There seemed to be anger there. And determination. And pain.

Certainly he was as handsome as his mother was beautiful—Justine caught herself. She must not dissemble.

'The others—' Her throat tightened at the thought of how Brenner's news would affect them. 'Halton—our butler—is fetching them. It will take a few moments, I am sure, to separate them from their friends.'

He glanced away. 'I understand you are engaged in a house party.'

She nodded. 'A few of their friends. Yes. We are having a little house party.'

He looked back at her, his expression disapproving. 'With their parents away, you engage in a house party?'

She lifted her chin. 'Why should they not have some enjoyment? Your brother and sisters are young and in need of occupation.'

His eyes flashed. 'I would not describe them as my brother and sisters.'

'Your half-siblings, then,' she corrected, feeling as if she were defending them.

'Who chaperons them?' he asked.

'I do.' She bristled at his disapproving tone. 'You cannot object to that. And, of course, some of the girls' friends have brought their own chaperons.'

Justine decided not to inform him that there were no parents in attendance at the house party. The girls' friends came from households too much like their own, with parents too busy with their own pleasure to attend a daughter's house party, not when some impoverished and dependent relation could perform the service.

She expected him to pursue the subject, but instead he glanced around the room and drummed his fingers on the table, as if he'd forgotten what they'd been discussing.

He is nervous, Justine realised. She warmed to him again, remembering how difficult this must be.

His green eyes fixed on hers once more. 'You know what I must say to them?' A worry line had formed between his brows and his breathing quickened.

'I do,' she managed.

He was tall, lean and physically intense, as if

inside him existed much pent-up energy begging to be released. He swiped a hand through his brown hair and paced the room. His misery resonated inside her.

Voices and footsteps sounded in the hall. The others were approaching.

In a moment all their lives would be for ever altered.

Chapter Two

Brenner stiffened as the protests of his mother's other children reached his ears. These young people were strangers to him. How dare his mother give him the duty to bring them such pain? He clenched his hand into a fist.

No doubt the Duke's vast wealth had given them a life of ease. They certainly had no need to worry about whether the harvest would be good enough or the income from investments high enough to pay all the expenses of an estate in need of repair. They probably had never experienced adversity.

And he, of all people, would change that. The idea sickened him.

They entered the parlour. Brenner expected to see the son and two daughters his mother bore, but there were three extra young men. Two Brenner recognised as the Duke's legitimate sons, the heir and the spare, whom he had glimpsed in society a time or two this past year.

By God, Brenner would have to tell his news to these two as well. The Duke's solicitor had been searching for the Duke's sons and, as of that morning when Brenner had been in the office, he had not located them.

Because they were here.

It was appalling that Brenner should be put in this position. There was still one extra young man. What more surprises were in store for him?

He glanced at them all again. One of the young ladies was the girl Brenner had seen earlier. The young man she'd been chasing had been the Duke's younger son, Brenner now realised.

This young lady walked right up to him. 'Are you Gerry? Halton said our brother had come.'

Brenner flinched at hearing the diminutive of his given name, even worse than being called Gerald.

Miss Savard stepped in. 'Yes, this is Viscount Brenner,' she told the girl. 'But do get in some order so I may make the introductions.'

They lined up, shoulder to shoulder, after some good-natured shoving among the young men. The Duke's heir was, of course, first.

Justine gestured to Brenner. 'Nicholas, may I present to you Viscount Brenner.' She cleared her throat. 'Lord Brenner, this is the Duke's eldest son.'

She, of course, realised the significance of Brenner's message to this young man.

Brenner bowed.

Nicholas's younger brother jostled him and laughed.

Justine silenced the young man with a severe look and went on to the next in line. 'The Duke's second son, Stephen Manning.'

Stephen extended his hand to be shaken. 'I've seen you, but never had the chance to meet you before.'

Brenner shook his hand. 'Lord Stephen.'

Stephen turned to the young man next to him. 'This is our friend, Drew. Lord Bassington. We've known him since school days. We wanted him to meet you, too.'

At least that mystery was solved. Brenner had feared there was another illegitimate son among the group. He shook Bassington's hand.

'Bassington,' he said.

The young man next to Bassington resembled the Duke's sons—and their father—except his hair was dark like his sisters' next to him. The young man's eyes startled him. They were so much like his own.

Justine introduced him. 'May I present Leo Fitz-manning.'

The young man smiled and extended his hand as well. 'This is too good. Glad to see you.'

The girl—young lady, really—next to him piped up. 'If only Mama were here. She would be over the moon.'

Justine quickly said, 'Miss Annalise Fitzmanning.'

Brenner felt as if he'd been socked in the chest. Annalise Fitzmanning was the image of the small miniature he'd found one day in a bureau drawer, one unknown to his father or it would have been destroyed. The miniature was of his mother.

'Miss Fitzmanning,' he managed, bowing.

She curtsied.

The young lady next to her, the one with the mussed gown from her race through the house, looked to be half in girlhood and half-grown.

She did not wait to be presented. 'Why are you all acting in such a ridiculous manner? She's Annalise. I'm Charlotte. We're your sisters and Leo is your brother.'

A muscle in Brenner's cheek twitched. A voice inside him wanted to shout *no*! Instead he bowed to her. 'Miss Charlotte.'

Justine stepped in again. 'Let us all be seated.'

'But the party…' Stephen began.

Justine seized his arm and propelled him toward a chair. 'The party can wait.' She turned to Bassington. 'Drew, perhaps you would like to return to the guests.'

'No.' Nicholas came to his side. 'Drew is like family. He belongs with us.'

Justine glanced at Brenner, who shrugged. Far be it from him to contradict the son of a duke.

Justine seated herself last, sitting between her half-sisters on a sofa. The young men lounged in the chairs, Stephen turning his around to straddle it and lean forward on its back. No one seemed in the least concerned about what Brenner would say to them.

No one but Justine. Her gaze caught his and he felt she comprehended his feelings. How was he to go on with this?

He struggled to remember the words he'd rehearsed on his way to Welbourne Manor. 'I have been charged to deliver to you some news.' He paused. This was too cold, too pompous for the enormity of what he must impart. He was the wrong messenger, the cruellest choice. 'I—I have news of the Duke and Duchess, news I am forced to bring to you.'

They all blinked up at him, still without a sign of trepidation. On the contrary, they seemed eager to hear what they must believe would be a message from their parents.

He closed his eyes. 'It is my duty to inform you of their deaths. From a fever. In Italy. Both—both of them. The Duke. The Duchess.'

'No!' Charlotte shrieked.

Brenner's eyes flew open again.

Justine held Charlotte down, trying to keep her in her seat.

Annalise wailed, 'It cannot be true!'

Nicholas turned pale. 'My God.'

'It isn't true.' His brother, Stephen, rose to his feet so fast he knocked the chair over. 'It isn't true. They are on their wedding trip.'

Leo peered at Brenner. 'What happened to them?'

Brenner answered him. 'They contracted a fever, a very virulent fever, and they were not able to recover from it.'

'A fever,' murmured Drew.

'They certainly did not. They never get fevers,' cried Annalise. She collapsed in tears against Justine.

'You are playing a cruel joke.' Charlotte burst into tears as well. 'And it is very bad of you.'

'It is no joke, Miss Charlotte,' he said.

Stephen rose. 'I knew it. I knew it.' He turned to his friend, Drew. 'I told you, didn't I, that I saw a magpie this morning. Did I not? Bad luck, I told you. A magpie always signifies bad luck.'

'That is all nonsense,' Drew responded. 'Superstition.' Only Drew and Justine remained in decent control.

Nicholas repeated. 'My father cannot be dead. He cannot.'

Leo groaned and buried his head in his hands. Stephen paced like a beast in a cage. 'It was an omen,' he muttered. 'An omen.'

Brenner gaped at them in numb shock.

He was totally unprepared for such an excess of emotion, would never have dared to show such lack of restraint. His father would have boxed his ears for it.

But he understood the pain of it. The announcement of the deaths of one's parents must be an enormous shock.

The memory flashed of his father telling him, 'Your mother's left us and she is never coming back.' He remembered the pain. Remembered he'd dared not show it.

The wailing grew louder. Charlotte tore at her hair. They were all moving, making noise, protesting, all but Justine. Stephen seized his chair and lifted it in the air as if to throw it.

'Enough!' Brenner shouted, his heart pounding. He pointed to Stephen. 'Sit down.'

Stephen sat.

He turned to the others. 'Be quiet. Now!'

They instantly fell silent.

Brenner scraped a hand through his hair. 'You are the sons and daughters of a duke. No matter how tragic this news, you must behave with decorum.' His eyes flashed. 'Do you think you are the only ones who have ever endured loss?' His voice cracked on this last word. He shook his head. 'Think—' he began again. 'Think what your father would say if he saw you now.'

In truth, Brenner had no idea what their father would say. He only knew his own father would be outraged.

All he really knew of the Duke was through his father, who wholly damned the man. The Duke's reputation had been a scandalous one even before he had run off with Brenner's mother. He, however, had been a part of the Prince Regent's fast set, so most members of the *ton* would not have dared to shun him completely.

'Lord Brenner is correct.' Justine spoke up, her voice firm. 'We must not abandon ourselves to our grief. Papa would laugh at us for making such a fuss.'

An amused father? That was an image Brenner could not imagine.

'Papa,' murmured Annalise. Tears ran down her cheeks. 'He is not dead.'

Brenner looked down at her and spoke low. 'I am sorry, Annalise.'

'Oh, my God.' Nicholas sat straight up. 'This—this means I am the—'

'You are the Duke now,' Stephen finished for him.

Nicholas stared at Brenner. 'But—but I do not wish to be the Duke. My father is the Duke.'

Brenner felt the young man's distress. The title was an enormous responsibility. 'You *are* the Duke now, no matter what you wish.' He tried to keep his tone mild. 'What you all must understand is you cannot wish this tragic news away.' Brenner knew only too well that wishes were useless. 'You can, however, behave in a manner befitting your station.' He fixed his gaze on Nicholas again. 'Especially you, Your Grace. Your first task ought to be setting an example for your brothers and sisters.'

Nicholas, as pale as paste, nodded.

Stephen whispered, 'Your Grace.' This whole family must get used to their brother being called *Your Grace*.

Gloom enveloped them, like a black cloud.

Charlotte looked directly at Brenner. 'What do we do now?'

They *all* looked to him.

Good God. As if he knew what to do.

He could read them the document in his pocket, the one that described how he was trustee over the Fitzmannings' finances, guardian over their persons until they reached their majority. He might also explain how he must approve Charlotte's and Annalise's choice of husbands. That had been part of his original plan. Place all this information on their shoulders and return home to ascertain how he could be responsible for them, yet still keep them at a distance.

Now, telling them all that merely seemed more cruelty.

He glanced at Justine, but she simply showed the same question in her eyes as the others.

He cleared his throat. 'It is probably best to ask your house-party guests to go home.' It was the only thing he could think to say.

Nicholas stood. 'I shall inform them of what has happened.'

Good, Brenner thought. *He sounds a bit like a duke.*

Stephen rose as well. 'I will tell the servants.'

'Yes, the servants,' Nicholas said. 'An excellent idea.'

Indeed, it was an excellent idea. Brenner had not even considered how this news would affect the servants.

He thought of another task for Nicholas. 'You need to pen a note to your father's solicitor and have it delivered right away. Put the man's anxiety about your whereabouts at ease and set a time to meet him as soon as possible.'

A flash of doubt crossed Nicholas's face, but he recovered. 'I shall do so immediately after informing our guests. I will call upon him tomorrow morning.'

Brenner relaxed. Order was restored and they had begun acting sensibly.

Drew stood. 'I'll go with Nicholas. Maybe I can be of some help with the guests.'

Nicholas opened the door of the room, and the two pug dogs ran inside, snorting as their small bodies waddled across the room. The smallest one ran directly to Charlotte, who scooped him up in her arms and held him against her cheek. The pup licked off her salty tears.

The other dog sniffed around Brenner's feet. Justine picked that one up and put him in Charlotte's lap.

'The dogs are yours, then, Miss Charlotte?' Brenner remarked, needing something—anything—to say.

She nodded, holding up the puppy. 'This is Oliver.' She inclined her head to the other. 'And Octavia. Oliver is new. Nicholas gave him to me.'

'They are fine animals,' Brenner said.

Annalise turned sombre eyes towards Justine.

'May I be excused? Would it be all right if I went up to Mama's room? I want to be in Mama's room for a little while.'

His mother's room. Brenner could suddenly smell the flowers again. He had a vision of gaily coloured dresses strewn over a bed, sunlight streaming in a window, his mother laughing.

Justine glanced towards Brenner.

'You do not need my permission.' His voice was stiff with the sudden memory.

Justine turned to Annalise. 'Of course you may go, if it will comfort you.'

'I want to go, too.' Charlotte put the pug on the floor.

Leo had turned himself towards a window. He twisted back. 'I need to go outside.'

'Go, then.' Brenner sounded severe to his own ears.

Charlotte, Annalise and Leo hurried out of the room, the pugs following, their paws clicking on the marble floor of the hall. Watching them, Brenner experienced an unnerving sensation of being apart from them all, excluded from their company. Ridiculous, because he had no wish to be in their company.

He glanced at Justine, whose hands were clasped in her lap. Her eyes were lowered and he noticed how her long, thick lashes cast shadows on her cheeks.

She looked up at him.

'That cannot have been easy for them,' he remarked. 'I told them so clumsily.'

She gave a sad smile. 'There was no way to make such news easy. You did well.'

His nerves returned and he rubbed his hands together, trying to feel calm again. 'They did not even ask for proof.'

'Proof?' Justine appeared perplexed.

'That this news is real.'

Brenner could indeed be playing a cruel joke, as Charlotte had accused. That would make more sense than the cruel joke his mother had played on them all by making him the bearer of the news.

'They trust you,' Justine said.

Brenner had been brought up to be much more suspicious.

He rubbed his forehead. 'Are they always this trusting?'

Her expression turned thoughtful. 'They have been somewhat sheltered from deceit and cruelty, which is quite remarkable when you consider…well, when you consider the circumstances of their births.'

'The young Duke and his brother, as well?' These two shared some commonality with Brenner's situation, although they must have been just out of leading strings when the scandal of the divorce filled every newspaper and was on everyone's tongues.

Tiny lines creased her flawless brow as she considered this. 'We all have led somewhat idyllic lives.'

Brenner averted his gaze. 'Did the divorce

not—' he couldn't conceive how to say it '—affect the Duke's sons?'

She shook her head. 'Their mother, I believe, was content to stay at the ducal estate, and my father indulged her desire to have the boys with her often. I would say Nicholas and Stephen spent half their time with her and half here, wherever they wished. They have grown up quite carefree.' She paused. 'Until now.'

Brenner, by contrast, could not recall a time he had not had some worry or another. And now he'd been mandated to worry over the Fitzmannings as well.

His gaze drifted back to Justine and this time it was she who looked away. It suddenly occurred to him that this news had affected her as well.

'I am sorry, Miss Savard,' he said quietly.

She glanced back in surprise. 'Sorry? For what?'

'For your loss,' he responded. 'For being the person who imparted the news of it.'

Her eyes held his. 'You have also had a loss.'

'I?' He looked away again. 'It is not the same for me.'

'But—'

He feared she would debate the subject with him. She did not persist.

He stood. 'I have remained too long. Is there someone I might send to engage a hackney coach?'

'A hackney coach?' Her brows rose.

'My father has the use of our carriage. I am afraid

we are reduced to the one, which is of no consequence because I so rarely need one. I merely engage a hackney.' Good Lord, what difference did all this make? He was nattering.

She rose and put her hand on his arm. 'We shall have our coachman drive you home.'

Her touch retained its impact. Brenner told himself his emotions were merely strained from his duties as a harbinger of bad tidings.

She looked up at him, her skin so smooth his fingers wished to feel if it was as soft as it appeared. She was standing so close that her scent reached his nostrils, light and floral. Roses and jasmine and lavender, like the flowers that were in the hall and in this room. Like the scent of a distant memory.

'Would you stay and have dinner with us? I am certain the others will have questions for you. We will dine early and you may return to Town in time for any engagement you might have.'

He had no engagements. His father was in the country, hence the unavailability of the carriage. Brenner's evening would be a solitary one.

'I will return tomorrow,' he said. Tomorrow he had better tell them the rest of his involvement with them. 'I have more business to transact, but I did not wish to pile more concerns on the young people.' He spoke as if he were an old man instead of merely thirty-two. He felt old today, however. And as tender as if he were the one still in leading strings.

'I know.' Her fingers pressed more firmly. 'You

must tell them more about their mother's will, but, I agree that today is too soon. Dine with us, won't you?'

'You know the details of the will?' He was surprised.

'Your mother had me read it before they sailed.' She glanced away. 'It was almost as if she'd had a premonition.'

The timbre of her voice halted Brenner's thoughts as well as his breathing.

'Say you will stay for dinner,' she murmured once more.

How could he refuse her anything? She had been so noble and kind and helpful to him, like a lifeline that kept him from drowning in emotion and memory.

'Very well,' he said. 'I accept.'

Chapter Three

Justine sat across from Brenner at the dinner table and could not help but watch him.

At least watching kept her eyes from wandering to the empty chairs at the ends of the table, the chairs once reserved for the Duke and Duchess. No one, not even Nicholas, had presumed to sit in them.

She did not know precisely why she had pressed Lord Brenner to remain for dinner. Merely out of politeness? If that were the case, his initial refusal would have ended any obligation, but she had practically begged him to stay.

Perhaps she feared they needed his steadiness. Was it steadiness or his merely being pompous and stiff? She could not tell for certain. Besides, she did not need him to handle the excess of emotion in her brothers and sisters. She'd been soothing their tempers and calming their rowdiness practically her entire life. No, it was not his steadiness, but something more personal.

She'd needed him.

He sat next to Nicholas, conversing with him. Brenner's manner was such a contrast to Nicholas, his voice so clipped and formal. No one in the Duke of Manning's household was formal, not even the servants, who skated on a very fine edge of impertinence at times. Not that anyone would pay that any heed. The Duke and Duchess's house had been replete with indulgence and acceptance. A far wider range of behaviour had been tolerated here than would be tolerated in another household.

Like the noisy argument between Stephen and Charlotte over her dogs.

'They are always underfoot,' Stephen said. 'If they were black cats, we should be doomed with bad luck. They are a damned nuisance.'

'They are not.' Charlotte's knife clattered against her plate. 'You tease them and they think you want to play.'

'I do not tease them—' Stephen went on.

Justine would have silenced them both, but she knew they were merely distracting each other. Bickering was preferable to mournful silence.

Where they must all think of who was lost.

Justine pushed a small buttered prawn around her plate, trying very hard not to think of how much she would miss her father and the Duchess, nor of whether some provision had been made for her. The Duchess had confided all their arrangements for *her* children, and there was no question that the inheritance of Nicholas and Stephen would have been adressed even before they were born, but she did not know for certain if her father had made some provision for her.

She gave herself a mental shake. It was petty of her to think of herself.

Spearing the prawn with her fork, she brought it halfway to her mouth before deciding to return it to her plate. She glanced up.

And caught Brenner watching her. He quickly averted his gaze.

Nicholas, with an expansive wave of his hand, turned to Brenner. 'And another thing. The funeral.' Nicholas was nothing more than a satchel of nerves. 'I have no idea how to arrange a funeral. I need your help, Gerry.'

'I prefer to be called Brenner.' It had been about the hundredth time the poor man had made that statement.

The Duchess had always spoken of him as Gerry, though, and that was why they paid him no heed when he corrected them. They'd all spent years thinking of him as Gerry.

'I will, of course, render whatever assistance is in my power,' he said to Nicholas. 'But, frankly, you need no help from me. There are many capable men in your father's employ who will make the arrangements for you.'

'Lord,' exclaimed Nicholas. 'Will they expect me to tell them what to do?'

Justine thought she saw a swift smile tug at the corner of Brenner's mouth. 'I suspect they will tell you what to do, but make it seem as if you had thought of it.'

Nicholas dropped his head into his hands. 'It sounds so complicated!' He sat back again and lifted a piece of cooked carrot to his mouth. 'I dread making a mistake.'

'Will there not be funeral cards sent?' Annalise asked Brenner. Funeral cards served both as an announcement and an invitation to the funeral.

'I expect so,' Brenner replied.

'I would like to create their design.' She was seated at Brenner's right. 'Will you tell them, Gerry?'

It looked as if he gritted his teeth for a moment before answering her. 'I have no say in the matter.' He gestured towards Nicholas. 'Appeal to your brother.'

Annalise leaned over him to speak to Nicholas. 'Nicky, will you ask them if I may draw the design for the funeral card?'

Nicholas looked uncertain. 'I will try.'

Brenner broke in. 'You will *tell* them, not ask. That is how it will be now.'

'By God,' whispered Nicholas, 'why should anyone listen to me?'

Poor Nicky! He'd completed his studies at Oxford and had only a brief time for the carefree pursuits of a wealthy young lord. The heavy mantle of responsibility had now descended on his shoulders, and neither he nor any of them knew if he could bear it with as much careless ease as their father had done.

Brenner broke the mournful silence that had descended over the table. 'Do you draw, Miss Fitzmanning?'

Annalise shrugged. 'I do a little.'

Justine protested. 'Not a little. It is her favourite diversion. Papa even allowed her to convert one of the sunny rooms above stairs into a studio.' A place where Annalise spent most of her time and where the others respected her wish that it be hers alone. No one entered, not even the maids, unless Annalise allowed it.

A duke's daughter who was so serious about her art would be considered an oddity. Justine tried to ascertain if Brenner's expression meant he disapproved.

She wondered if he disapproved of them all—so many people did disapprove of them. His clipped words made it seem so, but he'd also said enough to dampen Nicholas's impending panic.

Earlier, after the servants learned of the Duke and Duchess's deaths, they had been all at sixes and sevens until Brenner suggested Nicholas assure them their employment would remain secure. After that, matters ran smoothly and all the guests were gone within two hours without any of them feeling they had been rushed.

Brenner had kept everyone calm, Justine

believed, even if she could not tell precisely what he was feeling inside.

At that moment, Thomas, one of the footmen, appeared at Justine's shoulder to pour more wine. 'Thank you, Thomas,' she whispered.

'Gerry?' Charlotte piped up.

He inhaled sharply, but did not correct her. 'Yes?'

'Do not funeral cards include verse?'

'Often, I believe.' He finished the wine remaining in his glass as Thomas worked his way around the table.

Charlotte crossed her arms over her chest. 'I want to write the verse.'

Nicholas rubbed his brow. 'I must demand that as well?'

'Yes, indeed.' Her jaw was set.

Nicholas tensed up again. Justine bit her lip, worried he would vent his emotions on Charlotte.

'Are you a poet, Miss Charlotte?' Brenner asked, and the stressful moment passed.

'Love poems,' Stephen sputtered, stifling a laugh.

Charlotte punched him in the arm. She quickly composed herself into a ladylike pose to answer Brenner. 'I am a writer of verse, among other things.'

'She writes a salacious diary.' Stephen grinned. 'All fictional.'

Justine glared at him.

'What sort of accomplishment do you possess, Lord Stephen?' Brenner asked in a mild voice.

Charlotte laughed aloud.

Justine blinked in surprise. Brenner had come to Charlotte's defence.

'None at all,' said Stephen cheerfully.

'Stephen is a master at discovering good-luck charms,' Charlotte giggled. 'And Leo is a horseman.'

'Are you?' Brenner turned to Leo and actually sounded approving. 'Riding or breeding?'

'Both,' Leo answered. 'I would like to breed horses for riding and racing, but you must know, Stephen shares this interest.'

Brenner turned back to Stephen. 'Do you, Lord Stephen?'

The younger man grew serious for a rare moment. 'I would like to establish a race course.'

Justine suspected he would be able to do exactly that. Their father had always appreciated good horseflesh and had often spoken with Leo and Stephen about horses. She only hoped they had been left money enough for such ventures.

'Gerry?' Charlotte asked again.

Justine saw the flash of irritation in Brenner's eyes. 'Yes, Miss Charlotte?'

'Why do you address us with such formality? I mean, *Miss* Charlotte, *Lord* Stephen…'

Brenner looked surprised. 'It is the correct way. I was brought up to speak in the correct way.'

Thomas filled his glass.

'We are not correct, then.' Charlotte sighed. 'We call almost everybody by their given names. Even

Uncle George, although we are not allowed to call him that if anyone outside the family is present.'

'Uncle George?' Brenner took another sip of wine.

'The Prince Regent,' Nicholas responded.

He paused mid-sip.

'His Royal Highness is a great friend of our father's,' Stephen explained. He lowered his head. '*Was* a great friend of our father's.'

They fell silent again, the mournful silence that shouted of a desire to dissolve into tears. Even the weather matched their gloom. The sky turned dark and rain battered the window panes.

The footmen removed the dishes and brought in the dessert. Their chef, Signore Napoli, had outdone himself, making a centrepiece of sugar-paste flowers that looked as if they had been picked from a garden instead of being a tasty treat, small cakes prettily decorated with gaily coloured sugar frosting, marzipan shaped like tiny fruits and, finally, sparkling crystal dishes of strawberry and pistachio ices.

Justine saw Brenner's eyes widen.

She dipped her spoon into the strawberry ice. 'We do not serve such opulent desserts as a general rule, Lord Brenner. These were meant for the house party.'

He also tasted his ice, the pistachio. Their gazes held, and she sensed pain inside him, pain and sadness. Not the raw grief with which the rest of them were dealing, but something different, something old. It drew her to him.

Annalise picked up a small cake. 'This was Mama's favourite.'

After that they consumed the dessert in gloomy silence. When Nicholas finished, he rose from his chair and threw down his napkin. 'Do you mind if we forgo brandy?' Brandy was always served to the gentlemen after the ladies left the room. 'I am certain Halton will serve you some wherever you wish, but I need to excuse myself. I wish to retire directly.'

'Nicholas!' Justine's scolding tone had no effect.

Stephen pulled out their chairs. 'I cannot stay either. This day has been too taxing.' Leo nodded his agreement and joined Stephen heading for the door.

Annalise and Charlotte stood up, too. 'I just want to go to my room,' Charlotte cried.

None of them gave Justine time to call them back. Brenner remained silent.

'I apologise, Lord Brenner,' she said after they'd all rushed out. 'That was unforgivably rude of them.'

'It has been a difficult day,' he said in his formal tone.

'Would you like brandy?' She tried to make up for her brothers' and sisters' slights. 'I would be willing to keep you company or to leave you alone. Whatever you desire. Or shall I have Halton send it to the drawing room?'

He shook his head. 'It is time I took my leave.'

Justine rose and walked to the window. The rain now fell in thick sheets. She could not even see the line of trees at the edge of the garden. 'You cannot go out in this weather.'

He looked alarmed. 'I must.' He walked to her side and stared out of the window.

He was tall, she realised again, perhaps a bit taller than Nicholas and the other boys. She felt his tension rise, again experiencing the uncanny notion that she could sense his feelings. She just did not know what precisely caused them.

'We cannot send the carriage out in this weather,' she protested.

'I am forced to agree.' He paused. 'I hope your guests were not caught in this.'

His remark surprised her. She'd thought he would be thinking only of himself. 'They mostly came from London or nearby in Richmond. I do not think any were far enough away to still be on the road.' She looked into his green eyes. 'I want to thank you for all your help today.'

He glanced away. 'I did nothing but bring bad news.'

She made him look at her. 'We no longer kill the messenger, you know.'

He smiled, a fleeting expression, and his gaze held hers for a moment longer.

She turned to look out of the window again. 'It shows no signs of stopping soon, does it?'

He shifted, but did not answer her.

'You must stay the night with us.'

Chapter Four

Brenner could not sleep in this house. Its ghosts haunted him, especially the ghost of his mother, whose memory he thought he'd banished when still a schoolboy.

Her presence was everywhere. The elegant décor was a reflection of her. His father had erased all traces of that elegance until Brenner had forgotten about gay colours, gold gilt. Flowers.

It seemed as if every room in this house had at least one vase of roses and jasmine and lavender. Even in this guest bedchamber. Their scent kept him awake, the scent and old memories that now refused to be quelled.

Brenner rose from the luxurious feather bed and donned the banyan that had once been worn by the Duke, the man his mother had chosen over him. The Duke haunted him as well.

He kicked aside the Duke's slippers, preferring

his bare feet, and picked up the small lamp on the bedside table. He'd left it burning; he'd not been sure why. It was a waste of oil, but now he was glad he did not have to try to make his way downstairs in darkness. He planned to go down to the Duke's library and hoped no one would mind if he borrowed one of the books on the floor-to-ceiling shelves that lined the walls.

The carpet was soft under his feet and the polished wood at its edge cool as he walked to the door and stepped into the landing.

More lamps burned on the landing. So much for his worry about wasting oil. He and his father never kept lamps or candles lit once the household retired for the night, but at Welbourne Manor such economy must not be a concern.

What might it have been like to grow up in this elegant house without worries about the cost of candles or colza oil or flowers? How carefree it must have been.

An image of a joyful young Justine entered his mind, a happy little girl skipping through this hallway and down the stairs, rather the way Charlotte and Stephen had teased and chased each other through the house earlier that day while a piano sounded from the floor above. Brenner imagined laughter and music and long days of ease.

When he'd troubled to think of the Fitzmannings in the past, he'd thought of them *en masse*, a single spoiled and indulged entity, indistinguishable from some of the pompous sons of wealthy lords he'd known in school. He'd not thought of the Fitzmannings as distinct individuals, each now struggling with grief in his or her own way.

Justine was even more of a surprise. She seemed to be the hub around which they all revolved. He still could not believe he'd never heard of her existence. She was too vital to have been overlooked.

Brenner descended the stairs to the ground floor and turned down yet another lighted hallway to the library, a long, narrow room with windows on one side and a wall of books on the other.

The door was ajar and, as he entered, he was surprised to see lamps lit in this room as well. Were there lighted lamps in all the rooms? He made a mental computation of the expense of oil and candles enough to light every room in this house every night. The sum was considerable.

Would every fireplace remain lit in winter? he wondered, adding more pounds to the sum for the cost of so much coal.

The library lamps were dim, and Brenner needed his small lamp to illuminate the titles on the leather spines of the books.

Three volumes of Miller's *Gardener's Dictionary*, he read. That might be sufficient to put him to sleep.

The Whole Duty of Man According to the Law of Nature by someone named Puffendorf. Brenner passed on that one, having had quite enough duty for one day.

Hors de Paris. Now here was a book that promised to be diverting.

He started to pull *Hors de Paris* from its place on the shelf when a rustling sound startled him. He turned around.

'Lord Brenner, is that you?' A voice—Justine's voice—came from a large over-stuffed sofa facing the cold fireplace. She sat up, though her feet were still tucked beneath her, her lovely face bathed in the soft lamplight.

He pushed the book back in place. 'Miss Savard.'

She did not answer.

He cleared his throat. 'I—I could not sleep and thought there would be no objection if I borrowed a book.'

Raising a white handkerchief to her face, she wiped her cheeks and sniffled. 'No objection. Forgive me for not offering you the use of the library before you retired.'

'How could you know I would wish to read?' He stepped closer. Had she been weeping? The idea alarmed him. The hub of a wheel must remain solid or the whole wagon would come crashing down.

She inhaled a shaky breath. 'My father liked this room. He often sat here to read.' She dabbed at the corner of her eyes.

'You are weeping.' He felt helpless.

She wiped her eyes again. 'Oh, a little.' Her voice cracked and a sob escaped.

Brenner set his lamp on a table and crouched

down in front of her. 'It is my doing, for bringing you such distressing news.'

She reached out and took his hand. 'I have already said I do not blame you.'

Her warm hand on his, her skin so soft, he could not help but clasp it tighter and rub his thumb against its smoothness.

'Your father's death has saddened you.' It seemed a paltry, foolish thing to say, but he could not think of anything else, not with the sensation of her flesh against his.

She was no more dressed than he. Her robe was open and the thin muslin nightdress she wore clung to her figure. Brenner was mindful of the fact that there would be nothing beneath that thin layer of muslin but her bare skin, skin as soft and silky as her hand. He wore nothing beneath the Duke's banyan, even though the footman who'd attended him left him one of the Duke's nightshirts. He could barely tolerate wearing the Duke's banyan, let alone sleeping in the man's nightshirt.

She sniffed, and his thoughts turned to her distress, forgetting about dukes and thin muslin nightdresses.

Almost.

Tears glistened in her eyes. 'I will miss them both terribly.' She began to sob in earnest.

He sat next to her on the sofa and put his arm around her shoulders. 'It is understandable that you would grieve their loss.'

She snuggled against him, clutching the lapel of his banyan. He held her close and let her weep against his heart, her tears dampening the thick silk of his garment.

She wept noisily against him, her sobs seeping into Brenner like her tears seeped into the banyan. He acutely felt her distress, the distress he'd caused her. He knew of no way to ease her suffering.

Two deep, shuddering breaths escaped, and she stilled for a moment before pulling away and wiping her face again.

'Oh, how foolish of me. How lost to all propriety. I do beg your forgiveness again, which is all I seem to be doing.' Her voice rose on this last word and it seemed as if a new bout of tears were about to burst forth.

She held up a hand and mustered some composure.

'There is nothing to forgive, Miss Savard,' Brenner said. 'A grieving person deserves comforting.' At least, he'd always supposed that was true, although he could not remember ever being comforted.

Except by his mother.

That thought struck him like a thick shaft running him through. The pain was so intense he could not breathe.

She did not seem to notice, thank God. She blew her nose with the now thoroughly soaked handkerchief. 'I wish I could say I am only crying from grief, but that would not be true.'

He forced his voice to work. 'What is it, then?'

She gave a long, deep sigh. 'Oh…it is foolish, I suppose. And selfish. I am thinking only of myself.'

Thinking only of herself? That seemed unlikely. 'Surely you exaggerate.'

She shook her head. 'I assure you. I am thinking only of myself, but—but I am just so worried.' Her voice rose again.

Before she broke down again, he quickly asked her, 'What worries you?'

She sighed again. 'Your mother told me how Leo and Annalise and Charlotte will be well provided for, and it goes without saying that Nicholas and Stephen will have an inheritance, but—' her voice trembled '—I do not know about me.'

He touched her hand. 'Surely your father made some provision for you.'

She moved her hand away and wrapped her robe around her. 'The thing is, he may not have thought of it.'

Brenner was outraged. 'He could not have been so lost to all decency.'

She waved a hand. 'No, you do not understand him. He was a very loving father. It is just that he might not have thought to make arrangements for me.'

'I cannot imagine such a lack of responsibility.' His poor impression of the Duke was completely reinforced.

She made a wan smile. 'Well, I think it would be

have been more careless than irresponsible. Your mother and my father were dear, loving people, but they mostly followed their own whims. The Duke hired solicitors and men of business to attend to the serious details of his station, and I do not know if those gentlemen would have thought of me.'

The solicitors had not mentioned her to Brenner. Perhaps they had not thought of her. 'Did your father not provide you with a dowry?'

She shrugged. 'He promised me a generous dowry when the time came, but never spoke of an amount. I do not know of any papers drawn up about it.'

'This is outrageous.' He could not comprehend how a parent could fail to make provision for a child's future, how a parent could merely forget about a child.

Yet, was that not precisely what his mother had done?

Except that she had not entirely forgotten about him. 'Wait a moment. The Duke and Duchess had time to concoct the arrangements for me to be trustee of the Fitzmannings' inheritance—surely that is the time they would have thought to arrange matters for you?'

She turned towards him and her robe fell open again. 'But, you see, that was a whim. Your mother was such an impulsive creature. She came upon a miniature of you before their trip. The miniature sparked the idea for this plan, which you must admit is very odd and not at all considerate of your feelings. What's more, she did not know your character. You might have refused, and then matters would be in even more disarray.'

Brenner became very still. 'My mother kept a miniature of me?'

Justine nodded. 'She did. And there is a portrait of her with you as a small child in one of the rooms. I will show it to you, if you like. Not now, but tomorrow.'

He could not take this in. 'I had no idea she even remembered my existence—that is, until this task was given to me.'

She took his hand again. 'Do not mistake me. I do not know if she thought of you often, but she did speak of you from time to time and of how she wished she could see you.'

He could not believe his ears. 'She wished to see me?'

She looked upon him with sympathy in her eyes. 'She always said she was forbidden to see you.'

Forbidden? No. His mother cared nothing for him; it is what his father had always told him.

'Brenner?'

He turned back.

She squeezed his hand. 'She did not forget you.'

His mind whirled. It was a new idea, a new version of the mother he'd worked so hard to forget.

No, it made no sense. 'If she wanted to see me, she might have done so after I reached my majority. My father could have nothing to say about it then.'

Justine's expression turned sympathetic again. 'Then you may see my point. Your mother and my father were generous and loving when the thought occurred to them, but they were equally as capable of putting out of mind everything but their own pleasure. I do not know if your mother ever thought of contacting you. I do not know if my father ever thought of providing for me. Some invitation may have arrived or some other entertainment to distract them.'

It was easier for Brenner to turn his thoughts back to her problem. 'Your brother can ask the solicitors tomorrow. They will know.' He meant today. It was well after midnight.

'Yes.' She released his hand. 'Poor Nicholas. He is all nerves at the idea of meeting those gentlemen alone.'

'Stephen will accompany him, will he not?'

She seemed to force a laugh. 'That does not reassure him. Stephen and Nicholas have had no responsibilities. They've both merely been young gentlemen about Town.' She reached out and touched his hand again. 'Will you help them, Brenner? Will you accompany them?'

'Me?' What possible assistance could he render a duke?

'Nicholas has not had to think much of estates and investments and the duties of a duke. He may forget something.' She pleaded with her eyes. 'Will you make certain Nicholas remembers to ask about me?'

He glanced down to her hand in his. To help her, at this moment he would do anything. 'I will accompany them.'

'Thank you!'

She threw her arms around his neck and gave him a hug that nearly placed her in his lap. His senses were powerfully aroused and it was all he could do not to seek her lips and lay her back upon the sofa.

'Justine,' he whispered.

Chapter Five

Her breath was warm against his ear. 'Brenner, we need you so much.'

Need. He was filled with need.

It felt as if only Justine could fill the emptiness inside him. His hands ached to stroke her, to remove the slim barrier of their clothing and be warmed and comforted by each other's flesh.

He felt her breath quicken.

And came to his senses.

How had he abandoned any semblance of gentlemanly behaviour? Anyone who came upon them now would think he was compromising her. His attraction to her did him no credit. She was half-sister to his siblings, for God's sake. She was also the daughter of a man he'd despised since the age of ten.

He eased her away, still feeling the ache of wanting her. 'Miss Savard, neither of us is properly dressed.'

She blinked and looked down at herself, as if the thought that she wore almost nothing had not occurred to her before this moment.

He tried to smile. 'We would not wish to give anyone the wrong impression, would we?'

She slipped away from him. 'It seems I must ask your forgiveness again, Lord Brenner.' Her quiet voice only made the void inside him grow larger.

He reached out for her, but quickly withdrew his hand. 'Your need for comfort requires no apology,' he murmured, then forced himself to stand. 'But I would not wish to put your reputation at risk.'

Her brows knitted and she glanced away.

'You must try to sleep.' He was foundering, grasping for anything to say. 'Can you sleep, do you think?'

She looked back at him. 'I suppose I must at least try.'

'Well.' He flexed his fingers. 'Shall we go above stairs, then?' He clamped his mouth shut. By God, it sounded as if he'd just invited her to his room.

He again felt awash in imagining how warm she would feel, how soft, how good she would smell, and how much he desired not to be alone.

She stood. 'Did you not wish to borrow a book?'

'Oh, yes.' He had forgotten.

He picked up the lamp and returned to the shelf he'd examined previously. His fingers passed over *Hors de Paris*.

He pulled out *The Whole Duty of Man* instead.

* * *

Justine's glance wandered to his bare feet. Even in the dim light she could tell they were high-arched, as if he were poised always for flight.

Or to rush to someone's aid.

She tightened her robe around her and retied the sash. She must have appalled him with her behaviour. To fling one's arms around a man upon the first day of acquaintance was quite shocking.

It was equally as wicked to notice he did not wear a nightshirt under her father's banyan and to wonder if he slept naked in bed. She gave herself a mental shake. A few moments of kindness from a man and she lost all sense of propriety.

At least Brenner was a gentleman. Not every man was, as she well knew.

She sighed. This was no time to dwell upon *that* sad affair.

She stood and waited for him to approach, her glance returning to his naked feet. Strong feet, she thought. A strong man. And a good one.

He joined her, and they walked out of the room together. She made certain she did not brush against him.

In the hallway he gestured to the wall lamp burning. 'I did not need my lamp, I discovered.' His voice sounded disapproving.

'Your mother did not like the darkness.' Justine's throat constricted as she thought of the Duchess sometimes wakeful at night and wandering the house.

He tensed. It seemed he always tensed at the mention of his mother. Her leaving him had hurt him, Justine guessed. She had never known her mother, but she'd lost her beloved foster mother when that woman had become too ill to care for her. Justine's father had brought her to Welbourne Manor, where she had become part of the family. Her life had been very happy.

For the most part.

If only she could know if her father had provided for her now, she could rest easy. If not, surely Nicholas would not throw her out? Surely she could still be useful to the family? She could at least watch over Charlotte and Annalise.

Brenner would decide who watched over Charlotte and Annalise. She glanced at him.

She and Brenner silently walked up the stairs to the floor where their bedchambers were located.

She stopped in front of her door. 'I bid you good night, Brenner.'

He glanced down at the floor, but finally at her. 'I will rise early,' he said. 'Will I see you before I return to London?'

She nodded, suddenly grateful that she naturally woke early. 'So it is good night, not goodbye.'

He surprised her by taking her hand and clasping it for a moment. 'Until morning, then.'

She opened her door and backed into the room. He did not move until she closed the door.

* * *

The next morning Brenner did accompany Nicholas and Stephen to the solicitor's offices. Afterwards, Nicholas and Stephen stayed in London, taking up residence in the ducal house on Park Lane. It was Brenner who returned to Welbourne Manor to tell Justine her father had, indeed, provided for her.

Her father, in fact, had generously provided for all of them. She, Leo, Annalise and Charlotte would be wealthy, wealthy enough to attract good marriage prospects, although marriage was not in Justine's future, she knew.

Leo, Annalise and Charlotte accepted with equanimity the news that Brenner was their guardian and trustee. Justine was not surprised. Brenner's steadiness made them all feel safe. He seemed to know just how much information they could absorb at any one time. He visited often over the next few days, each time explaining more of his role in their lives, each time making them feel safe and secure under his care.

Justine and her sisters spent their time preparing the mourning clothes they'd worn less than a year ago when poor Princess Charlotte and her dear little baby had died. Annalise created a hatchment bearing her parents' coats of arms to hang above the front door, a sign of their loss. She also designed the funeral card, with her mother's favourite flowers, elements of her father's crest, an image of Saint

Mark's in Venice and a ship in full sail. Charlotte wrote the memorial poem, a heartfelt verse surprisingly mature for such a young girl. Her verse said her parents were 'for ever a-sail on heav'n's seas'.

Brenner made certain Nicholas informed the solicitor that Annalise's design and Charlotte's verse must be used for the funeral card.

To Justine's great pleasure, Brenner confided in her, talked to her about the solicitors, about Charlotte, Annalise and Leo. Sometimes it seemed as if he needed her approval. She more than approved of him. Justine's admiration of Brenner grew with each day. Even in her grief, her heart gladdened when he appeared, and she enjoyed the time she spent in his company.

By the time a week had passed, the funeral cards had been engraved, printed, and sent out. Black gloves and hat bands had been purchased, and all the pomp and ceremony befitting the funerals of a duke and duchess were arranged.

The funeral and interment would take place at the parish church near the Manning ducal estate. Nicholas, Stephen and Leo would attend, escorting the carriage transporting the coffins. Brenner saw no reason to accompany them. He'd mourned his mother long ago.

During the week Nicholas and Stephen had only occasionally visited Welbourne Manor, so Justine was surprised to see Nicholas just a few days before they were due to leave for the funeral.

must say and do. Merely to see him among them would give them strength.

Would give Justine strength.

Nicholas's voice rose the loudest. 'You must come. There's nothing else for it.'

Brenner held up both hands. 'Very well. I will attend.'

He caught Justine's eye and their gazes held a brief moment.

Chapter Six

Two days later the reception took place. Annalise and Charlotte's funeral-card design was adapted for the invitations and delivered to all persons of quality in London, Richmond and as far as Brighton, the seaside town where many of the *beau monde* spent their summers. Because His Royal Highness would appear at the reception, anyone who could reach London in time was expected to attend.

Not only had Nicholas insisted Brenner be there, the fledgling Duke also insisted Brenner join the Duke's children in the reception line. Brenner stood between Stephen and Justine.

More than a week had passed since he'd so briefly held her in his arms, but at times the memory returned so vividly he could almost still feel her softness and her warmth. He'd spent much more time at Welbourne Manor than he'd ever expected, but Justine's presence made him look forward to

walking through Welbourne's door. His heart gladdened at seeing her smile, watching her graceful
gestures, or noticing how sunlight lit her cinnamon-
hued hair with streaks of gold.

They formed the reception line in Welbourne's
large hall, the first room he'd seen at Welbourne.
Mourning dictated everyone wear black, so the room
with its throngs of guests looked like a Mayfair ball
from which all colour had been leached. Brenner
tried to guess who among them attended because of
true grief and who did so merely to impress the
Prince Regent.

A gentleman with whom Brenner had a nodding
acquaintance was announced. Roger Kinney and his
wife passed through the line, Kinney repeating the
same words so many others had uttered, 'My sincere
condolences.' The gentleman barely took notice of
Brenner when he uttered the words to him. He'd
shown only slightly more animation addressing the
new Duke.

When he came to Justine he paused, casting a
quick glance at his wife, who moved on ahead.
Kinney then gave Justine his full attention. 'Justine,
my dear.' He did not shake her hand, but lifted it to
his lips, placing a kiss on her black glove. 'I am so
very sorry for your loss. How tragic for you.'

Brenner's eyes narrowed.

Justine pulled back. 'Mr Kinney.'

Kinney's gaze swept the length of her. 'When
you are able to break away, we must speak.'

Brenner gritted his teeth.

'I do not think so,' responded Justine, all warmth absent from her voice.

Kinney moved on, and the next person began speaking to Brenner. There was no opportunity to ask Justine about the exchange.

The butler's loud voice announced the next caller, 'The Earl of Linwall.'

Brenner's father was the last person Brenner had expected to see in this house. His father waited his turn to offer condolences he surely could not mean.

'So good of you to come, sir.' Nicholas energetically shook Brenner's father's hand, and Brenner thought he might have discovered who had invited him.

'It is exceedingly kind of you,' Stephen added.

Lord Linwall moved on to Brenner and his polite expression disappeared. 'What the devil are you doing here?' his father said fiercely.

Brenner had intended to explain to his father about all of this—that is, unless, of course, he could have devised a way to say nothing at all.

'I might ask you the same question.' Brenner bristled.

His father's eyes flashed. 'I would not dare offend His Royal Highness.'

Undoubtedly many of the people present had come because of the Prince Regent. 'Will you stay in town tonight?' Brenner asked.

'Yes,' was the terse reply.

'I will explain to you this evening, then.' Brenner turned to Justine. 'Miss Savard, allow me to present my father, Lord Linwall.'

She smiled and curtsied. 'An honour, sir.'

His father looked puzzled.

'Miss Savard is the eldest of the late Duke's daughters,' Brenner explained.

'Ah.' Understanding dawned. 'Another daughter. Different mother. Had no idea.'

It was rudely said, and it angered Brenner. His father proceeded to Leo and Annalise and Charlotte, who treated him like a long-lost uncle.

'Gerry has been so good to us,' Brenner heard Charlotte say.

His father glanced back at him with a thunderous expression.

The two girls kept his father trapped while they extolled Brenner's virtues and asked about his health and the comfort of his travel. Where had the Fitz-mannings learned such generosity of spirit?

'His Royal Highness, the Prince Regent,' Halton announced.

A buzz went through the crowd, and the way parted for the Prince. The Prince Regent was an imposing figure. Dressed in the mourning garb typical of the other gentlemen, His Royal Highness still managed to project an aura of power that set him apart.

When His Royal Highness spoke to Nicholas, however, he appeared warmly personal. Brenner could not hear what the Prince said, but it brought tears to Nicholas's and Stephen's eyes. The Prince took their hands and squeezed and patted them, his sympathy and grief genuinely displayed.

Nicholas stepped out of the reception line when the Regent came to Brenner. 'Your Royal Highness, allow me to present to you the Duchess's son, Lord Brenner.'

The Regent's eyes lit up.

Brenner bowed. 'Your Royal Highness,' he said. 'I am deeply honoured.'

The Prince waved a dismissive hand and patted Brenner's arm. 'Your mother was a great favourite of mine. A wonderful woman. I will miss her most acutely.'

Brenner bowed again. 'Thank you, Your Royal Highness,' he mumbled, taken aback by the sincere statement.

The Prince then saw Justine and put his arms around her. He gathered Leo, Annalise and Charlotte in similar embraces. 'My dear ones.' Tears streamed down his face. 'How shall we ever do without them?'

Brenner heard Charlotte whisper 'Uncle George' in the Prince's ear.

'Brenner has helped us,' Leo told the Prince. 'I do not know what we should have done without him.'

'He knew just what to do,' Charlotte said. 'And he let Annalise and me design the funeral card.'

The Prince then engaged them in a discussion of

the engraving and the verse, but when that was done, he returned to Brenner.

'You have my gratitude for helping these dear ones,' His Royal Highness said to him. 'You must let us know if we may be of any assistance at all.'

Brenner bowed yet again. 'You are too generous.'

Brenner meant his words. There was no doubt that the Prince Regent was indeed a close friend to this family and would continue to act so.

The Prince greeted one or two of the other guests before departing. The room remained silent for a moment after he left, as if he'd taken all the energy from it with him.

The reception line broke up after that and the guests partook of the refreshments available.

Brenner's father approached him. 'I am leaving, but I expect that explanation tonight.' He did not wait for Brenner's reply.

People who had never taken any notice of Brenner at other social gatherings made an effort to speak to him now. Royal favour did have its effect.

Brenner noticed that Mrs Kinney stood talking with some other ladies. He looked around for Mr Kinney and did not find him. Or Justine.

Brenner walked through the hall out to the terrace that overlooked the Thames. He glimpsed Kinney with Justine at the corner of the house. Kinney had his hand clasped around Justine's arm.

Brenner moved closer.

'When can I see you, Justine?' he heard Kinney ask. 'My regard for you is unchanged.'

Justine tried to pull away. 'You cannot see me. If you call upon me, I will refuse to see you.'

'You cannot mean that.' Kinney pulled her around the corner.

Brenner quickened his step. 'Release her!' he demanded.

Kinney started, and Justine wrenched herself from his grip. She ran to Brenner's side.

Kinney smiled. 'You have interrupted a private conversation, Lord Brenner.'

'Hardly a *desired* conversation, Kinney.' Brenner spoke the words with sarcasm. And anger. 'You are not to impose on this lady again, do I make myself clear?'

'Lady?' Kinney gave a laugh. 'How are you in a position to speak for this…lady?'

Brenner's hand curled into a fist. 'As a member of her family.'

Justine stood behind him and he felt her hand upon his back.

'I suggest you collect your wife and leave, sir,' Brenner went on. 'Unless you would prefer this tale to reach His Royal Highness's ears.'

Kinney looked alarmed, then pursed his lips. 'Always hiding behind the Prince Regent.' He bowed and walked towards the door, stopping next to Justine. 'I merely wished to renew our acquaintance.' He glanced at Brenner. 'But I see how it is.'

'You are married,' Justine snapped. 'That is how it is. And I take pity upon your wife.'

Kinney merely gave her a sardonic smile before continuing to the door.

Justine breathed a sigh of relief. 'I do not know what I should have done had you not intervened.'

Brenner wanted to ask her about Kinney, but what gave him the right?

She seemed to read his thoughts. 'When I was much younger, he courted me.' She glanced out towards the river. 'Until I discovered he was a scoundrel. I'd hoped I had seen the last of him.'

'You have seen the last of him,' Brenner vowed. 'Or he will answer to me.'

She gazed into his eyes. 'Again, I thank you.' A breeze caught a loose strand of her hair, making it dance around her face. She tucked it behind her ear. 'Do not tell anyone of this,' she asked him. 'Please?'

At that moment Brenner would have promised her anything. 'I give you my word.'

They re-entered the house together.

Chapter Seven

All the way back to town Brenner dreaded the inevitable confrontation with his father. He rode with Nicholas and Stephen in the Duke's carriage, only half-attending to their effusive thanks for his attendance at the reception. On the morrow Nicholas and Stephen would travel to the ducal estate for the funeral service and interment at the parish church. It was an estate his mother had never visited, Brenner learned. It would be her final resting place.

When the carriage stopped at the town house he shared with his father, Brenner squared his shoulders and entered the house.

What a contrast to Welbourne Manor. No candle lit the front hall and, even though night had not yet fallen, everything looked grey.

One of the footmen greeted him and took his hat and gloves. 'His lordship said that you were to join him in the drawing room, my Lord.'

Brenner groaned inwardly. 'Thank you, I shall do so.'

The drawing room was directly off the front hall, and he suspected his father had been watching for the carriage. There was no way to delay. He entered the room.

His father sat stiffly in one of the chairs, a glass of brandy in his hands. 'You took your time.'

Brenner walked over to the side table where a single lamp burned. This room was every bit as dreary as the hall. He poured himself some brandy. 'I needed to wait until the new Duke chose to leave.'

His father scowled. 'Never thought I would see the day you'd ride in that carriage. Or stand in that house, bold as you please.'

Brenner chose a chair across from his father. 'I said I would explain—'

'What?' His father's voice rose. 'Did they leave you a fortune, is that it? Now you want to hob-nob with them?'

Brenner fought to remain calm. He understood his father's wounds went deep, so deep the humiliation of his marriage's end was still raw. It would likely never heal.

'There is no fortune…' He explained, as clearly and concisely as he was able, about his mother's will and the duty she had imposed upon him.

His father's face grew redder as Brenner spoke. He half-rose from the chair. 'She made you guardian? Trustee to her bastard children?'

Brenner had heard his father refer to the Fitzman-nings as bastards for most of his life. For the first time he felt the flare of anger. It was on the tip of his tongue to tell his father to remain civil.

He thought better of it.

'It defies understanding, I agree,' he said instead. 'But there it is.'

His father sat down again and waved his hand. 'Well, hire someone to do it for you. The Duke's damned solicitor. Would serve the man right. Charge the cost to their estates. No doubt they can afford it.'

'I cannot do that,' Brenner protested. That, however, had been his original plan. 'It is my duty.'

'Duty?' His father laughed, a bitter sound.

Brenner shot back, 'Have you not always taught me that duty is seldom what you choose to do, but something you must do?' Good Lord, Brenner had heard that statement too many times to count. Had not his father thrown duty to the family name in his face when Brenner had wished to purchase a commission in the army so he could fight Napoleon?

'This is a different matter,' his father snapped. 'You are being disloyal to me.'

Brenner leaned towards his father. 'I would never be disloyal to you,' he said in a low voice. 'But I will be the son you taught me to be. I will do my duty to you and to the Fitzmannings.'

His father's face turned red at the mention of their names. 'It is a scandalous household. Those sons of his show every indication of being as much the libertine as *he* was.' His father always referred to the late Duke as *he*. 'And that other one, that *Justine Savard*, who knows where she came from—'

'Enough!' Brenner stood. 'I will not hear you speak so.' *Not of Justine*, he added silently. 'Like it or not, this responsibility has been required of me and I will fulfil it.'

The Fitzmannings depended upon him. Although given every advantage money could buy, they were ill-equipped to manage the sudden shift in their lives. They needed guidance and protection and it was up to Brenner to provide it.

'In fact—' Brenner made a sudden decision '—tomorrow the new Duke, his brother and half-brother leave for the funeral. I intend to stay at Welbourne Manor. I cannot leave the young ladies in my charge unprotected.'

Brenner had intended to stop by the Manor often to make certain all was well and to complete some of the tasks still required of him, but he had no wish to spend his evenings listening to his father rail against him for doing so. He'd pack a bag and move in with them. He was their guardian; they could not refuse him.

Besides, he had a notion they would like his company much more than his father would.

'You cannot do that,' his father shouted. 'You have responsibilities to me, as well.'

'I will fulfil them, I assure you,' he said heatedly. 'I will call upon your man of business as often as I do when I am staying here.' He fixed his father with an intent look. 'I promised you I would oversee all the finances and I will keep that promise. You, in return, must keep yours.'

His father did not play cards nor wager on horses, but he did fall for every wild financial scheme that came his way. He'd poured so much money into this or that nefarious investment that their capital had been seriously depleted. Brenner had taken over and his father had promised never to invest without his son's approval.

'I keep my promises,' his father muttered.

Brenner sat back in the chair and rubbed his brow. 'You ought to go back to the country house. Stay for the harvest or do some hunting.'

'I will stay here and I demand you do the same,' his father huffed.

Brenner bit back a contentious retort. 'I'll check on you, then, from time to time, to make certain you are all right, but I will stay at Welbourne Manor while I am needed there.'

Justine and her sisters sat with Leo in the drawing room, waiting for Nicholas and Stephen to fetch him for the trip to the ducal estate. The brothers might be away as long as a month. It felt like another loss.

The door opened and Nicholas and Stephen entered. Followed by Brenner.

Her day brightened at the sight of him.

'Are you going with them, Gerry?' Charlotte asked.

'No.' He smiled at her.

'Well,' Charlotte went on, 'you should stay with us, then. You are our guardian and you should guard us. Especially at night, because everyone knows the most danger is at night—'

Justine stopped her. 'Charlotte! It is not your place to say such things.'

She feared Brenner would be annoyed, but his eyes twinkled with amusement. 'It is a good thing I packed a trunk, then.'

'You are staying?' Charlotte cried.

'I am staying,' he answered.

Charlotte threw her arms around his neck. 'I am so glad of it!'

Brenner laughed awkwardly, but he gave Charlotte a hug in return. Justine envied her.

When she released him, Brenner explained, 'There are matters we might more easily accomplish if I remain at Welbourne Manor. I'll stay until Leo returns.' He tossed Charlotte an impish look. 'Then Leo may guard you.'

Justine watched him being pulled this way and that while her brothers and sisters all needed his attention. Nicholas asked for last-minute advice. Stephen made a jest. Leo reminded him of some household matter they had not previously discussed. Charlotte and Annalise begged to know what tasks would be required of them, Annalise with dismay, Charlotte with curiosity.

Justine gave a silent thanks to Brenner for coming

to stay with them. She needed him. This was another unbearable day, the day her brothers must leave to accompany the bodies of her father and the Duchess to their final resting place. The finality of it was so very painful.

A half-hour later Brenner stood at Justine's side when she and her sisters waved a tearful goodbye to their brothers. The young men left on horseback and would meet the carriage carrying the coffins in Richmond. For the rest of the journey, they would ride at its side.

When the three riders had disappeared down the road, Annalise swung around to Brenner, defiance in her eyes. 'I am going to think of Mama and Papa as being in Venice, not in—in boxes that will go into the ground!'

He leaned back in surprise. Annalise ran back into the house.

'Do not fret, Brenner.' Charlotte sniffled. 'She will retire to her studio room and paint gloomy pictures for a few days. It is her nature.' She sighed. 'I still wish I could have gone with them.'

'Ladies do not attend funerals,' Brenner told her.

'Sometimes they do,' she insisted.

Her pugs, Oliver and Octavia, looked up at her with their bulbous eyes.

'Come on, my precious ones. Let us go for a walk.' She led the pugs towards the garden.

Justine's pulse quickened as it always did when

she happened to be alone with Brenner, even at this sad moment. 'You mentioned a task for them, did you not? Shall I call them back?'

His gaze touched her, and she felt herself grow warm even though the morning breeze from the Thames brought its usual chill. It was as if he wrapped a blanket around her, making her feel safe and secure.

'It can wait.' His eyes lingered, but he eventually looked away. 'I frankly do not know how to occupy my time today.'

She took a breath. 'May I help with the task you spoke of to Charlotte and Annalise'

His brow furrowed in concern. 'It is to locate certain of the Duchess's personal possessions and make sure they are given to whom she bequeathed them.' He gazed out at the road. 'Perhaps it is too soon for such a task.'

Justine tried to imagine searching through the Duchess's things. Tears stung her eyes at the thought. 'Perhaps.'

Their gazes touched again.

He quickly glanced away. 'Something more mundane, then. Like…' he seemed to search his thoughts '…like household accounts. Leo wished me to examine household accounts.' His gaze returned.

She smiled. 'I will assist you.'

It would help her to spend the day in a distracting occupation, or was that an excuse? All she knew was, if she spent the day with Brenner, it would keep her grief at bay.

Chapter Eight

After two days at Welbourne Manor, Brenner became impatient to tackle the list of items in his mother's bequest. He had no great desire to rummage through his mother's belongings. Indeed, he could barely manage reading the pages of items listed. Jewellery. Linens. Silver. Porcelain. Crystal. It was a task best dispensed with as soon as possible.

When he'd made the impulsive decision to stay at Welbourne Manor, he'd only thought of seeing Justine, sharing meals with her, talking with her. He had forgotten that his mother's essence, her memory, her ghost was everywhere in this house. At times he fancied he would discover her around a corner, smiling, asking, 'Gerry? Would you like to take a walk in the garden?'

Somehow touching her precious belongings made her seem even more real to him. The sheer number of items she treasured enough to mention was daunting. To read them brought old resentments, old pain. His mother had chosen these trinkets over him.

This morning he marched down the stairs to the breakfast room with a resolve to dispense with the task once and for all.

'Good morning, Brenner.' Justine, alone in the room, smiled up at him from the breakfast table. The light from the window made her appear like some Da Vinci madonna.

His breath caught. 'Good morning,' he managed, his gaze lingering a moment too long. He quickly turned to the sideboard to serve himself with breakfast. 'I trust you are well this morning, Miss Savard.' Lord, he sounded like a pompous old man. Like his father, in fact.

'Yes, thank you,' she responded.

His emotions in her presence had become hopelessly tangled. Too often he remembered how she'd felt in his arms and too often he had the raw carnal impulse to hold her again. At the same time, a part of him felt serene in her company, as if he was where he truly belonged.

He could barely remember feeling anything before he'd first stepped into Welbourne Manor. He suspected he'd become so practised in controlling his emotions, he'd rendered himself numb.

He sat at the table. 'I thought perhaps we might tackle the Duchess's list today. What do you think?' At least he could successfully hide his disordered emotions from her.

'I am willing.' Her smile was uncertain. 'Annalise and Charlotte will be down presently. You can propose the idea to them.'

He glanced down at his food. The youngest Fitzmannings had remained sullen and reclusive. Even Charlotte's good humour had dissolved into bouts of temper. It seemed to Brenner that they were in danger of wallowing in their sorrows.

'Would you like me to ask them?' Justine added.

He looked up and saw a sympathetic expression on her lovely face. It was most unsettling when Justine read his mind. There were some thoughts about her he did not wish her to know.

Her gaze captured his once more. Her eyes fascinated him, such a light grey circled in such a dark blue.

Annalise and Charlotte entered the breakfast room, Charlotte shooing the pugs from the door so she could close it. She was already squabbling with her sister.

'Why can I not borrow your black ribbon?' Charlotte complained. 'I need it to tie back my hair, and it is not as if you are using it.'

'I lent you a ribbon before and your dog chewed it. This is my only black one.' Annalise pushed by her sister to reach the sideboard.

'That was before. Oliver won't chew it. I've trained him.' She tossed her loose hair off her shoulders as if to demonstrate how desperately she needed this ribbon. 'Anyway, it is just a ribbon, hardly a precious item.'

Annalise glared at her. 'But it is *my* ribbon and I do not wish to lend it.'

They sounded like the yapping pugs.

'Good God,' Brenner muttered. 'Is there only one black ribbon in this house?'

Justine seemed unruffled. 'I have a black ribbon you may use, Charlotte.'

'Thank you, Justine,' Charlotte responded in a very dramatic tone, accented by glaring at Annalise.

The drama continued as they jostled each other for the sparest of breakfasts, one slice of toasted bread and a dab of raspberry jam. When they sat, they both grabbed for the pot of chocolate at the same time and a jousting match of hands caused Brenner to reach over and remove the pot before it was sent flying.

'Enough of this nonsense!' he snapped.

They both leaned back in their chairs and folded their arms across their chests.

'I dislike being shouted at,' Annalise said with a pout.

'Then behave like a lady,' Brenner shot back.

Charlotte laughed.

Brenner swung around to her. 'You are included in that admonition, Miss Charlotte.'

'*Miss* Charlotte,' she repeated disdainfully. Her eyes shot daggers at him. 'Gerry. Gerry. Gerry.'

By now they were all aware how using this name annoyed him.

'Charlotte!' Justine cried. 'You are being childish. Both of you know how to behave better than this.'

The room fell silent.

After a pause, Brenner poured chocolate for each of the girls. 'I make allowances for your grief.' He tried to keep his voice as mild as possible. 'But, you would do better to practise decorum. When you are out in the world, society will not be so tolerant.'

'They will want to criticise us,' Annalise said in a depressed tone.

Brenner averted his gaze. 'Perhaps.'

Charlotte sat up straight. 'Because we are by-blows? I'll wager that is it.'

'Charlotte!' Justine's voice rose in shock.

'Well, we are by-blows.' She looked defiant.

Brenner frowned. Such plain speaking and defiance would not serve them well when it came time to arrange marriages.

'If you behave like ladies, you are more apt to be accepted as such,' he said in a firm tone. 'But if you act like hoydens, people will say it is due to the circumstances of your births.'

'We know how to behave, do we not, Justine?' Annalise said. 'We have been brought up properly.'

Justine glanced at Brenner before answering. 'You, indeed, have learned proper behaviour,' she answered in a careful voice. 'But you have also been allowed a great deal more freedom than other young ladies of your station.'

'We behaved properly at the reception, did we not?' Charlotte asked.

Brenner remembered their lack of restraint with the Prince Regent, but he said, 'You did very well.'

Annalise and Charlotte lapsed into twin expressions of sheer sadness, and his heart lurched at the sight.

He took a sip of his tea and changed the subject. 'If you ladies are able to spare me some time, I would very much like to inventory the items your mother bequeathed to you.'

They both paled and their mouths dropped.

'Go through Mama's possessions?' Annalise's voice rose to a high squeak. 'I cannot do it. I cannot.' She covered her mouth with her hand. 'Please allow me to paint. I must paint.'

A fit of weeping was imminent, Brenner could see. His father would have given him a prime thrashing for such a display.

'Annalise, calm yourself,' Brenner said.

'If Annalise is not going to help, then neither am I,' Charlotte cried, folding her arms again.

Brenner looked at Justine, but she merely raised her brows, communicating, he felt, that she had no better idea than he how to solve this.

He placed both hands on the table in a feeble attempt to steady himself, as he composed some very severe words for them, but they looked so young and so vulnerable, it would be like kicking Charlotte's dogs, something he often thought of, but would never do. Eventually they would have to move beyond grief, but perhaps not today.

'Very well,' he finally said. 'Not today, then.'

Freed from the onerous task, Annalise and Charlotte settled pleasantly into the rest of breakfast. After some less emotional conversation, they asked to be excused. They would, no doubt, retreat to their own pursuits and not be seen again until dinner.

Brenner was once again alone with Justine, her gaze resting lightly on him.

'You are a severe taskmaster, Lord Brenner.' She smiled at him, and he felt as if the sunlight had joined them inside the room.

He rolled his eyes. 'I feel as if I am Gulliver in the land of the Lilliputians.'

Her smile widened. 'They are not small.'

'No, but they are warlike.' He took another sip of tea.

Justine spoke. 'I will assist you in the task, if you desire it.'

He glanced up at her.

She blinked, as if his gaze had struck her with force. 'I should be able to locate the items on the Duchess's list.'

Justine, always ready to help, whether it be with a ribbon or anything else requested of her.

'Thank you.' His voice came out lower than intended.

Colour rose in her cheeks. 'Shall we meet in the Duchess's sitting room?'

His heartbeat accelerated, but he did not know if it was due to anticipation of Justine's company or to his reluctance to see and handle his mother's most intimate possessions.

He set his jaw. 'I do not know the room.'

She gave a nervous laugh. 'I ought to have given you a tour of the house before this. It quite slipped my mind.'

Again he spoke in a low voice. 'Would you meet me in the library in half an hour?' He knew the library's location.

She lifted her gaze. 'In half an hour.'

Chapter Nine

Brenner walked into the library cursing his haste. He ought not to crave Justine's companionship so much he rushed to meet her. He needed to return to his former, ordered life, where he had only his father's problems to worry over.

He rubbed his face. It would be at least two years before he could return to his own life, when Charlotte was old enough to marry. When the girls married and Leo reached his majority, Brenner would have no further reason to involve himself with any of them. By that time the Linwall farms would be making a profit and the investments restored. He could think about marriage for himself.

Justine's image flew into his mind.

He could never contemplate marriage to Justine. Never. Not with her ties to the Duke and his mother. He would be for ever involved with people he'd never even wished to meet, the children his mother had loved and his father detested.

He could not muster up precisely the same rancour he once felt towards Leo and Annalise and Charlotte, though. He rather liked them, even though they had no toughness of spirit. Too indulged. He could not describe it exactly, even to himself, but what he held most against them was that they made him remember his mother.

He glanced at the library clock on top of the mantel. Ten minutes early. He paced the room, skimming the book titles, computing how many books there were, trying to estimate precisely what the Duke's library would be worth. Another staggering amount.

He sat. On the sofa where he and Justine had embraced, he realised too late. Never mind. He was not a moonstruck schoolboy. He had work to do.

Brenner pulled the Duchess's list from his coat pocket and used the glow from the ever-lit lamp to try again to read it all the way through.

It was a tedious list, itemising porcelains, silver, lace, crystal, brooches, combs, linens…pages and pages. Ten at least. He counted the number of items on a page and multiplied that number by ten. Two hundred and fifty items to locate and to assure were given to whom they'd been bequeathed. He skimmed the names next to each item, checking quickly through each page.

Justine's name did not appear.

Her name had not appeared on the part of the will that had bequeathed certain things to favoured servants and two or three friends.

He almost crushed the paper in his fist, furious at his mother all over again. She had not seen fit to give Justine a trinket or two? Selfish woman!

The door opened and Justine entered. Brenner rose from the chair.

'You are here already,' she said brightly. 'And I thought I would be early.'

He'd just seen her at breakfast, but it was like gazing at her anew.

'I was perusing the list.' He always seemed to say idiotic things around her. 'I estimate two hundred and fifty items to locate.'

She laughed, but it seemed more of a nervous laugh than an amused one. 'At least that many. Your mother loved pretty things.'

And she undoubtedly had plenty of the Duke's money to purchase them with. And still she'd not assigned even one to Justine.

'May I see the list?' she asked.

He handed it to her and watched her read, looking for some sign that she saw what he'd seen. That his mother had not thought of her.

'It is in Wenden's hand.' She looked up at him. 'Wenden was your mother's lady's maid.'

Yes, he knew that. The maid was still recuperating in Venice. Both she and the Duke's valet had caught the same fever, but it had not killed them. The

Duke's men of business had already sent money for them to return when well enough to make the journey.

But never mind the maid. What about the absence of Justine's name?

She gave no discernible reaction. 'She has organised it by room. This shall not be as difficult as I thought. We can start in here, as a matter of fact.' She handed the list back to him and took out a graphite pencil from a drawer. 'You can mark off what we find.'

They cleared spaces on a table to place the items, a space for Leo's items, one for Annalise, one for Charlotte. Brenner intended to turn them over immediately, mostly because once he gave them to their new owners, he was done with the items.

Because it was Justine who would locate them, Brenner barely had to touch any of them, which was quite acceptable to him. He called out the first item. Justine found it and placed it in the proper space.

There were very few of the Duchess's items in the library. Bound volumes of *The Lady's Magazine*, a few novels and volumes of poetry, the mantel clock, and two porcelain vases that contained the expected lavender, roses and jasmine.

They moved on to the great room and a series of smaller drawing rooms.

Brenner frowned, surveying what they'd collected in the fifth room. Justine still remained cheerful despite the growing numbers of items, none of which were for her.

He glanced at the next item on the list. 'Flower pyramid,' he called out. His brows rose. What the devil was a flower pyramid?

She walked directly to a side table where cuttings of lavender, roses and jasmine had been placed in a strange blue-and-white vase, shaped like a... pyramid, with increasingly smaller tiers. The open mouths of blue-and-white monsters on the corners of each tier held the flower stems.

Justine picked it up. 'Who is it for?'

He double-checked the list. 'Annalise.'

She nodded.

Brenner was leaning against the table where she placed the vase among Annalise's other new possessions. She brushed against him.

Before she could move away he caught her arm. 'I cannot help but notice the Duchess has given nothing to you.'

Colour rose in her face and she paused before speaking. 'Why would she? I am not her daughter.'

Brenner looked into her eyes, searching, he told himself, for evidence that the Duchess's slight hurt her as much as it angered him. Her expression did not change.

'But you grew up here, did you not? Did she not act like a mother to you?' He grew angry with himself for asking about his mother's character. He did not want to know her.

But he did want to know Justine.

She glanced away. 'She was under no obligation

to treat me as a daughter, Brenner.' He thought he heard a tinge of emotion in her soft voice, emotion she was trying to hide.

As he hid his emotions.

She covered his hand with her own, and again looked up into his eyes. 'She was kind to me.'

It was his turn to look away. He could not think of his mother as kind, not after the turmoil she had caused by deserting him.

He took a breath. It was easier at the moment to think of the slight she had given Justine, who obviously was a vital part of this household. The hub of the wheel, for God's sake. Could not his mother have given her something? A small snuffbox? A candlestick? Something?

Her fingers tightened around his hand, and he looked back into her eyes.

Her gaze remained steady, as if she were determined not to feel pain. 'My father did his duty by bequeathing me enough for a very comfortable living. No one else has any obligation to me.'

Obligation. The second time she'd used the word.

Their gazes held, and her hand still held his. They were so close Brenner could feel the heat of her body, see the brightness of her eyes, the lush fullness of her pink lips. How would those lips taste? he wondered.

She lowered her lashes and moved away. 'What is next on the list?'

Good that she put distance between them, because he'd been unable to.

He straightened and cleared his throat as he glanced back at the list. 'Pair of Meissen kittens.'

She started for the door. 'Those are in your mother's sitting room.'

He followed reluctantly. Thus far the bits and pieces his mother valued, the beautiful, the whimsical, the *valuable*, were scattered in the more public rooms. He'd been able to tolerate the glimpses of her those items forced him to see, but they were about to enter her private rooms, rooms where her presence would be more vivid.

They entered her bedchamber to reach her private sitting room. He'd expected a dark and gloomy room, reflecting her death, but the curtains were open and her bedchamber was light and airy, with painted Chinese wallpaper decorating the walls with brightly hued flowers. The furniture was gilded wood and here, again, were vases of fresh flowers.

He gestured to one of them. 'Fresh flowers?'

Justine smiled sadly. 'She loved her flowers. I suppose that is why the maids put them here.'

In his father's house the servants would be scolded for such an excess.

She opened the door to the sitting room. 'I believe it is their way of honouring her memory.'

He frowned. He'd not expected his frivolous mother to earn the loyalty of servants.

They stepped into the sitting room, decorated with the same wallpaper, the same gilt furniture. His gaze, however, was immediately drawn to a painting that dominated the room, a painting he'd seen his father destroy when he'd been ten.

Justine stood next to him as he stared at it. 'This is the portrait I told you about, the portrait of you and your mother.'

His mother, big as life, in a white, gauzy gown and powdered hair. He, little more than a babe, was seated on her lap, his hair in curls, young enough to be wearing a dress much like hers. The background was a flower garden, a profusion of lavender and roses and jasmine.

'Is—is this a copy?' he managed.

Justine looked up at the painting. 'My father had Hoppner paint it for your mother. She always said this copy was true to the original.'

The original had hung in the Linwall country house before his father had slashed it and had thrown the shredded pieces in the fireplace.

She walked over to a gilded desk and took something from its drawer. She placed a miniature portrait in his hand.

A miniature of him when he'd been an impish schoolboy.

His hand closed around it. He lowered himself on to a couch, suddenly feeling as if his legs would not hold him.

'Your mother wanted you to have these.' She sat beside him. 'The portrait and the miniature. I have the letter that puts it in writing.'

He stared at her, unable to comprehend what she was saying.

She placed a hand on his back. 'She missed you, Brenner,' she murmured.

His eyes stung with tears and his throat twisted painfully, but he'd be damned if he'd weep now after so many years. Justine put her arm around him and held him close while he fought for air.

He felt as if he were ten years old again, home from school for the summer, a day much like this one. He'd come in from out of doors, from the sunny morning to the relative coolness of their country house. His father had been standing in the hall.

'She's left us.' His father sat. 'And may she rot in hell for it.'

Brenner clung to Justine as if his sanity depended upon it. The pain hit him afresh. He needed Justine's comfort. Needed her.

She held him in an embrace, silent as he fought his grief. She ran her fingers through his hair and held him together. Suddenly something in him shifted and he no longer felt like that abandoned ten-year-old boy. He felt like a man and he was acutely aware of his desire for the woman in his arms.

Footsteps sounded in the hallway and brought him to his senses. 'Justine! Gerry!' It sounded like Charlotte. 'Some man has called upon you.'

Brenner pulled away, and Justine straightened her clothes. He rose and gave her his hand to help her up. When he pulled her up, he also held her in a quick but silent embrace before they walked out of the room and into the hall.

Charlotte ran up to them, the two pugs scrambling to catch up to her. 'A man is here from Papa's solicitor. He has boxes for you, Gerry.'

'You answered the door, Charlotte?' he asked in a disapproving tone. It was not proper for the daughter of a duke to answer the door.

'Well, I was just walking by it,' she responded defensively.

They descended the stairs, the pugs hopping after them, to where the man waited in the hall. Brenner recognised him as one of the solicitor's clerks.

'Lord Brenner.' The man bowed and handed Brenner an envelope. 'We extend our apologies. These were in our safe and quite overlooked.' He indicated a stack of four flat velvet cases. 'There is a letter to explain it all, a letter from the Duchess.'

Chapter Ten

Now what task did the solicitors have for him? Something so important they'd sent one of their men to see to it. Brenner looked at the stack of cases.

'I must beg your leave, sir.' The clerk edged towards the door. 'The hackney coach is waiting.'

'Certainly,' Brenner responded.

As Brenner closed the door, Annalise appeared on the stairs. 'Who came to call?'

Charlotte answered her. 'A man from Papa's solicitor. He brought Gerry a stack of cases.'

Four identical cases, each flat and covered in black velvet.

'Can we open them?' Charlotte asked.

Brenner shrugged. 'We might as well.'

With Brenner carrying the jewellery cases and Charlotte's pugs following, they all went to the small drawing room where Justine had first taken him to meet the Fitzmannings. The girls sat themselves on the sofa, Justine between them, as they had done that first day. The pugs started growling and huffing and sparring with each other at Charlotte's feet.

Brenner lowered himself into a chair adjacent to the sofa, placing the cases on the side table. He opened the letter.

It was written in his mother's hand. He recognised it immediately even though he had not seen more than her signature in over twenty years. The stab of emotion returned. The letter was addressed to the solicitors and predated the will making him trustee and guardian.

'What does it say?' asked Charlotte.

'It tells me what I must do with the contents of the boxes,' he replied.

'What is in them?' she asked.

Brenner handed the top box to Charlotte. 'Open it.'

She undid the gold latch and opened the velvet case. 'A diamond necklace,' she exclaimed.

'Four diamond necklaces,' Brenner said. 'One in each box.'

This necklace resembled a string of tiny flowers, a garland of diamonds.

Charlotte sighed. 'It is so beautiful.'

'Let me see it,' Annalise asked.

Charlotte removed the necklace from the box and handed it to Annalise.

Justine's eyes shone with admiration. 'I have never seen anything so lovely.'

Neither had Brenner, but he was looking at Justine, who was enthralled with the necklace.

Annalise handed it to her and Justine held it so that the sun's rays caught in the diamonds' facets. Her eyes sparkled like the jewels and her face flushed.

Brenner's breath caught.

'Why are there four of them?' Annalise took the necklace from Justine's hands.

He glanced back down to the letter. 'The necklaces are for your wedding days.'

'They are for us?' Charlotte clasped her hands together in excitement. 'But there are four. Which one is mine?'

Brenner's mind was whirling. 'The boxes are numbered.'

The Duchess had listed her four children and placed a number by each of their names. Brenner's name headed the list.

'What number is on that box?' he asked.

Charlotte, pushing her dogs away from her feet, turned the box over and found the number embossed in gold. 'Number one.'

Brenner folded the letter and put it in his pocket. 'Then that one is Justine's.' He cleared his throat and spoke more firmly. 'Necklace number one is Justine's.'

Justine looked up. 'Mine?' Her heart pounded.

Brenner smiled. 'Yours.' He took the necklace from Annalise and placed it in Justine's hand, closing her fingers around it.

She glanced at him, expecting him to say he'd been mistaken. He merely continued to smile. Justine weighed the diamonds in her hand. They were cool to the touch. The necklace was delicate, but extravagant at the same time. She felt awed by it, and it was hers.

The Duchess had not forgotten her.

Justine had lied to Brenner. She had been crushed to learn the Duchess had left her nothing on the list. Pages listing figurines, porcelain boxes, paintings, this and that, but nothing for her. It had hurt terribly. Justine had loved the Duchess like a mother and it had devastated her that the Duchess had given her nothing.

All that pain now disappeared. The necklace had changed everything. Justine stared down at the beautiful diamonds. Her eyes filled with tears. The Duchess had not forgotten her after all.

'Let us see the others.' Charlotte bounced eagerly in her seat.

'Open them,' Brenner told her. 'They are numbered according to age.'

'Whose is number two?' asked Annalise.

'Leo's.' Brenner handed Charlotte the box.

Charlotte's eyes danced with mirth. 'Leo will look very silly in a diamond necklace.' Both she and Annalise giggled.

'Obviously,' Justine broke in, 'it will be for his bride.'

They giggled even more. 'We do comprehend that, Justine,' Annalise assured her.

While Charlotte opened Leo's box, Justine examined her necklace again. She glanced up to see Brenner gazing at her, his expression enigmatic.

'Leo's is pretty, too.' Charlotte held it up.

'It is different, though,' Annalise added, touching it. 'But both necklaces look like tiny flowers.'

'Open yours.' Charlotte handed box number three to Annalise. 'I'm opening mine.'

The two girls opened boxes three and four, exclaiming over their beauty and comparing the differences. The necklaces were the same length and similar in design. Justine would wager they used the same number of jewels, for the same number of carats.

The Duchess had placed her on an equal footing with Leo, Annalise and Charlotte. Justine closed her eyes and savoured the moment.

It mattered not at all that she would never have a wedding day upon which to wear her beautiful diamonds. Even if she never wore them, she would treasure the necklace for the rest of her life.

'Put it on,' Brenner said while Annalise and Charlotte were comparing their two necklaces, each concluding theirs was the finer.

Justine held his gaze for a moment before placing the strand of sparkling flowers around her neck. When she fastened it, she looked up to see approval in his eyes.

'Oh, Justine, it looks beautiful on you,' Charlotte cried. 'Wait here. I'll get a mirror.' She ran out, her little dogs in pursuit.

Justine glanced at Brenner again. 'How does it look?'

He paused a moment before answering. 'It becomes you.'

The compliment made her senses flare and greatly added to her happiness.

A few minutes later Charlotte returned with her pugs, whose excitement had grown. She handed Justine a mirror.

Justine gazed at the diamonds glittering against her neck. They did indeed look like a sparkling garland of diamond flowers.

'Well?' Charlotte arched a brow. 'What is your assessment?'

Justine grinned at her. 'I believe I love them.'

Annalise laughed. 'I love mine, too.'

She put her necklace on, and she and Charlotte stood up and posed, taking turns looking at themselves in the mirror. The dogs thought it was a game and ran around their ankles.

'I love how it catches the light and how many colours it makes. I must remember that if I ever paint diamonds.' Annalise took the necklace off again and dangled it in the air, watching how the diamonds broke the sunlight into all the colours of the rainbow.

Charlotte came over to her. 'Here, try on Leo's necklace.'

Charlotte put Leo's diamond necklace around her sister's neck, but she had some difficulty fastening it.

'Don't pinch me.' Annalise's hand flew up to the nape of her neck. She dropped her own diamond necklace and bent down to pick it up.

'Wait,' cried Charlotte, 'your hair is caught.'

Justine rose to see if she could help. She, Annalise and Charlotte all struggled to free Annalise's hair from the clasp of the necklace.

Suddenly Brenner shot to his feet. 'Charlotte! The dog!'

By the time Brenner gave the warning, little Oliver was scampering out of the doorway, necklace dangling from his mouth, Octavia chasing him.

'My necklace!' Annalise cried.

Brenner dashed off after the dog. Charlotte and Annalise, holding Leo's necklace at her throat, raced behind. Justine followed. In the hall, they all stopped.

'Where did he go?' Justine asked.

'We lost him.' Brenner sounded annoyed.

Annalise looked about to cry.

'I think he went above stairs.' Charlotte started for the door.

The door facing the river was open to let in the cool breeze. Brenner walked towards it. 'I'll look outside.'

An hour later they had found neither dog nor necklace. The other necklaces were locked away in the Duke's safe. Annalise was despondent. Justine and Charlotte sat with her on the bed in her bedchamber.

'I am so sorry.' Charlotte's voice trembled. 'I will give you my necklace.'

'No, that would not be right.' Annalise sniffled. 'Mama gave that necklace to you, not to me. It is my fault. I dropped it.'

'But I made you drop it when Leo's necklace got caught.' Tears also rolled down Charlotte's cheeks.

Ordinarily Justine would give up one of her possessions to mollify Annalise or Charlotte. Guilt niggled at her for not doing so now.

'I am certain we will find your necklace,' she tried to reassure Annalise. 'Do not worry.'

'But Oliver carried it outside.' That much they now knew.

Brenner was still outside, searching for the necklace. He'd enlisted the aid of the footmen as well. They were searching every inch.

Annalise rose. 'I want to go to my studio. I have to draw my necklace while I still remember it.'

Justine left Annalise's bedroom and walked out to the garden to see if she could assist in the search.

She found Brenner seated on a bench near the pond, his head lowered into his hands. She stopped some distance away and just watched him in this unguarded moment.

Her heart ached for him.

She'd forgotten that his day had also been a tumult of emotion. She approached quietly and he did not look up until she was within three feet of him.

'We have not located the necklace.' He looked angry. 'I blame myself. I should have been more vigilant.'

'May I sit?' she asked.

He straightened and moved to give her room.

She sat and touched his arm. 'It is no one's fault. We must simply have faith that the necklace will be found.'

He sat very still, looking into her eyes. Eventually she placed her hand in her lap, and he gazed out towards the garden. 'A diamond necklace is a great temptation. My father would be certain a servant would steal such a valuable piece.'

The idea had never occurred to her. 'I would be very shocked if any of our servants did such a thing.' Her hand still tingled from touching him.

His forehead creased. 'Are your servants so loyal?'

She gazed at him again. 'They are. I believe your mother and my father were carelessly benevolent towards them. Our servants have had a freedom I imagine is absent in other houses.'

He rubbed his face. 'Your household is not what I imagined it to be.'

She wondered how he'd imagined them while he grew up alone with his father. They'd grown up thinking of him as a brother, because the Duchess always referred to him that way, but surely his father would not have been so generous? Brenner's father seemed a bitter and resentful man.

But she suspected Brenner was too tender at the moment for a discussion of his mother and father.

'Annalise retreated to her studio to draw the necklace,' she said instead.

He attempted a smile. 'It is good she has such a pastime.'

She went on, 'I suspect Charlotte is writing a play about the episode. A very dramatic one.'

He reached for her hand. To have his strong fingers wrapped around hers caused a burst of sensation inside her, making her want more, making her want his arms around her, his lips against hers—

She caught herself. Scandalous to think such thoughts about him.

He withdrew his hand and crossed his arms over his chest. 'Perhaps we should continue with the Duchess's list.'

'Are you sure, Brenner?' It had not been easy for him to go through his mother's things. She wanted to ease his pain, not witness its return.

'I prefer to finish the task and be done with it.' His voice was firm.

Chapter Eleven

Brenner followed Justine back to his mother's bed-chamber, where his mother's scent still mingled with the scent of the flowers, back into the sitting room dominated by her life-sized portrait. The miniature of himself as a child still lay next to the list on the table where he'd dropped it as if it had been a hot coal. He picked up the list and slipped the miniature into his coat pocket.

He scanned the list. 'Where did we leave off?'

Justine stood close, brushing his arm as she read. He was aware of her and his eyes refused to focus on the words.

'Here it is.' She pointed to the item below the last one he'd marked off. 'Brass-and-bronze Argand lamp.'

She turned and fetched the lamp from a pretty gilded writing table.

'For Leo,' Brenner said.

It helped him to focus on the task, to stare at the paper instead of the portrait, to think of possessions instead of how prettily she moved.

'Next?' She looked at him.

'Gold-plated desk set,' he read.

He noticed her mood had brightened since earlier in the day, even with the loss of Annalise's necklace.

She located the desk set.

They kept up the rhythm, Brenner reading the item on the list and Justine finding it.

While she searched drawers for a quizzing glass, Brenner watched her. 'Did you like your diamond necklace?'

She turned to him, smiling. 'Oh, yes.'

He held in his own smile at her obvious pleasure. He'd made the right decision. After all, he did not need or desire his mother's necklace for a future wife. There were the Linwall jewels—the entailed ones, all the others having been sold—for his future wife to wear. Justine need never know that it had been his name next to box number one, not hers.

He crossed his arms over his chest. 'The Duchess did not forget you, after all.'

She walked over to him. 'I was not truthful earlier. I wanted her to remember me. She was like a mother to me.' Her voice cracked and she swallowed.

They finished in the sitting room and moved to the room he dreaded most. His mother's bedroom.

His mother seemed too real to him in her bed-chamber. He fancied she would at any moment step out of the painting in the sitting room and sweep into the room with a swish of her voluminous silk skirts. She would seat herself at the dressing table and powder her face with a large feather puff.

And she would be laughing at the antics of her little boy.

He shut his eyes at the vivid memory, opening them to stare at the list. 'Gilded hairbrush.'

Good God. Was everything his mother owned gilded? It seemed excessively pretentious. His father would never have stood for such extravagance, even if he'd had the money to buy such an item.

She must have been miserable with his father.

As they progressed through the rest of the list, Justine had to search through drawers for the items. Fans and handkerchiefs and gloves. Items his mother had touched, had worn.

Justine knelt next to a chest of drawers—gilded, naturally—searching for a red silk miser purse. She gasped.

'What is it?' Brenner asked.

She turned to him, holding a packet of letters in her hand. 'Letters. The top one has your name on it.'

He crossed the room and took the letters from her hand, staring at them as he helped Justine to her feet. His name was on the envelope, written in his mother's hand. He looked at Justine, too taken aback to know what to do.

She touched the pale blue ribbon that tied the letters together. 'Open it, Brenner.'

'I do not know…' His voice faded into indecision. This truly seemed like coming face to face with his mother's ghost.

'You ought to see what she wrote.'

She was right. Perhaps his mother explained why she had chosen him as guardian and trustee. Or perhaps she explained why she had left him without a word from her. Some apology was certainly due to him.

'I cannot read them in here. Come with me.' Brenner walked back into his mother's sitting room and lowered himself on to the settee. Justine sat next to him.

He untied the packet and glimpsed some of the other envelopes. 'They are all addressed to me.'

He turned the first envelope over. Its seal was unbroken. His fingers shook as he broke it and opened the first letter.

It was dated a month after his mother had run off with the Duke.

My dearest Gerry, the letter began. *Mama is so sorry she had to leave you without saying goodbye. I hope to see you soon when your papa will allow it. I miss you so very much…*

It went on to talk about things she had seen and done that would have been of interest to a ten-year-old boy, and she asked him pertinent questions about his activities. At the end of the letter, she repeated how much she missed him.

The second letter was dated about two weeks

later, still expressing the hope that she would see him soon. Letter after letter, perhaps thirty letters in all, spanning years, becoming successively more despondent, successively more hopeless, successively further apart.

Brenner could hear her voice in her words, could see her laughing with him, playing a game of chase in the garden. He could see her sitting with him, telling him of some adventure, making an outing to Ranelagh Gardens seem like a storybook adventure.

It became more difficult to breathe, his throat ached and he furiously blinked away tears.

'I never saw these,' he told Justine. 'I—I thought she did not think to write to me.'

'She wrote you many letters,' Justine whispered.

He was perilously close to breaking down. Indeed, he was certain his emotions would have shattered had not Justine been at his side, reading along with him, touching his hand when she'd not yet finished a page.

'These were never delivered to me.' He feared he knew why.

The last letter in the pile gave the verification. It was written by his father to his mother. In the cruellest language possible, his father quoted the divorce papers, which apparently stated that his mother was to have no contact with her son whatsoever. His father wrote that Brenner had refused to read her letters, that Brenner had said she was dead to him from now on.

Brenner threw the paper down and rose from the settee. 'That blackguard.'

Justine picked up the page he'd dropped.

'He never told me.' He paced in front of her. 'I never said she was dead to me. He said it all the time.'

He turned towards the door. 'I am going to have this out with him.'

She came after him. 'No, Brenner. You must calm yourself.' She seized his arm to hold him back. 'Do not go to him in the heat of emotion.'

He started to pull away from her, but she grabbed hold of his other arm as well.

'Think about it.' She tried to shake him, but he held on to her as well, his hands on her shoulders. 'It was a long time ago.'

He intended to merely push her away, to rush to the carriage house and have a horse saddled so he could ride into Mayfair and confront his father, but she was too close, too earnest in her pleas.

He gazed down into her captivating eyes. 'I have spent years believing she cared nothing for me.'

She put her arms around him, hugging him close to her. 'I know.'

Even in his misery and rage he realised perhaps she did know. She'd had a mother, too, who'd left her. He pulled away, again looking into her face. 'Did—did your mother ever write to you? Visit you?'

Pain flashed through her eyes. 'My mother sent

me to a wet nurse on the day I was born. My father told me only that she'd come from a French aristocratic family and she'd fled the Revolution. She had a chance to marry respectably, but not if she bore some other man's baby.' She blinked and averted her gaze. 'I do not even know her name.'

It was Brenner's turn to hold her. 'Poor Justine.'

He felt her body shudder against his and he lifted her chin to see tears falling from her eyes. He held her tight again, but his own pain would not be denied.

He fought for air as his own weeping began. Justine backed them towards the couch where they clung together, releasing the pain inside each of them until they were drained of it. They both pulled away at the same time.

Brenner took a neat handkerchief from his pocket and offered it to Justine. She gently stilled his hand, finding her own lace-edged handkerchief, black like her gown.

She laughed softly as she wiped her eyes. 'I suppose we both needed that.'

He caressed her cheek with his thumb. 'I would say we are a matched set.'

Justine took a deep breath. 'We cannot blame them.'

He was certainly not ready to absolve his father of blame, but he did not wish to talk of him any more.

His eyes fixed on her full pink lips, slightly

parted. He leaned forward and she tilted her head up. He placed his lips upon hers, intending only a kiss of gratitude for her wisdom and strength.

As soon as he tasted her, he knew he'd lied to himself. He wanted her. All of her. Not only her strength, but her heart and, at this moment, the pleasures of her body.

She deepened the kiss, exciting him further. He slid his hand down the length of her neck to cup her breast. She moaned and the kiss took on a more urgent nature.

Brenner was nearly beyond thinking when he pulled away to remove his coat and waistcoat. When he returned to her, he sought her lips again, and desire flared even hotter when she pulled his shirt from his trousers and slipped her hands underneath to rub his bare skin.

He gently lay her on her back and covered her with his body. Their excitement was fevered now, but neither issued a caution. When Brenner thought to pull away, she urged him forward; when he responded to her, she asked for more. Soon they were a tangle of legs, crumbled clothing and no will to turn back.

He wanted to plunge inside her and connect himself to her for ever, but he had a thread of self-control, enough to ask her if she was certain she wanted this.

She lifted her hips before the words were formed in his mouth. 'Now, Brenner,' she murmured. 'I want you now.'

He entered her and truly was lost to all reason. The sensation of her, her scent, the feel of her breath against his skin, the small sounds she made, the eagerness with which she met each thrust, drove him on.

He had not realised how empty he'd felt until fulfilled by Justine. At this moment, loving Justine, joining with her, body and soul, Brenner felt completed and whole and nothing else mattered to him. He spilled his seed inside her and felt her convulse around him. The peak of their pleasure quickly ebbed.

Reality returned.

He had seduced her, made love to her, had taken advantage of her when her emotions were in the most tender state. What could he say to her now?

She looked upon him with a shocked expression. 'Brenner,' she murmured as if speaking an apology.

'Gerry! Justine! Where are you?' Charlotte's voice sounded in the hall.

'Good God!' Brenner cried. Whatever happened to Charlotte hiding herself away?

They rose quickly. Justine straightened her gown and Brenner hurriedly tucked in his shirt and put on his waistcoat and coat.

'I'll go ahead,' Justine said, hurrying out of the door to encounter Charlotte. It bought him enough time to do up his buttons and try to smooth his hair and to bring some order to his neckcloth.

Justine had just reached the bedchamber door when Charlotte opened it. 'There you are. Why did you not answer me?'

Justine spoke a bit breathlessly. 'We did. Did you not hear us?'

Charlotte shook her head. 'What were you doing, anyway?'

Brenner emerged from the sitting room. 'What you and Annalise refused to do. We've been sorting out your mother's possessions.'

She looked from one to the other. 'You look like you've been rolling around or something.'

Brenner exchanged a quick glance with Justine. 'The work is taxing with only two people.'

Charlotte rolled her eyes. 'Well, Halton said I should find you and tell you that the necklace has not been found and the footmen have abandoned the search. Cook says that dinner will be served in an hour. I've told Annalise, but she says she will not eat.'

'Tell her I expect her at dinner,' Brenner responded. He looked towards Justine. 'Have we finished for the day?'

She flushed and looked down. 'I will just take a moment to tidy things.'

Brenner turned to Charlotte again and said a bit too sharply. 'Well, go and tell Annalise she must come to dinner.'

'I do not know why you are acting so mean!' Charlotte huffed, but she left the room.

Brenner looked at Justine.

She did not meet his eye. 'I'll tidy up here, Brenner.'

He could hardly think. 'We will talk later?'

She nodded.

Chapter Twelve

Justine hurried to her bedchamber, leaning on the closed door behind her.

She could not believe what she had done. Making love to Brenner. She'd not wished to resist him. In fact, she was certain she had encouraged him. She'd wanted that special feeling of closeness with him, that closeness that had gone so horribly wrong once before.

God help her, she could still feel Brenner inside her, that glorious sensation, that intensity of excitement, that demand for release. She ached to repeat it again with him.

Brenner had looked shocked when it was over, and certainly it was she who had shocked him. How could she face him over dinner when they must pretend nothing had happened between them?

She cleaned herself as best she could and rang for her maid to dress her hair and help her change into her black dinner dress. All the while she thought of Brenner, of making love with him. Of possibly having created a child with him.

When she was presentable again she descended the stairs.

Brenner waited for her in the hall. 'Let me speak to you now.'

She'd hoped to delay this conversation. Her thoughts were not in order, her emotions were a shambles. They walked through the grand hall to the outside into the still warm day. A breeze came in from the river, which sparkled in the sunshine even though it was nearly five o'clock.

Brenner glanced around as if to assure himself they were alone.

She would not wait. 'Brenner, about this afternoon—'

He held up a hand. 'Say no more. I offer you my sincere apology for—for taking advantage of you. I fully comprehend that I have compromised you; therefore, I will marry you.'

'Marry me?' She could not be more shocked.

Such words were ones she had once thought her happiness depended upon, but she never expected them to be spoken by Brenner. She expected him to call her a wanton woman, fit only for a brothel.

He kept talking. 'I am fully prepared to accept my responsibility.' His voice was flat and his face mask-like, as if he were hiding his true emotions from her.

He could not wish to marry her, not appearing and sounding like that.

She closed her eyes and tried to imagine what it would be like to marry him. Without love between them, it would be bleak. Lonelier than being alone.

She lifted her chin. 'Brenner, you do not really wish to marry me. It is all over your face how little you desire it. Do not let what happened between us spoil your happiness.'

At least some expression now showed in his face. Confusion. 'Happiness? I do not see the relevance. I took advantage of you. I compromised you. I will do the right thing.'

Emotions swirled inside her: hatred of herself for her carnal weakness, humiliation that it should be Brenner who had discovered it, anger at him for so obviously detesting the idea of marrying her. But another emotion struck daggers in the others.

She loved him.

Because she loved him, she'd been weak, but he should not have to suffer for it.

She started to reach for him, to touch his cheek, but withdrew her hand. 'Oh, Brenner.' Her voice came out like a sigh. 'I am the one at fault for what happened between us.'

His stony demeanour returned. 'It was my responsibility. My duty is clear.'

'It was not your responsibility.' He would force her to speak out loud what she found painful to even remember. 'Surely you could tell that this was not the first time?'

He gazed downwards.

Her cheeks burned. 'I have lost any pretensions to respectability.'

His eyes narrowed. 'Who was the man?'

She waved a hand and turned away. 'Does it matter? I have no desire to speak of it.'

'It was Kinney.' He sounded disapproving.

Halton appeared in the doorway. 'Dinner is served.'

Brenner ran a hand through his hair. 'We must talk more after dinner.'

There was nothing more Justine wished to say. She knew only that she would not be the cause of more unhappiness in this man's life.

None of his conversation with Justine had gone the way Brenner thought it would. He thought she would be angry at him. He thought she would be relieved he was willing to marry her. He had no notion what it meant that she had not agreed.

He offered her his arm and escorted her to the dining room, aware the whole time of her fingers on his sleeve.

Charlotte and Annalise were already seated. They'd chosen chairs next to each other so Brenner and Justine had no choice but to sit opposite them and next to each other. Close enough to touch.

Good God, Brenner hoped he would not touch her, because he wanted to. Very much.

He held the chair for her and she brushed against his fingers when she lowered herself into her seat.

It was not until he'd placed his napkin on his lap that he realised the air was thick with tension not his own. He glanced at Annalise and Charlotte.

Annalise pointedly turned towards Justine. 'Jussy,' she said in an affronted tone, 'I do not see why I should be *forced* to come to dinner when I *explicitly* said I did not wish to come.'

'She yelled at *me* for it,' complained Charlotte. 'That is the last time I ever deliver messages.'

Brenner had no patience for this. 'You should not be delivering messages, Charlotte. Or answering the door. Those are tasks best left for the servants.'

'Well, you asked me to deliver your message to Annalise,' Charlotte snapped.

'You are being impertinent, Charlotte.' He did not wish to deal with their childish tempers, not when he'd just asked Justine to marry him and she had refused.

'Jussy—' Annalise pointedly ignored Brenner again '—I am desolated over my lost necklace.' She shot a glance at Charlotte. 'My *stolen* necklace, I should say. I do not see why I could not have a plate sent up to my studio. I wanted to be alone.'

'It was not my decision to make,' Justine told her.

Bear up, Annalise, Brenner thought. It helped nothing to wallow in her disappointment.

'Stop saying you are desolated,' Charlotte cried. 'I know it was my fault you lost your necklace—'

'Had my necklace *stolen*,' Annalise broke in.

Brenner felt a headache building.

The soup was served.

Annalise finally looked directly at Brenner. 'You should make Charlotte confine the pugs rather than give them the run of the house.' She made it sound as if it were his fault Oliver had carried off her necklace.

'They do not have the run of the house!' Charlotte's voice rose. 'Otherwise they would be here in the dining room.'

Annalise lifted her nose. 'I am surprised they are not.'

Charlotte threw down her spoon. 'Oh, why don't you just take my silly necklace and be quiet about it!'

'Because I want *my* necklace!' Annalise cried.

'Good God!' Brenner raised his voice even louder than the two of them. 'Stop this caterwauling!'

Both girls blinked at him in surprise.

They needed to learn a bit of control. Had not the last couple of weeks taught them that life would not always be easy?

'This hoydenish behavior does not belong at the dinner table,' he scolded. 'It must cease this instant. We have been through this before.'

Annalise tossed him a defiant look. 'Might I remind you, *Gerry,* I did not wish to come to the dinner table.'

He felt Justine stiffen next to him.

'You are acting rudely, Annalise,' he told her. 'I suggest you develop some decorum.'

Justine squirmed in her chair.

'Decorum?' Annalise's voice rose an octave. 'I just had my diamond necklace snatched away and lost, the necklace my *mother* wanted me to have—'

'Oh, remind us of the necklace again,' Charlotte muttered.

Brenner slapped his hand on the table. 'This is enough! We are eating dinner.'

Charlotte turned on him. 'You can't tell us what to do, Gerry.'

This defiance did the girls no credit. He leaned towards them both and spoke in a firm, even voice. 'I am your guardian. That gives me the right to tell you what to do.'

'It does not give you the right to act as if you are superior to us!' Charlotte cried.

Annalise shot to her feet. 'I cannot bear to be here another minute!'

'Sit down!' Brenner shouted.

'Brenner,' Justine spoke in a low voice.

'One moment, Justine.' He levelled his gaze at Annalise. 'You need to appreciate that I am in charge of you. I do not wish to exert authority—'

Her eyes flashed. 'Authority? What could you do to me? Nothing.'

Annalise could not behave like this and expect to move in polite society. Brenner lost all patience with the lot of them. 'I could lock you out of your studio, for one thing.' Not that he would ever do such a thing, but Annalise did not need to know that.

Annalise paled. 'You would not dare.'

'Brenner,' Justine spoke louder.

He silenced her with his hand.

'You cannot lock Annalise out of her studio!' Charlotte flung an arm around her sister.

Justine stood. 'Brenner,' she said in an insistent tone, 'I would speak with you for a moment.'

She walked out of the room, and he had no choice but to follow her.

Once out of the room and out of earshot of Annalise and Charlotte, she swung around to face him. 'Have you a maggot in your brain? You are making everything worse. You are being overbearing. Do not forget these two young ladies just lost both their parents.'

'They cannot use that as an excuse for impertinent behaviour. Bad things occur, and they must learn to bear them, because behaviour such as that will cause them much criticism.' This seemed self-evident to him.

'You must give them time,' she insisted.

He crossed his arms over his chest. 'I have given them time. Now they must simply bear it and develop some self-control.'

'You merely make them defiant.' She straightened. 'I will not have it.'

'You are not responsible for them, Justine. I am.' He did not wish to argue with her, but she must understand what was at stake here. He walked away a few paces and turned back to her. 'It is my responsibility to see them married. Do you not think I want to see them married well? If they wish to attract proper suitors, they must behave in a proper manner.'

'They are still young, Brenner,' she countered.

'Annalise is of a marriageable age. Your father ought to have had her presented this Season.'

She gave him an exasperated look. 'He could not do so. He and your mother took their wedding trip.'

He kept her gaze. 'He and my mother should have thought of Annalise. Your father did not attend to your marriage either,' he went on. 'Did he not care if you married?'

Her face turned red. She took a step towards him, hands on her hips. 'You did not know him.'

'I know he did not see you married. How old are you, Justine? Twenty-three? Twenty-four? When did he intend to help you?' He was making her angry, he knew. What he did not know was why.

Because she did not want to marry him, perhaps?

She swung away from him. 'I already told you I was ruined. Why do you discuss this with me? I cannot be married.'

He turned her around to face him and kept his hands on her shoulders. 'Justine,' he said earnestly, 'I did not mean to speak so harshly. I do not wish to quarrel with you.'

She looked up into his eyes. 'Oh, Brenner. You should go back to your home and forget about us.'

She would send him away? His insides turned cold. 'You do not wish me to stay, Justine?'

She averted her gaze. 'Perhaps it would be best if you did not. You cannot be happy here.'

He released her, turned on his heel, and walked towards the stairs. He would leave that very night, since that was what she wished.

Justine walked back into the dining room and burst into tears. A few minutes later, she, Charlotte and Annalise watched Brenner leave in one of the coaches.

Chapter Thirteen

Brenner's ride in the carriage to Mayfair was spent in a state of abject misery. He'd done everything wrong, failed miserably at doing his duty to his half-sisters and, most of all, to Justine.

He entered the dark town house and climbed the stairs. As he passed his father's bedchamber, he noticed a faint light under the door. He knocked and entered before waiting for permission.

His father, dressed in a nightshirt, sat in a chair sipping brandy and reading a book by lamplight. He looked up at Brenner's entrance.

'You just burst in? Is that the kind of behaviour that is acceptable at that house?' His father's voice dripped with rancour.

The thing about emotions, once unleashed, was that they were hard to rein in again. Brenner was not certain he even desired to do so.

'I did learn something at *that house*.' He mocked his father's tone.

His father gave a disparaging laugh and returned to his book.

As if that would stop him now. 'I discovered letters, Father. Letters addressed to me.'

His father lowered his book.

Brenner set his chin. 'I read my mother's letters to me.' Letters that included the hope that she would soon be allowed to visit him. 'You kept them from me.'

His father sputtered. 'How dare you criticise me after what your mother did to you? Leaving you like that.'

Brenner forced his voice to remain steady. 'She wrote that she wanted to visit me. You prevented the visits. You kept her from me and made me think it was she who did not care to see me.'

His father waved a hand. 'Lies. She always said whatever she wanted you to think. The fact of it is, she ran off and I did what was best for you.'

'You are lying,' Brenner said. 'There was also a letter from you saying that you kept me from her to hurt her. You were not thinking of my welfare.'

His father rose from his chair, his eyes bulging. 'Did you think I would reward her for leaving us like that? She ran off. She left us, and I'd be damned if I didn't try to pay her back any way I could.'

Brenner just gaped at him before turning on his heel and heading to the door.

Before he left the room, he turned back. 'You

taught me to do my duty even when it was distasteful, so you need not fear I will not do my duty by you. I'll continue to save your estate from ruin and keep you out of the poor house, but beyond that I promise nothing.' He opened the door and walked out.

The next morning he stumbled down the stairs after a sleepless night. He hesitated at the door of the dining room, knowing his father would be seated there. There was no sense avoiding him, however.

Brenner opened the door.

His father did not even look up from his *Morning Post*.

Brenner walked to the sideboard with an appetite only for a piece of toasted bread. He picked up a slice and stared at it. It reminded him of Annalise and Charlotte.

He brought his plate to the table and sat. There was no pot of chocolate at this table and no scent of flowers in the room, no smiling Justine making him feel welcome. Even the day was bleak and overcast.

Brenner poured his tea and leaned his head in his hands.

'Do not put your elbows on the table,' his father said.

Brenner looked up. He ought not to have been surprised. He'd been hearing messages like that at the dining table his whole life. What he wished to hear was a word of apology, some acknowledgement of the wrong his father had done him.

'You did not even ask me about my health,' his father muttered, rattling the page of the newspaper. 'I could have been on my deathbed for all you would have known.'

He'd never realised the depth of his father's selfishness. 'You knew where I was, had you need of me.'

His father put the paper down. 'I would never have sent a message to that house.'

'Then I suppose it is fortunate you were not on your deathbed,' Brenner retorted.

'That's enough,' his father snapped. 'I will not stand for impertinence. I expect more decorum from you at this table.'

Brenner gaped at him. His father sounded just as his son had sounded the night before. No wonder Annalise and Charlotte wished to defy him.

He felt the clenching of anger inside him, an anger he would not express, because it would only make matters worse.

As Justine would have said.

The pain of losing her struck him anew.

His father chewed on a piece of ham, not quite swallowing before he spoke. 'You are a fool to connect yourself to that household. How do you expect to make your way in the world if you associate with that sort?'

Brenner's own thoughts from the night before reverberated inside him. What his father was saying was not that much different from what he'd said about Annalise and Charlotte making a good marriage.

He levelled a gaze at his father. 'If the Prince Regent connects himself with them, how can I be faulted for it?'

'Hmmph. The Regent.' His father rolled his eyes. 'Now there is a person to make one's model. No one would receive him if he were not the Regent.'

Brenner, feeling his anger escalate, took a sip of tea.

Mere days ago he would have spouted the same opinion of the Regent as his father, the opinion having been learned at his father's knee. True, the Prince was a frivolous, extravagant man who always spent beyond his means, but he'd shown himself to be a warm, loving friend to the Fitzmannings. Besides, the Prince's life had its own unhappiness. His Highness had been prevented from legally marrying Mrs Fitzherbert, the woman he loved, and had been instead forced to marry the vulgar Caroline of Brunswick.

Brenner put down his cup and stared out of the window. The sky had lightened momentarily, and Brenner felt as if the clouds in his mind had also blown away.

His father jabbed at the air with his finger. 'The scandal of that house will taint you, you mark my words.'

At this point Brenner was more worried that his acting like his father had tainted Annalise, Charlotte…and Justine. He felt sick inside that he'd treated them exactly as his father treated him. Scolding them and presenting the world as an unfriendly place was not the way to help his brother and sisters make their way in the world.

Moreover, acting like his father had made him ashamed of his feelings towards Justine, his desire to love her and make love to her. He ought to have proposed to her happily, in anticipation of the joy they could have together.

He glanced at his father and now saw a lonely, bitter man, a frightening vision of what he himself would become some day.

Unless he could devise a way to return to Justine and his sisters and beg their forgiveness.

He'd almost become a part of them, that happy, carefree, motley household. Beginning with news of their parents' deaths, he'd brought them nothing but unhappiness. Why would they ever wish to see him again?

His father's butler appeared in the doorway. 'Lord Brenner, there is a person named Halton requesting to speak to you.'

Halton? Had something happened to Justine?

'Who is Halton?' his father complained. 'He is interrupting breakfast.'

'Not yours, Father.' Brenner rose from his chair. 'I will see him.'

Halton stood stiffly in the hall of the town house, twirling his hat in his hands.

'What is it, Halton?' Brenner asked as soon as he was in earshot. 'Has something happened?'

The man's face took on a worried expression. 'The young ladies,' he began, 'Miss Fitzmanning and Miss Charlotte. They have run away.'

'Run away?' All sorts of terrible things that could befall them flashed through Brenner's mind.

Halton pursed his lips. 'I took it upon myself to inform you and beg you to return to the Manor with me. Miss Savard is sick with worry.' He emphasised these last words.

'I will come at once.' Brenner grabbed his hat and followed Halton out of the door to where one of the Duke's carriages waited. The coachman showed a sober expression. As soon as they settled in the coach, it started off, gaining great speed when they reached the open road.

'Why did they run away?' Brenner asked.

'I do not know, sir,' Halton replied. 'I believe it had something to do with the conflict between you yesterday.'

Good God. Had he upset them so much?

Justine sat in the small parlour that held too many memories of Brenner. Annalise and Charlotte had sent a message that they desired her to wait for them there. Characteristically, they were not here at the appointed time.

Justine had done a great deal of thinking through-out the night. Goodness knows, she had done no sleeping. She'd so regretted arguing with Brenner about Annalise and Charlotte. He'd been correct. They greatly needed to improve their behaviour. They needed to develop sufficient control over their emotions so they would not make the same mistakes she had made.

Her mistakes had driven away the only man she could ever love.

She might have at least been able to see him often, to be his friend. Now she suspected he would stay far away from her lest he be ensnared by her again and feel forced to propose marriage to her.

She covered her face with her hands, trying not to weep again. Surely she had no more tears left after the previous night?

This room faced the Thames and reminded her of when Brenner said he would marry her. Would she ever look upon the Thames again without thinking of that moment?

She heard footsteps on the marble floor of the grand hall and turned, expecting a footman to tell her Charlotte and Annalise would be delayed.

But Brenner strode in the room.

'Where are they?' he said right away. 'Do you have any idea where they have gone?'

Brenner had returned. Her legs nearly gave out with the relief of seeing him again.

But he was talking nonsense. 'Where who has gone?'

'Annalise and Charlotte.' He looked frantic. 'They have run away.'

'Run away!'

At that moment, giggles sounded outside the door and a key turned in the lock.

Brenner tried the door. 'We are locked in.'

Justine pressed her temple. 'Why?'

Yapping dogs and girlish giggles could be heard through the windows. Justine and Brenner hurried to look out.

There stood Annalise, Charlotte and Halton on the grass, wearing grins on their faces. Halton made a deep bow and Annalise lifted the door key so they could see it. They all ran off, Charlotte turning to wave as Octavia and Oliver jumped around her feet. A moment later they could hear them entering the grand hall, the pugs yapping as they crossed the room and their footsteps faded.

Justine turned to Brenner. 'I do not know what this is all about.'

His brow was furrowed. 'Halton fetched me, saying the girls had run away.'

'But they have not run away.' None of this made sense.

Slowly a smile grew on his face, and his eyes sparkled green. He broke into loud, unrestrained laughter. It was a glorious sound she had not heard before and she could not help but enjoy it.

'You still cannot guess?' he managed.

She was mystified. 'I—I am sorry they tricked

you into returning, but I knew nothing of it.' She was not sorry that he'd returned, however. She merely wished for him not to leave again.

'I am not sorry at all.' He struggled to sound sober. 'Tell me, what happened last night after I left?'

'I told them you had gone because I quarrelled with you.' That was essentially the truth.

'Did you tell them all that transpired between us?' he asked.

'No!' The idea of doing so horrified her. 'I would never tell, Brenner.' She had, of course, wept in front of them as if her heart was broken, which it had been.

He grinned. 'Our sisters are clever girls. Hoyden-ish, undisciplined, defiant, but clever. I suspect they worked it out.'

Our sisters? She blinked. 'Worked what out?'

He seized her hands and pulled her into an embrace, holding her tight. 'That I am a fool. That I blinded myself to my true feelings.' He released her, but held her face so that she gazed into his eyes, warm and soft. 'I made a mess of it yesterday, Justine. What I needed to tell you is that I am in love with you. I believe I have loved you from the time of our first meeting. I do not regret making love to you, only that I did not wait until marrying you to do so. I care nothing if it is my duty or not, I want to marry you.'

She was stunned speechless. Was it truly possible that he could love her?

His eyes were earnest and sincere. And adoring. He inclined his head and lowered his lips to hers.

She gasped and flung her arms around his neck, pressing against him, seizing his kiss.

He broke apart and leaned his forehead on hers. 'So, Justine, will you marry me?'

'Yes!' she cried. 'Oh, yes.'

Epilogue

Spring 1819

The day was as fine as spring could be in England. Azure skies, gardens in bloom, crisp fresh air. Welbourne Manor was abuzz with activity. Gone were the hatchment, black clothes and sad faces. Servants bustled to and fro, and soon carriages would arrive. This was a day of joy.

This was Justine and Brenner's wedding day.

They were to be married by special license in the Great Room of Welbourne Manor, the formal drawing room gleaming with mirrors and gilding and carved friezes and panels. The room's beauty was enhanced by dozens of vases filled with early roses, lavender and jasmine. His Royal Highness, the Prince Regent, was expected to attend and would give away the bride. Because the Regent would be present and playing such an important role, Brenner's father would also attend.

Brenner stood talking with Nicholas, Stephen and Leo. Nicholas, the new Duke of Manning, would be his best man. He excused himself and hurried to fetch a velvet box from the house safe. With the box in hand, he climbed the stairs to his mother's bedchamber where Justine was getting ready.

He knocked on the door.

Charlotte opened it. 'Oh, Gerry! We wanted you to wait and be surprised at how pretty Justine looks.'

He kissed Charlotte on the cheek and held up the velvet box. 'I have an errand.'

'The necklace!' She stepped aside.

Justine turned and smiled at him.

She looked like an angel in her white dress, as beautiful as a woman could be.

Annalise rose from a chair. 'I'm sketching her, so you can remember what she looked like today.'

'How could I forget?' He embraced Annalise.

But it was Justine he was drawn to.

She reached out her hands to him. 'I am all nerves. How are you faring?'

He kissed her quickly on the lips. 'I am eager to become a married man.'

She laughed.

He lifted the velvet box. 'I brought your diamond necklace.'

The door to the sitting room was open and Brenner had a clear view of the portrait of his mother. It made him feel as if she were watching them.

He rubbed his thumb against the velvet box. *You should have given the necklace to her,* he said silently.

He opened the box and removed the necklace, placing it around Justine's neck. She made a quick glance towards his mother's portrait and fingered the lovely diamonds.

'They suit you,' he said.

She grinned. 'You have said so before.'

He stepped back, but saw Justine touch the necklace again and he was glad he'd given it to her. His mother might never have known it, but the necklace was always Justine's.

Two hours later in the great room Brenner heard the vicar speak the words, 'I now pronounce you man and wife.' Afterwards Leo, Annalise and Charlotte ran up to them. Nicholas shook his hand and embraced Justine. Stephen clapped him on the back. Even the Prince Regent gave him a robust shake of the hand.

When all the guests had left, he and Justine were still surrounded by family. Brenner gazed at them all, grateful to be a part of them. It struck him how much his life had been changed. This family had been his mother's wedding gift to him, more precious than the diamonds circling Justine's neck.

He took Justine in his arms and swung her around until they were both giddy with laughter.

It was a good beginning for a happily ever after.

* * * * *

Annalise and the
Scandalous Rake

by
Deb Marlowe

Dear Reader,

It is such a thrill to be involved in this anthology, in large part because I got to collaborate with two of my dearest writing friends. Diane, Amanda and I first came together on a tour that paid tribute to the Regency, so it is fitting that we should bring a little bit of it to life for you now. We had such fun coming up with our Fitzmannings.

We met in Williamsburg, Virginia, where this lovely, unruly family was born, and we spent months e-mailing each other and getting to know them better. I know that we have all thoroughly enjoyed the time we spent with Justine, Annalise and Charlotte. We sincerely hope that you do too!

Deb

To my Mom,
who loves a good novella! This one is for you.

Chapter One

Anticipation skittered down Ned Milford's spine. He could scarcely believe his luck. Cultivating an acquaintance with the unruly young men of the Fitzmanning Miscellany had been a stroke of genius, for now sunlight flashed off the shining wheels of his phaeton as he swept through the gates of Welbourne Manor. With pleasure Ned noted that the grounds appeared to be as elaborate, extensive and well maintained as rumour painted them. He could only hope that the rest of the estate and the notorious family it housed lived up to their scandalous reputations. He was counting on this trip to supply fodder for a month's work.

Beside him, his manservant shivered and out of the corner of his eye Ned caught the older man making a surreptitious sign against evil.

'What the matter with you, Cardle? You'd think those were the gates of Hell, the way you've been carrying on about this house party.'

'Might as well be, sir, if half of what I've heard turns out to be true.'

'Don't turn old womanish on me now, man. It's a right rare privilege to be asked out here. And you—of all people—should know better than to hold truck with gossip.'

'A little servant's gossip is one thing, sir, and there's usually no harm in taking advantage of such to fill your belly and warm your bed, but this place is another matter altogether.' Cardle's head had sunk between his shoulders and he looked about warily. 'You've heard the stories: secret meetings of dark societies, political intrigue—' he lowered his voice to a dramatic whisper '—and *orgies*.' He shuddered. 'I'd bet every stick and stone on the estate is tainted with years of debauchery and mischief, and likely a lot worse, that's gone on here.'

'Nonsense. If half of that were true, I'd have seen some sign of it in those boys. And I haven't. Perhaps they do possess a taste for scandal broth and a talent for mischief, but underneath it all they are naught but typical young bloods of the *ton*.' He raised a brow at Cardle. 'And that is no worse than I have been accused of.'

Truthfully, Ned had been surprised to find that he liked the young men. Nicholas, the newly minted Duke of Manning, had a more serious demeanour than his brother, droll Lord Stephen Manning or even his more earnest half-brother, Leo Fitzmanning, but they all possessed a sharp wit and an easy, comfortable way about them. They all quite obviously cared for each other as well, a quality that Ned had not experienced in his own family, and certainly had never come up against in his trawls through society.

'No,' he said firmly. 'This is a house party like any other. The only difference is the hefty sum that this one will bring us. Imagine the broadsheets that will come of this! If I don't witness a new situation to work into a caricature every day, then I'll eat my hat—and that doesn't even take into account the gossip that will be bandied about. We'll find material for many a print from this, I tell you, enough to keep Dubbock from our backs for a month or more.'

Ned glanced behind them, to where his meagre luggage was strapped. 'Speaking of which, you've packed my supplies in the saddlebag, have you not?'

'Yes, sir. Like always.'

'Don't let that bag out of your sight for a minute, Cardle. We'll have to be extremely careful here. These boys—indeed, all of the Fitzmanning Miscellany, if rumour is to be believed—are as wild as a kettle of cats—and twice as mischievous. If anyone could dig up the truth, it would be this bunch.'

Ned ignored the tiny part of him that wondered if perhaps that would be such a catastrophe. The secret delight he'd felt in his career as Prattle, the celebrated caricaturist, had long since faded. But his publisher's enchantment with the coin he brought in had only increased with his popularity—just as the *ton*'s curiosity had grown with each new broadsheet. Who could he be, the *beau monde* wondered, this man who caught wind of society's every sin and sketched it in exquisite detail? How did he learn of every secret rendezvous, each gaming-hell brawl, and every Bond Street snub? They loved to speculate, just as they delighted in the mockery of his pen and feared that they might somehow become its next victim.

Lord, but what an uproar there would be if the polite world discovered that the anonymous cartoonist was one of their own! Ned would likely be shunned as a betrayer of his class. He might even become as notorious as the family that had invited him here. And though he knew he could weather the scandal with little regret, it was always one simple question that stopped him from simply giving up his nefarious career: what the hell else could he do with his life?

He cast such sober thoughts away as he reached a gravel drive and drew his phaeton up before a gleaming Palladian villa. Just beyond he could see the sunlight glinting off the Thames. A groom came running to take the horses' heads. Jumping down, Ned had a few quiet words with him regarding their care. He was happy to see Cardle drape the saddlebag of supplies over his shoulder as a footman emerged from the house to help with the luggage. All in all, it was a disappointingly normal arrival at the infamous Welbourne Manor.

relling down on him. With a shout he jumped out of the way and the two chased each other around the entrance hall like a pair of puppies chasing their tails.

Oaths and dire threats echoed up the stairwell and before long curious servants began to gather upstairs and peer down over the railing. Far from alarmed, they called out advice from overhead and began placing bets on the outcome. Ned, delighted, paused on the first landing to take it all in. He had leaned against the banister to enjoy the spectacle and to plan the caricature he could draw of the frenzied scene—when he saw her.

He drew himself up, the chaos forgotten—perhaps because she looked so completely unaffected by it all. She leaned over the banister, her large dark eyes taking in the scene at a glance. Colour-stained fingers gripped the wood in front of her. For just a second, Ned felt the heat of her gaze drift over him. He stared, entranced by the faintest flicker of mischief on her otherwise composed face—and there he stopped. Her face. He'd never seen, let alone sketched, another like it. Wide cheekbones, high and proud. A lovely oval shape saved from perfection by a divertingly pointed chin. Loose dark hair, drawn into a long plait, made a lovely frame for a most interesting picture. His right forefinger twitched as he watched her. His mind whirled, already mentally setting her unique beauty to paper.

'Stephen,' she called. Her tone was calm, but firm.

Ned glanced down to see that the young man was poised to charge up the stairs, his brother in full pursuit.

'Don't do it, Stephen. You know it is bad luck to pass someone on the stairs.'

Stephen pulled himself up short. 'What?' he said uncertainly. 'What was that, Annalise?' he called.

'You'd do best to just give the letter back to Nick. The gentleman is wearing an opal in his cravat, Stephen. You don't want to risk it.'

All the uproarious mischief had drained out of the young man. He stared at Ned, horrified. 'I say, Ned, is your birthday in October?'

Amused, Ned glanced up at the poised girl, then back down. 'No, sorry old chap. I was born in April.'

Stephen backed away from the stairs. He handed the paper over to his brother, who snatched it and stomped away without meeting anyone's gaze. 'You're taking a risk, Ned, wearing that thing,' Stephen called. 'Never wear an opal if it's not your birthstone—it attracts the worst luck!' He shuddered. 'Go on up to your room and take that opal off straight away, there's a good fellow. Then I'll tell you what the rest of that letter said.'

'All right, then.' Ned smiled. He glanced up to congratulate the girl, but she had already gone. Something flickered inside of him, a whirl of interest, stirring to life. 'Stephen,' he called. 'Who was that?'

'Who was who?' Stephen asked.

Ned nodded upwards. 'Your sister, perhaps?'

'Oh, yes,' Stephen answered. He gave a negligent wave of his hand—as if a raucous conflict brought to a halt by a girl's few select words was an everyday event. 'That's just Annalise.' He cast his infectious grin up at Ned. 'God's teeth, but I'm glad you're here, Ned! We're going to have a bang-up time of it!'

'Yes,' Ned said with another glance up at the empty banister. 'I do believe you are correct.'

She was lost. Finally she had achieved that perfect state of concentration, that elusive blurring of time and identity. Annalise Fitzmanning no longer existed. She was nothing but light and colour and the precise stroke of the brush over canvas. Utterly content, she abandoned all sense of time, place and self.

Until the determined knock sounded upon the door.

She ignored it. It had taken her long enough to reach a productive state after the commotion in the hall, but at last the image in her head was springing to life under her hand. In any case, her siblings and all of the servants at Welbourne should know better than to disturb her in her studio.

'Annalise!'

She jumped. Her brush jerked, leaving a dis-coloured smear across her painting. 'Brenner?'

'Yes. May I come in?'

Annalise grimaced. Her half-brother had arrived

back from town early, which likely meant that he was fully immersed in his 'head of the family' role—and she had a good idea just what had set him off. 'I'll be right out,' she called.

'I would prefer to come in,' he returned.

She set down her palette in resignation. 'Of course, do come in.'

The door swung wide and Annalise sighed. Marriage had been kind to Brenner. His manner had lightened considerably in the last year, but at this moment he looked as dour as she'd ever seen him. He didn't enter fully into the room, but stayed in the shadow by the door.

'I had a visit from Lady Blackthorne this morning.'

'How nice,' she said blandly. She took up a knife and scraped away the discordant streak of paint. 'Justine and I only recently paid her a call.'

Brenner's gaze remained fixed on her. 'So I heard.' He crossed his arms. 'Annalise, you know that Justine and I wish for you to establish yourself a little in society. Justine chose to begin with Lady Blackthorne because of her connections, and because she has interests similar to yours. She is very proud of her art collection and particularly of the long gallery of ancestral portraits.'

'Yes, I viewed them when we visited.'

'She seems to think you did more than that. She said you painted black moustaches and devil's horns on all of her ancestors.'

'She said that?' Annalise set down the knife and

idly took up her brush again. She could see the tension in her brother's frame.

'Yes. Is it true?'

'No.'

His shoulders slumped in relief.

'I used charcoal. It will all brush right off.'

He stiffened again. 'Annalise! Why would you pull such a stroke? My God, you are nearly as bad as your brothers. Despite my lectures and labours, they are continually mocked in the damned broadsheets—and now you'll likely end up there as well! Do you not see? You've jeopardised your chances almost before you've begun!'

Annalise dropped the brush and rounded on him. 'Didn't Justine tell you how horrid Lady Blackthorne was?'

'Everyone knows how horrid she is! But she is a force to be reckoned with in society. Her good opinion is nearly essential.'

'Her good opinion is nearly unattainable—at least for me. We'd not been seated for five minutes before she began to rail about the loose morals of the highest nobility and how unsavoury it is for the rest of the *ton* to deal with the consequences.'

Brenner's mouth abruptly closed. 'She said that— to you and to Justine?' he asked after a moment.

'Yes. And worse—she said that it was perfectly correct for the Royal Academy to forbid female painters to show at the Summer Exhibition.'

Brenner rolled his eyes. 'Ah, *now* I begin to

understand.' He finally took a step further into her studio. 'Come, we must talk a moment. Is there a place for us to sit? It's hard to believe that this is the first time I've been in here.'

His gaze wandered and she saw him take in the bank of windows, the light and airy aspect of her hideaway, the organised stacks of supplies and blank canvases, and, at last, the rows of completed works leaning against the far wall. He kept his gaze politely averted from the painting she'd been working on, but she could sense his curiosity.

'Would you like to see Stephen's birthday present?' she invited with a sweep of her hand towards a covered easel. 'If you will promise not to tell, that is. I want it to be a surprise.'

'Of course.'

Annalise led him over. Her heartbeat accelerated as she drew the oilcloth away. She watched carefully for his reaction.

It was everything she could have hoped. At first his eyebrows lifted and his face lit up with the pleasure of recognition. Then he grew more serious and he stepped closer to the painting. For long moments he ran a searching gaze over it, until admiration broke through and shone clear in his expression. 'Annalise,' he said low, and the reverence in his voice filled her with joy, 'this is remarkable.'

She could not hide her pleasure. 'Thank you.'

'Truly, my dear. I knew, of course, of your passion, but I had no idea you were so skilled.'

She clutched the easel tightly. His words were like water to her parched soul, but she kept her face and voice composed. 'Do you think Stephen will like it?'

'How could he not? The blend of light and shadow, it is magnificent. I nearly expect him to walk off the canvas. And I can see that you have highlighted his superstitious nature. Though I don't understand some of the symbolism, I'm sure he will.'

Annalise shrugged. 'I meant at first to paint something more ironic—mock his beliefs a little. But I could not. Instead, I've used all portents of good fortune—he looks over his right shoulder at the new moon, he carries white heather, has a ladybird alight on his shoulder and coal has fallen in his path—all indicators of good luck.'

'He will enjoy the joke,' Brenner agreed, 'and he will be proud to show this off for the rest of his life.' He smiled his approval and Annalise's heart lifted. 'Do you have more?'

'Of course.' She led him to the rows of leaning canvases and watched as he spent long, silent minutes absorbed in her work. Annalise felt a surprising mix of agony, pleasure and satisfaction as she watched him. Pleasure won out, though, as the expression on his face told her what his silence did not, and it quickly turned to ecstasy when he finally turned to her and spoke. 'I had no idea. These cannot be hidden away in here, my dear. They must be seen.'

Bitterness stole away a piece of her happiness. 'But the Royal Academy…'

'Forget them.'

She blinked. Hope bloomed as Brenner abruptly turned away and began to pace along the east windows.

'It would appear that we've both been neglectful, Annalise. I have failed to discover just how deep your passion and talent run.' He held up a hand as she started to speak. 'And you have neglected to consider a life outside this studio. You have hidden behind your brothers and sisters for too long. I propose we rectify these problems with a compromise.'

She stood, still and silent. Waiting.

'I will do my best to arrange a private, invitational showing of your work…'

She could not suppress her gasp of delight.

'But you must agree to *try*, Annalise—try to envision and pursue a life outside the walls of Welbourne Manor.'

Her racing thoughts had still not moved beyond those magical words—*private showing*.

'I'm not speaking in generalities,' Brenner warned. 'I've invited Lord Peter Blackthorne to the house party.'

'Oh, Brenner,' she groaned.

'Just listen, please. He's well acquainted with your brothers, so it does not look out of the ordinary. He would make a very good match for you, my dear. He comes from the highest society, but he's a second son, so he would not lightly dismiss the money you would bring. Obviously he is not as stodgy as his mother, or he would not have accepted. He does share her interest in art, I hear.' Brenner sighed. 'Please, just give him a chance. That's all I ask.'

The vision of a showing hung, glorious and tempting before her. But could she do what Brenner asked? Annalise was not a stranger to polite society; she was just accustomed enough to know she did not enjoy it. Her mother had taken her about a bit, before she died. There had been snubs and cutting remarks then, too. And though her dashing, glamorous mother had laughed it off, Annalise had felt the rejection deeply. The Fitzmanning Miscellany was a joke, a blot on the shining surface of the *ton*. She had no desire to subject herself to more of their scorn and derision.

But Brenner had only asked her to give Lord Peter a chance. She hesitated—and in her mind's eye flashed a brief vision of the handsome stranger on the stairs this afternoon. Perhaps she wouldn't be so reluctant had Lord Peter possessed vivid green eyes and a smile full of wry good humour.

She waved the thought away. Lord Peter might have a sober demeanour and the unfortunate tendency to refer to his dinner in every conversation, but Brenner only asked her to give him a chance, not her promise or her hand. And she could face him here at Welbourne, rather than in the treacherous drawing rooms of the beau monde. Slowly she nodded.

'Good, then,' Brenner said with satisfaction. 'Lord Peter arrives tonight.'

Chapter Two

'You might as well stop right there.'

Ned paused, his pencil hovering over the rough sketch he'd started. He'd learned—the hard way—to listen when Cardle spoke with the Voice of Doom.

'Why? I think I've captured the devilry in Stephen's eye quite nicely.'

'There were no other witnesses to the event, sir. You and I were the only ones to see that particular scene. It would be a dead give-away.'

'Nonsense.' Ned pointed to the sketch. 'I took great care to include myself. See? Not too flattering an image, either. And just look at the gallery of servants gathered. Any one of them might have been bribed to describe the scene.'

Cardle heaved a morose sigh that perfectly complemented the Voice of Doom. 'No. They would not have been bribed. You were right, sir. We are going to have to tread very carefully while we are here.'

Ned straightened. 'Why? What's happened?'

'Nothing's happened—and that's at the heart of the problem.' The manservant shook his head. 'Things are not…usual…below stairs.' The manservant frowned.. 'I admit, I expected the situation downstairs to be as loose and debauched as it's rumoured to be above. Instead I've found the opposite, if you can credit such a thing.'

'Tell me,' Ned said.

'The maids are not giggling over padded corsets or freckle creams. The footmen are not making bets on who will be the first gentleman to cast up his accounts or to be found in a bed other than his own. They don't gossip at all—at least, not about the family. I was informed quite firmly that the upper servants have nearly had the raising of the young people and they won't hear a word spoken against a one of them.' Cardle rolled his eyes in Ned's direction. 'They were only too happy to discuss your rakish reputation, however.'

Damn. Ned pursed his lips and ran an appraising eye over the sketch. Unerringly, his gaze was drawn to the upper banister. He hadn't sketched Stephen's sister into the scene. He'd begun to, but his fingers had hesitated, and he'd suffered a strong desire to keep the vision of dark beauty, knowing eyes and that intriguing hint of mischief to himself. He'd drawn a maid in that spot instead.

With regret he flipped the sketch book closed. 'Oh, well, Dubbock likely would not have been satisfied with that one in any case. He made it clear he was expecting something racy to come from this house party.' He tossed the book aside and stood. 'But it's a damned good thing you found this out so early in the game. We'll both have to be careful not to make a fatal misstep.' Ned grinned. 'I'd give you a raise, if you weren't already so damned expensive.'

'I'm worth every penny, sir,' Cardle said, straight-faced, as he carefully laid out evening clothes upon the bed. 'Now tuck away your things, for the footmen are bringing up a bath.'

Ned did as he was bid and allowed Cardle to deck him out in full evening regalia, right down to satin breeches and a modest emerald stickpin in his cravat. He was grateful he had by the time the gentlemen joined the ladies in the drawing room after dinner.

The meal had been top-notch, the company genial and varied. Ned paused just inside the doorway. Satisfaction thrummed in his veins as he paused to let his gaze drift over the room. Nowhere else in England could he have come across such a disparate collection of people. In the corner the infamous Lord Rackham gathered gentlemen for a card game. Ned had heard at dinner that the old roué had been a close friend of the old Duke. Nearby sat Lady Brenner with a knot of eminently respectable ladies, and just a few feet from them stood a group of rakish London bucks. Politicians and profligates, lords and Lotharios… His jaw dropped. By the pianoforte stood a patroness of Almack's, and Ned could have

countess took Ned's arm. 'Have you met everyone, Mr Milford?'

Grateful to have the conversation turned, Ned seized his chance. 'No, as a matter of fact, I have not. Familiar as I am with the young men of your family, I've yet to meet the ladies.'

'Ah, well, let me remedy—' The Viscountess broke off in mid-sentence. 'Oh, dear.' She let Ned go and touched her husband's sleeve once more. 'Darling, Nicholas is wearing an incredibly sly and satisfied expression. I would guess he's dreamed up some sort of revenge for the trick Stephen played on him today. Perhaps you should head him off before we have a full-scale war erupting?'

Brenner made a quick farewell and left them. Lady Brenner watched him go before meeting Ned's gaze with a rueful one of her own. 'I do apologise, Mr Milford, but I think I had best go and send Stephen to request the tea tray.' Her eyes narrowed and her mouth curled. 'But Annalise is just over by the window. Why don't you introduce yourself? As you may have guessed, we don't stand on ceremony here at Welbourne.'

Ned hesitated and the lady's smile grew into a full-blown challenge. 'Come now, sir, my husband has branded you a hero. Annalise might have a slight reputation for being prickly, but surely you aren't afraid of a mere girl?'

'I'm no hero,' Ned said. 'But I'm enough up to snuff to know when I'm being manipulated by a beautiful woman.' He lowered his voice. 'And I'm enough of a cad to admit that I enjoy it.'

'I'm happy to oblige you, then,' the Viscountess answered in a conspiratorial tone. Her expression changed, just for a fleeting instant, as she gazed over at her sister-in-law. Concern, perhaps? Or worry? But then her smile was back as she lifted a brow in his direction. 'I wish you luck,' she said, and then she was gone.

He glanced back at Annalise Fitzmanning. She had turned her attention elsewhere. Here was his chance.

She noticed his approach. Ned could tell by the sudden acceleration of her breathing, the swallow she forced down and her determined effort to focus on the passing waiter, the group near her, anything *but* the direction from which he advanced. She was not smiling now. In fact, as he drew near—she bolted. Age-old instinct drew him to a stop. His senses heightened as she made for the door.

'Miss Fitzmanning,' he called.

She hesitated, but only for a moment.

He refused to chase her. 'Forgive my bad manners, but I'm afraid your sister-in-law made it impossible for me not to come over and introduce myself.'

That brought her up short. She turned to face him and, captivated, he stared. Up close her features looked irregular. The large eyes, oval face and pointed chin appeared to be somehow slightly mismatched—and yet terribly interesting.

'Insulted your manhood, did she?' she asked. 'I'm afraid Justine will go to any lengths to force me to meet an eligible gentleman.'

Ned blinked. When she spoke, everything changed. In animation the landscape of her face shifted, blended into a harmonious beauty that shocked him a little. He had the sudden, wild urge to make her laugh. He wanted to see what effect a wide grin and laughing eyes would have on that incredible face.

He bestowed upon her his most charming smile. 'That, and presented the assignment as if it were a Herculean task.' He leaned towards her.

She stiffened.

'Annalise!' It was one of the girls he'd seen flitting around the drawing room like a cheerful little wren. 'Won't you introduce me?' she asked with a sparkling smile in his direction.

'I might, if I knew the gentleman's name,' Annalise Fitzmanning said with irony.

Ned promptly bowed. 'Milford, ladies. Mr Ned Milford, at your service.'

'As Justine has already acquainted you with my name, please allow me to introduce my scapegrace of a sister.' A note of fondness crept into the lady's tone. 'Miss Charlotte Fitzmanning.'

The young girl bobbed prettily. 'Oh, but it is indeed a pleasure, Mr Milford. We've heard much of you from our brothers.'

Ned frowned with mock severity. 'Don't you believe a word of it, Miss Fitzmanning.'

Charlotte bit back a smile. 'As a general rule I disbelieve nearly everything they tell me. But as they were all unfailingly complimentary where you are concerned, I will make an exception.'

He bowed. 'Your generosity is appreciated.'

'Ah, but it is *your* generosity I mean to take advantage of, sir.' She tilted her head and gazed at him in a coquettish manner. 'Can I ask you for the loan of a small, personal item?'

'Charlotte!' her sister gasped.

'Don't grow all rigid now, Annalise,' Charlotte pleaded. 'You've planned a birthday surprise for Stephen, and I want to do the same.'

Amused, Ned watched the girl deliberately turn and twinkle up at him. This one was going to be dangerous in a year or two.

'Any little thing will do, Mr Milford. It's only temporary and it's for a good cause. My friend Miss Halford and I are asking everyone to help us.'

He was already unfastening his cravat pin. 'No gentleman could resist a request from such a charming young lady.' He winked at her. 'You should have asked for something bigger.'

'Perhaps next time I shall,' she said, clutching the emerald stickpin in delight. 'But this is perfect! Thank you, Mr Milford, you should have it back soon enough.' With a curtsy and a breathless giggle she was off to rejoin her friend.

Ned stared after her. 'A difficult age,' he remarked r sister. 'But she appears to be a lovely girl.'

No response. He glanced over to find Annalise staring intently over his head. He sighed as he realised that easy charm might have won over the younger Miss Fitzmanning, but the elder was going to require something more.

He puzzled a moment, until he saw that her focus was centred not over his head, but upon it.

Ah. Of course. Relief surged in his chest. He didn't stop to ponder why.

'Burnt umber,' he said.

Her eyes flew to his face. 'I beg your pardon?'

'My hair. Burnt umber, primarily, with a few streaks of mixed red ochre and bronze.'

She gaped at him.

'My sister is an artist as well,' he explained. 'Watercolours. She spent a long time experimenting before she got the colour right. I recognised the signs of your frustration.'

Her face closed suddenly, as if she'd shuttered the window to her soul.

He shrugged. 'All the men in my family are cursed with this shade.'

Her gaze strayed back to his head. 'It's a lovely colour,' she said. She hesitated. 'Would you mind…?'

'What? Oh, yes, of course. You wish to see it in the light?' Obligingly he took a step back, towards the nearest lamp and back again. 'Tricky stuff, is it not?'

'The way it changes… It's lovely,' she repeated. She snapped her mouth abruptly shut and glanced across the room. 'Justine told you that I am an artist?'

'No.' Ned laughed. 'She only warned me that you were prickly.'

The lady rolled her expressive eyes. 'She would.' She bit her lip. 'Then may I ask how you reached that conclusion?'

'I noticed the colour on your fingers earlier,' he gestured towards her now immaculate hands, 'when you so adroitly settled the fracas in the hall. And tonight when I entered, you stood a little apart, watching the others carefully. I could almost see you composing a scene in your mind.'

Her gaze narrowed. 'You are very observant, Mr Milford. Not many people see in such detail. Perhaps you are an artist yourself?'

He entertained a fleeting wish to tell her the truth. The whole truth. For the briefest moment he considered lobbing it like a mortar into the centre of the house party and letting the shards fall where they may. To be free of careful concealment, lies and pretence? It was a shimmering mirage of relief he'd never before contemplated and suddenly wished he could reach for.

He gave her a rueful smile instead. 'No, I am merely a student of human nature. Although I have a passion for art, alas, I lack the talent to truly create it.' He paused, surprised at himself. Though he'd ...ted that particular half-truth before, he'd never ... with such a wistful tone.

Just as he'd never received such a look of heart-felt sympathy in response.

'I did, however, collect quite an eager following in my school days, with my, ah…pointed… lampoons of our school masters.'

Now it was his turn to snap his mouth shut. That was a titbit he'd carefully kept to himself since Prattle's emergence.

'But oils in particular eluded me,' he said in an effort to divert her. 'Is that your preferred medium?'

'It is,' she said shortly. She'd become distracted as a brace of footmen entered the room, carrying an easel and what must surely be a covered painting. 'As you shall see soon enough. Do please excuse me.' She took a step away, but, hesitating, turned back. 'Perhaps I could give you a lesson in oils, some time during your stay.'

He should refuse. She stirred to life things in him that would perhaps best be left asleep. He should focus his attention on her brothers and concentrate on finding something that would please Dubbock.

'I would enjoy that,' he answered.

Annalise thought she'd been uncomfortable earlier, when Ned Milford had deliberately sought her out. She'd always thought of herself as the quiet Fitzmanning, content to lurk behind her more flamboyant siblings, to observe their interactions and record the best—and occasionally the worst—of them in oil and canvas. It was a restful role, as familiar as the stained smock she donned each morning, but one that left her feeling woefully inadequate when approached by a handsome, polished gentleman.

And he had, hadn't he? Deliberately sought her out, that is. Like a general surveying a field of battle, he'd raked the room with his gaze. She'd felt a surge of recognition when she had seen him making mental notes of the social terrain, but his intense green eyes had not faltered until they'd fallen on her. *Mission accomplished*, his body language had shouted, or perhaps *target sighted*—and he'd run that sharp-eyed gaze over every inch of her, in a completely masculine and leisurely manner.

It was puzzling. And exhilarating. Even as they'd spoken—empty social banter—she'd felt the weight of his narrowed gaze and the pulse-pounding, tingling response it had called forth. But then he'd guessed at her artistic interests and she'd felt something else from him—empathy and understanding. She'd nearly shivered at the raw, exposed feeling that had skidded down her spine.

And that had been as nothing compared to what she felt now.

For Ned Milford now stood, bent close in frowning concentration, directly in front of Stephen's portrait. And she, who rarely felt a moment's doubt regarding her own skill, had to wrench her twisting hands apart as she awaited his judgement.

In an attempt to distract herself, she turned away to examine the rest of the room. Stephen had adored the surprise. He'd laughed and hugged her and called for champagne to toast his sister's talent. Her family had been enthusiastic in their praise as well. Now she carefully eyed the other guests, but there were no dark looks or discontented mutterings. No one appeared to be offended or outraged at the idea of a mere girl presuming to paint. Annalise allowed a little of the tension to drain from her shoulders. Until she sneaked a glance over her shoulder back in the direction of the easel.

'I love it,' Stephen said, close to her ear.

She tried to control her jumpy nerves as he handed her a glass of champagne.

'I'll hang it in my rooms and gain a little luck every time I look at it, Annalise,' he said fondly. 'You couldn't have given me a better gift.'

'I'm so glad you like it.' She smiled at her brother. 'Though I was sorely tempted to go in the other direction and mock you a bit.'

'And perhaps you should have, at that, Miss Fitzmanning.'

She and Stephen turned to find Lord Peter Blackthorne heartily smiling down on them. Tall and proud, Lord Peter cut a dashing figure. But his thickening middle and the close-cropped style he adopted for his tight black curls made him look older than his five and twenty years. Annalise had met him on several occasions, and he'd always been attentive, if pompous in his manner.

'Many happy wishes on the day, Lord Stephen. I do apologise for the lateness of my arrival,' he continued, 'but I found myself unavoidably delayed on the road from London.'

'Not at all,' Stephen said in the same false hearty tone. 'Glad you could join us, my lord. Trouble with your cattle?'

'No, nothing so dreary. It's just that I stopped at the Red Hand in Walham for my nuncheon. There I had such a game pie as I've never before experienced. Such a light pastry crust. An exquisite balance of meats! Well, of course I had to have the receipt, and as I found the cook to be quite illiterate, there was nothing to be done but to have him make another while I made careful notes.'

Annalise bit the inside of her cheek.

'Nothing else to be done,' Stephen gravely agreed.

'Such a shame that you missed dinner,' Annalise remarked before Stephen could go further. She fought to keep the hopeful note from her voice. 'I'm sure we could have a light tray sent up to your rooms, sir.'

'No need, thank you. I've already done just that. Had the cook send me up a little of everything he served for dinner. I must say, he lived up to his reputation. I've long heard tales of the exquisite chef you keep here at Welbourne. French, is he not?'

'Signore Napoli is Italian and very skilled,' she assured him.

'As are you, dear girl,' he said with a stiff little

bow. He gestured towards the painting. 'Your work, I gather?' At her nod, he continued. 'Charming, indeed.'

He tilted his head and regarded her in a considering manner. 'Though I stand by my earlier remark. Perhaps you ought not to encourage your brother, either in his gambling or in his absurd superstitions. Do you know that I encountered him on Bond Street not long ago, in the most reprehensible state?' He leaned in close and spoke low. 'He wore his cravat untied and his coat turned inside out, right there on the streets of London!'

'I was having a bang-up run of luck!' Stephen protested. 'Would you have me risk it?'

'I would have you abandon such notions altogether,' Blackthorne replied. 'Certainly I would not have you expose the fairer members of your family to such nonsense.' He nodded at someone past Annalise's shoulder. 'Only let me ask Mr Milford and I'm sure he'll agree with me wholeheartedly.'

'Only if you are singing Miss Fitzmanning's praises.' The gentleman joined their group and reverently took Annalise's hand. She swallowed. Abruptly all the shivery feelings that had earlier run down her spine reversed course. A thrilling wave rushed up her back and lifted all the fine hairs on her head.

'I am humbled indeed, Miss Fitzmanning.' He bent low over her hand. 'If this is an example of your talent, then I cannot wait to see more.'

His words, and the smile that went with them, curled luxuriantly about her heart. 'Thank you,' she breathed. There was no good reason for his opinion to matter where others' had not, but there it was. It did. And she did not care to question it—not when he looked at her with such heat in his eyes.

'I cannot fault your judgement, sir,' Lord Blackthorne opined, 'but I take leave to caution you, Miss Fitzmanning. With talent comes responsibility. I am convinced you must wish to use your abilities to improve the world about you.'

What she wished at this moment was to use her skills to paint Mr Milford—in sun and in shadow and every shade in between. She longed to capture the glory of his hair and the chiselled planes and valleys of his face. And perhaps once she had, she might wish to touch him with her paint-stained fingers...

Annalise took a drink of her wine and recalled herself firmly to the conversation.

Stephen laughed. 'Annalise knows dashed little about the world about her, Blackthorne. She spends all her time in her studio.' He raised a hand to signal for a footman. 'Besides which, it's my birthday. Loosen your corset a little, sir, and don't prose on like somebody's mother.'

'Stephen!' Annalise objected.

But Mr Milford kept her from continuing. 'I'll disagree with you, Stephen, and venture to guess your sister is wiser than you suspect. Clearly she has eyes that see into the heart of a man. I think you'd be surprised to discover what she knows,' he told her brother.

'I take leave to disagree with you as well.' Lord Peter doggedly pursued his subject. 'I refuse to be offended, Mr Fitzmanning, since it was my own mother who taught me that we should strive to leave the world a better place than when we entered it. Your sister possesses the ability to move others, to perhaps sway their thoughts or emotions. That is an ability I fancy I know something about,' he said with humility.

'Aye, I have heard rumours that you have moved the Commons with your oration,' Stephen replied, beckoning again for the tray of drinks. He turned back, and finding Lord Peter's eyes turned modestly down, he mouthed, *to sleep*, and, closing his eyes, let his head drop to his shoulder.

Annalise bit down hard on her lip. Next to her, Mr Milford gave a violent cough.

'Your mother mentioned that she would like to see you pursue a political path, Lord Peter,' Annalise managed.

'Yes, she's a cousin to Lord Sidmouth, you might recall, and has long been after me to follow in his illustrious path. I admit that I was reluctant at first. I thought perhaps the Church might be a better fit for me and felt it was a perfectly respectable choice for a second son.'

Stephen raised his glass. 'I am in perfect sympathy with you, sir. Certainly I can see you exercising your skills from the pulpit and enjoying the simple pleasures of the parsonage.'

'Yes, but lately I am come round to my mother's thinking. Without doubt our government could make use of another voice in support of reason and order.' Lord Peter shot a loaded look in Annalise's direction. 'But there are other reasons. I confess I'm fond of fine things.'

'Such as fine chefs?' Stephen asked.

'Of course, but that is but one among many considerations. Women, in particular, are fond of large houses and larger parties and all the trappings that go with a life of social consequence.' His heavy, speaking gaze was still locked on Annalise. 'I've come to realise that a career in the Home Office is more likely to attract…er, I suppose I mean *support* such a lifestyle.'

'The Home Office?' Mr Milford repeated. Annalise thought she detected a current of irritation in his voice. 'Your skills must be great indeed—many men might wish to work for the government, but not many seek to aim so high.'

'Indeed, I hope that my skills will serve,' Lord Peter answered, his eyes still fixed on Annalise's face. She was beginning to grow more uncomfortable by the second.

'But of course I must prove myself,' he continued. 'My mother has consulted with her illustrious cousin and together they have devised some very specific trials through which I may prove my readiness.'

'Well, I'm sure we all wish you success,' Mr Milford said. Annalise noted with interest that his colour had grown higher. 'But that sounds uncomfortably reminiscent of my days at Eton.' He raised a brow. 'I do hope neither your mother nor her cousin will take a birch rod to you, should you perform lower than their expectations.'

Abruptly he turned and bowed low over Annalise's hand. 'As we are fortunately both graduated from the schoolroom, perhaps you will talk to me a little of the symbolism you've incorporated into your brother's portrait?'

Furiously fighting back a blush, Annalise agreed and laid a hand on his arm. With a nod toward Lord Peter's darkening expression and a twitch of her mouth towards her grinning brother, she allowed Ned Milford to lead her away.

Chapter Three

'Everyone, if I could have your attention?' Miss Charlotte Fitzmanning called. Mid-day sun bathed the marbled entrance hall as she dashed up the stairs to address the assembled guests, a fresh and pretty sight in her vivid green riding habit. One of her little pugs lay content in her arms, the other followed her, to collapse panting at her feet. 'Now that everyone has had their nuncheon, I'd like to share *my* birthday surprise for Stephen.'

'Are you going to give him Oliver?' Leo called out.

'No!' she exclaimed, cuddling the dog closer. 'It's something he will *enjoy*.'

'Perhaps you should challenge him to a race, then, Charlotte, and actually let him win.' Nicholas laughed.

'I'd rather she challenge you,' Stephen mocked. He and his officer friend—Captain Monroe, Ned recalled—had only just made their way into the entrance hall. 'It would indeed be a treat to watch her outride you once more.'

'Hush, you two.' She turned to the group at large. 'Some of you will know—what did Stephen enjoy more than anything, when he was a child?'

Around him in the crowd, Ned heard all of her brothers groan.

'Yes, indeed, a scavenger hunt!' she crowed. 'And it shall also serve as the afternoon's entertainment, so you may thank me instead of pulling such faces.'

Ned caught a few more moans added to the chorus, but at the foot of the stairs, Charlotte's friend Miss Halford gamely applauded.

'Well, I admit I was afraid of such a reaction,' Charlotte said with a grin. 'But I need your help.' She lifted the dog to face the crowd. 'You see, my Oliver is a bit of a magpie. He has a love of shiny things and the troublesome habit of taking them and squirreling them away. Some months ago, he hid a valuable necklace of gold and diamonds, and, despite our best efforts, we've been unable to find it. But with so many fresh eyes to help us today, we are sure to be successful.'

'Will the person who finds it be allowed to keep it?' called Lord Andrew Bassington.

Charlotte flushed a little. 'No—for it's meant to go to Annalise upon her marriage.'

Ned's interest peaked.

'But I will give you several reasons to play along,'

Charlotte continued. 'First, you will recall that two evenings past many of you loaned Miss Halford or me a small, personal piece of property.' She grinned at the resultant muttering. 'Yes, indeed, I've hidden them, and along with the diamond necklace, they will make up the list of treasures to be found. So now many of you have a vested interest in participating. The more who do so, the greater the chance that you will recover your possessions.'

Miss Halford began to circulate through the crowd, handing out lists.

'Second,' Charlotte said, 'the two players who find the highest number of items on the list will win a chance to engage Nicholas and Stephen in a rousing game of billiards tonight. The rest of you are cordially invited to attend a reading of my poetry in the drawing room this evening after dinner.'

Ned laughed. She'd hit upon a sure-fire way to get all the young bucks to play along.

'Should a *lady* place in the top two…' here Charlotte paused and shot Miss Halford a pointed look '…and should she not wish to play billiards, then she may reserve a dance with Stephen, or reserve the chance at some other boon from him.' Charlotte drew a deep breath. 'And last, but never least, I'm hoping to persuade Annalise to grant a sketch to the person who recovers the necklace. More information will follow, once I've tracked her down and browbeaten her into agreeing.'

Laughter rang out, and Ned saw that most of the

guests had been convinced to play along. With disgust he watched Lord Peter call loudly for a list. 'Where may we look?' the portly prig called.

'Anywhere at all,' Charlotte answered. 'Nowhere is out of bounds, save Annalise's studio.' She quirked a smile at Lord Peter. 'Certainly you may search the kitchens.'

'The bedrooms?' asked Lord Bassington.

'As long as you don't go alone,' Charlotte countered.

'I'll take the stables,' Nicholas stated.

Nearly everyone had entered into the spirit of the thing, but Ned found himself incapable of it. Guests dispersed in all directions, but he dragged himself up to his room to fetch his sketchbook.

Cardle was there, and already aware of the plans for the rest of the day. 'The staff don't hold out much hope,' he informed Ned. 'But they believe your best bet to find the thing is outside.' He handed Ned his book and waved him away. 'And if you don't find diamonds, you just might scare up a pair of lovers or two in the shrubbery. Dubbock would like that.'

It was likely true, but Ned couldn't drum up any enthusiasm for the prospect. Brooding and silent, he headed out.

This house party was not playing out as he'd expected. The Fitzmannings had casual manners and an exuberant enthusiasm, but so far he'd seen nothing remotely shocking or lascivious. That is to say—nothing useful.

The rest of the guests had been particularly disobliging as well. Those willing to gossip had shared nothing he hadn't heard before and the only thing remotely scandalous that he'd seen himself was Lord Rackham pinching the maids. He scowled. Now, could he find a maid in the south of England who had not already been pinched by the old rakehell? That would be noteworthy.

But truthfully, he had not been his normal, keen-eyed self the past few days. Prinny himself might have shown up and danced a jig on the dining-room table and Ned would have missed it. He'd been too preoccupied observing Annalise Fitzmanning.

There was just something…diverting about her. What a conundrum she was. Her brothers, in particular, accused her of spending too much time in her studio, teased her about her dull existence and lack of worldly knowledge, but Ned thought he'd rarely met anyone who interpreted people so accurately. Generally she hung back in company, but in more than one instance he'd seen her insert herself to smooth a social gaffe, or put a guest at ease. He didn't think anyone else noticed how much she contributed to keeping the tone of the party on an even keel.

She interested him—and as he reached the welcoming shade of the Welbourne home wood, he privately admitted that it had been a dreadfully long time since anything like curiosity had kindled within him.

He'd only gone a short distance from the house when he stumbled upon a lovely private pond. Sunlight shimmered off the water and over the grassy bank. At one end a pier jutted into the water and all about stood convenient groupings of shade trees. Flipping open his sketchbook, Ned settled against the base of a spreading maple. As he began to draw the charming scene before him, he tried to narrow down the point in his life when he'd become so unutterably bored.

It was true, wasn't it? It had been too long since he'd lost himself to interest or excitement. Not since his early days as Prattle, when scrying out the *ton*'s secrets had presented a deliciously naughty challenge. But he'd reached a point, somewhere since then, when he'd seen too much. In searching out the worst of his fellow man, he'd allowed himself to become tired and jaded.

It was a personal price he'd paid, and likely well deserved. But something about this house party was awakening him to just how steep it might be. Worse than that, though, was the echo of Viscount Brenner's words in his head.

We're struggling to secure the future of this family, and every broadsheet mocking their antics increases the odds against us.

For the first time Ned began to wonder at the price that others might have paid along with him.

Something rustled in the wood nearby. Ned recalled himself and glanced critically down at his open book. He stifled a curse. Not even when he'd begun to question the consequences of his work could he disengage from it.

He'd drawn a rough rendition of the landscape before him, but in the top corner of the page he'd etched out a figure. A detailed sketch of Lady Blackthorne, complete with a slender rod bent between her hands.

Disgusted, he tossed the book aside and crossed to the edge of the bank. For long moments he stared sightlessly, allowing the soft lap of the water and its reflected sparkle to soothe him. A pair of dragonflies danced across the surface, engaging in the most obvious flirtation he'd seen since he'd arrived. He snorted and as they shifted towards him he squatted to watch their antics. Gradually though, his attention shifted. There was something odd about the scattering of rocks submerged before him; a different sort of sparkle... Surely not? He bent closer to the water to investigate, reached—

'You've got her proportions wrong,' said a voice behind him. 'You need a little less in the front and rather more in the back.'

Ned whirled around. Annalise Fitzmanning leaned against the maple, her neck craned to examine the sketch he'd left on the ground.

'Lady Blackthorne, I mean. But the pond is lovely,' she said with a smile. 'And I particularly like the way you've captured the movement of the water.' She peered closer. 'That's very clever—your lines perfectly capture the moment when the little waves are about to break and spill over themselves.'

Panic thundered in his chest. Quickly he strode over and closed the cover—before she could catch sight of any of his other sketches.

'Thank you.' He breathed a little easier with the book in his hand. 'As you can see, I'm no artist, but admiring your work inspired me to try my hand at it again.'

'I didn't mean to intrude.' She heaved a sigh. 'It's a lovely spot, isn't it?'

Ned caught the wistful note in her remark. 'It is indeed. Would you care to join me?'

'Thank you, yes,' she answered with relief. Glancing back in the direction of the house, she found a spot beneath the shelter of the trees. As she settled herself, the fashionably low neckline of her blue camlet day gown gaped away from her a bit. It granted him a delicious glimpse down the front of her bodice.

A gentleman would take a seat and give up such a vantage. Instead, Ned leaned against the tree. He smiled. Ah, yes. This angle bared at least another half inch of her more-than-adequate bosom. 'Are you hiding, Miss Fitzmanning?' he asked. 'From everyone in general or someone in particular? I confess, I would never have thought to call you craven.'

'Sorry to disappoint, but I've just discovered a massive yellow streak running down my spine.' She grimaced up at him. 'As you would, too, were you to endure what I have for the past two days.'

He assumed a shocked expression. 'Surely you don't refer to Lord Peter's solicitous attentions? I noticed that he condescended to adjust your stirrup to the correct length this morning—'

'Yes, apparently I've been riding incorrectly for years,' she interjected.

'And, of course, I was present when he so kindly read you that lecture on the proper use of your talents.' He fought back a smile and crossed his arms in front of him. 'Should you not be flattered?' Leaning forward, he could keep his grin at bay no longer. 'He *is* on a path towards a life of social consequence, you know.'

'Flattered? Indeed, yes. Any woman would be— any one who does not mind being regarded as an obstacle on that path.'

He frowned. 'An obstacle?'

'Yes! Clearly *I* am the test that Lady Blackthorne and Lord Sidmouth have put him to.'

There was no helping it—Ned let loose a startled laugh. 'Do you think so?'

'Without doubt,' she answered firmly. 'It's obvious he's been asked to improve me—as if I were a shoddy estate he was interested in purchasing.' She rubbed her brow and looked up at Ned with a jaundiced eye. 'Besides my deficiencies in those areas you've mentioned, I've also been kindly instructed on the most elegant fashion to descend a staircase and a more efficient way to hold a battle-dore racket.'

'Ah, he's anticipating tomorrow's big tournament, is he?'

'Yes, and far too much else besides! The worst came this morning at breakfast, when I was informed that it is entirely unacceptable for me to dislike kippers.'

'Well, to give him credit, his borough is in Cornwall. All those fisheries, you know. It wouldn't do to offend the electorate.'

'Well, *I* am offended, and it is Brenner who is anticipating too much if he thinks I would quietly accept such a match!' she said with heat.

'Tell him all that you've told me and I'm sure he'd see the unsuitability of it,' Ned said easily. 'You cannot blame him, though, for wishing to see you settled in life.'

'I'm perfectly settled, and satisfied with the way things are.'

'But I thought every girl your age must be contemplating marriage. In fact, I rather expected you to be at the forefront of today's scavenger hunt. I understood the missing necklace to be yours?' He looked away, towards the water, before turning to gauge her reaction.

She held silent a long moment. 'Yes, mine on the occasion of my marriage.' Her fingers rooted in the layer of old leaves beneath them, all of her attention focused there. Perhaps she thought to find her treasure beneath them. His mouth curved. He cast another glance towards the pond and wondered just how to—

'The necklace belonged to my mother,' she continued. 'The conditions were set out in her will.'

'It's a handsome legacy she's left you, then. Are you not eager to have it found?'

'No.' She spoke sharply now. 'In fact, I was relieved when Oliver stole the necklace away. Part of me never wants the thing found at all.'

Perplexed, he kept silent. Thoughts of billiards and poetry danced in his head and he glanced rather longingly back towards the pond.

'You cannot understand,' she said with despair. 'My brothers and sisters do not, and they know—' She paused to breathe deep and let her gaze fall to her lap. 'They were raised in the same circumstances.'

Abruptly, Ned took a seat on the ground. He was close enough to touch her, but he carefully did not. 'I've siblings of my own, Miss Fitzmanning. I know perfectly well that they can look at the same object as you and see something entirely different.' He craned his neck to look in her face. 'Perhaps it might be easier to share your trouble with a stranger. Shared burdens and all that.'

She shook her head. 'No, you are unlikely to see... I'm sure you had a perfectly normal childhood.'

'Yes, indeed, if you count being packed off to

school at a tender age and then left to my own devices.' He grimaced. 'My father read me a list of behaviours deemed unacceptable for the family's good name and counted his duty done.' Shrugging, he coaxed, 'There, now I've spilled a secret. It would be bad form were you not to do the same. I promise I'm a good listener.'

Her head reared up. 'We've already established how well you see, Mr Milford. I suspect that if you are half as good a listener, then you could be very dangerous indeed.'

He hesitated. 'Not in this case. You have my word on it.'

She stared at him for a long time. He waited, and put the minutes to good use wondering if he'd ever seen so many delightful shades of brown as mixed in her eyes.

'I'm sure it's nothing but childish fancy,' she said eventually, with a wave of her hand. 'You see, our parents were gone from Welbourne for long stretches of time. For months, at times.' She made a face. 'I'm sure you're aware, Mr Milford, that my parents were *fast*, and extremely fashionable.'

'Only to the extent that the rest of England is aware.' Ned smiled.

'Exactly. And while they were off setting fashion, we children were left here, alone.' Her mouth drooped. 'I missed them dreadfully, for there was so much pleasure and delight and fun when we were together.'

Suddenly she leaned towards him and very determinedly met his gaze. 'You are aware of the nature of my parents' relationship?'

Mesmerised, he stared. And very nobly kept his eyes from straying downwards. 'Yes.'

Intent, she searched his face. For what? Judgement? Scorn? He could have laughed at the irony. She wouldn't find it in him.

Apparently satisfied, she withdrew a little. 'They were on their wedding trip when they died.'

He nodded.

'They were so happy. Thrilled to be truly together at last, and excited to be travelling back to Italy where they had first met and fallen in love. I was happy for them, of course, but not that they were leaving for another extended trip.' She sighed. 'When Brenner brought us the terrible news, I refused to believe it at first. Foolishly, I thought that if I did not accept it, that it could not be true.' Her eyes filled. 'It was easy to pretend that they were just off on another adventure, to convince myself that they would be back some day, wearing smiles, handing out hugs and extravagant presents, filling the house again with love and laughter.'

'And that will change if the necklace is found?'

'Yes.' Her head dropped. 'Every time I see it, I'll have to face the fact that my mother is never coming back.' Her voice lowered to a whisper. 'And that I'll never fulfil her expectations.'

'Her expectations?' Ned considered that. 'Miss

Fitzmanning, surely you don't think that Lord Peter will be your one and only chance at marriage?'

He recoiled from the sizzle of her scornful look. 'I'm the illegitimate daughter of notoriously scandalous parents, Mr Milford.' She gestured towards his sketchbook. 'And in the words of Lord Peter's mother, I have the amazing cheek to fancy myself a painter. Candidates for my hand are unlikely to be lining up at the gates.'

'Don't be so quick to discount your charms, my dear. Or the charm of your substantial dowry. Or even your brothers' influence. There are as many reasons to marry as there are marriages.'

She snorted. 'Oh, yes. Perhaps I shall marry for dynastic reasons, or perhaps for property or influence. After all, my mother entered a loveless, practical marriage the first time, and it worked out so well for her.'

He clapped his mouth shut. 'Well, you've routed me on that one. I can think of no suitable rejoinder.' He rose to his feet and extended his hand. 'And since that is the case, let me be the first to wish you a long and happy spinsterhood.'

Her mouth gaped open. And then she laughed.

And he froze.

This was the first time, Ned realised. The first time he'd seen her eyes light up and her mouth curl. The first time he'd witnessed her features melded together in glorious accord to produce exquisite beauty.

Unbelievable what a change came over her face. Unheard of what effect her throaty, rasping laughter had on his body. It pounded a beat upon his ear that was quickly taken up by his pulse. It echoed through him, finally taking up residence in his stirring nether regions.

So easily she did it, awakened these sensations within him—without any apparent effort at all. And she had called him potentially dangerous? Clearly the intelligent thing for him to do would be to steer clear, to leave her to the tender ministrations of Lord Peter Blackthorne.

'You were right.' She smiled up at him as she took his hand and climbed to her feet. 'I do feel better.'

Ah, well. When had he ever chosen the intelligent path?

He did not relinquish her hand. He used it to pull her in, close enough so that he could feel the warmth of her. 'At the risk of repeating Lord Peter's mistake and anticipating too much—may I ask if you'll be my partner in battledore tomorrow?'

Her smiled dimmed. Her breath came a little faster. His own had gone shallow, as if he'd just run a race—and lost. He ran his gaze over the appealing lift of her brow and the curious angle of her chin. His index finger twitched.

'I should like that,' she said.

His finger trembled again and he lifted it, traced the pink and tender shell of her ear, the unique sweep of her jaw. Her pulse leapt beneath her skin, triggering his own. Slowly he tilted her chin up, waiting for her to object, to step back, to slap his hand away.

She did none of those eminently sensible things. Which left him free to do the entirely impractical thing.

Baby soft, the skin of her lips. Her whole body trembled when he touched her there. Feather light, he opened her.

He leaned in. Her eyes closed, even as she stood straight against him, strung as tight as a bow. He pressed his mouth to hers. It was a soft kiss, sweet and chaste. And yet he was hot and hard and as ready as he'd ever been in his life.

She drew back a little. Sighed. Their breath mingled a moment before she slowly backed away.

'Oh,' she breathed. Her dark eyes were full of wonder and something that looked like fear. He took a step towards her, but she only shook her head. His outstretched hand fell to his side as she turned to disappear into the wood.

Chapter Four

Annalise had given Ned Milford the wrong answer. *I should like that*, she'd said when he'd asked her to partner him in Stephen's ridiculous battledore tournament. Wrong. Unwise. She definitely should *not* like that idea.

But she did. Despite the fact that she always avoided such play when people other than her family were present. Despite the fact that when she did participate, she nearly always teamed up with Leo or Charlotte. Despite the fact she was rarely comfortable associating so closely with anyone outside her own family circle.

But then, she wasn't exactly comfortable in Ned Milford's presence, was she? No, not comfortable— especially not since he'd *kissed* her. But that hadn't stopped her from reliving that incredible moment, from brushing her fingertips repeatedly against her lips, from practically wallowing in the sensations that he'd aroused within her.

It didn't stop her from partnering him, or from thoroughly enjoying it. They laughed in breathless fun as they batted the shuttlecock back and forth. He was athletic and graceful and Annalise blushed even as she struggled to work in tandem with him, to learn his body's cues as he wielded his racket with ease. They didn't win—Stephen and Miss Halford trounced the rest of them with an astounding two hundred and seventy-nine bats—but they acquitted themselves decently with a respectable eighty-four.

And before it was over she'd agreed to be his dinner partner. Later still, when Justine had the rugs rolled back for dancing, they danced a waltz together. And for the first time in her life, Annalise found her natural reserve had deserted her.

She suffered a wave of gooseflesh every time his arm brushed hers at dinner. She barely ate and rarely spoke, so busy was she breathing deep, absorbing the scent of him: soap, primarily, but she also detected a whiff of the spirits he'd had before dinner and something faintly metallic. She stared and stared at his hands, trying to fix their shape, their strength, the exact spacing of the masculine hairs on the back, for when she would paint him. For she would paint him, she knew, and hands were so difficult.

When he put his arms around her in the dance, all thought of painting flew from her head—and when was the last time that had happened? But rational thought held not a chance. She was too aware of his warmth, of the protective circle of his arms about her, of the tight wariness inside of her easing. Always, it seemed, there had been a part of her she'd held back, kept safe and protected. It opened, occasionally, when she was at work. But now she felt it unfurling and basking in the warmth of Ned Milford's smile.

She dared not show a bit of it, though. Annalise clamped down hard on her awakening emotions. She fought to keep her body from trembling and her face from reflecting all the tumult inside of her. Neither he nor her siblings must ever suspect how thoroughly he'd shattered her.

She discovered soon enough just how thoroughly she had failed.

'I'll admit it,' Justine whispered to her the next morning as she and Annalise arranged a mass of fresh-cut blooms from the garden. 'I thought he was little more than a charming rogue.'

'Who?' Annalise asked. She stabbed a rose into her vase and deliberately did not meet Justine's gaze.

'He's asked everywhere, of course,' Justine continued. 'And seen almost as many places as he's asked, but I admit I've heard some rumours of... high-spirited behaviour, shall we say?'

'Who are we saying it about?' Annalise asked again.

'He's been everything he should be this week, though. I find him quite delightful, in fact.'

Distinctly uncomfortable, Annalise shuddered at the sly smile that Justine cast her way.

'Certainly the two of you appear to be getting along swimmingly,' her half-sister said.

'Justine—' Annalise lowered her voice to a whisper again '—are you speaking of Lord Peter Blackthorne?'

'Heavens, no!' Justine tilted her head. 'Unless you find you prefer him, after all?' She shook her head. 'No, I was referring to your Mr Milford.'

Aghast, Annalise dropped her armful of greenery. Oh, Lord, she'd failed. Instant heat flooded her. Had all of her impassioned thoughts and inarticulate longings been apparent for everyone to see? But what did Justine—and all the rest of them—know? Not of that kiss, surely? 'Justine! He is *not* my Mr Milford!'

Justine bit back a smile. 'Just as you say, my dear.'

Annalise stared at her a moment. 'If you will excuse me,' she said hoarsely, 'I believe I've a canvas upstairs that needs stretching.' And with her face flaming and her heart warring between pain and pleasure, she retreated to her studio. She spent several hours there, pouring out her conflicted feelings in oil and girding her loins for what was coming. For if she was any judge of her family, Justine's comments were only the beginning.

Never had she been so sorry to be right. She was glad she'd prepared herself, though, for it was the only thing that kept her from spraying tea all over Charlotte later that afternoon. 'Are you going to marry Mr Milford?' her sister asked, all innocence. 'I think you should, for then Brenner will have to let me order that rose-coloured organza from Justine's modiste. It would be just the thing for a wedding.'

Later in the evening, Annalise merely blushed when it was Leo's turn. 'I knew you'd like him,' he said as they played at cards. He nodded across the room and she followed his gaze to the table where Mr Milford was taking his turn being fleeced by Lord Rackham. 'Never doubted it, since the day he dragged me to Mr Turner's gallery in Harley Street. Thought I'd never get him out of there—he sounded just like you, going on about form and shadow and colour.'

By the next day's picnic luncheon, Annalise was perfectly composed when Nicholas decided to chime in with his opinion. They were seated together on a blanket and her older half-brother was making substantial inroads on a plate of sandwiches. 'As handy with his fives as any man I've seen,' Nicholas said around a mouthful of devilled ham.

'Excuse me?' she asked calmly. 'Between the sandwich and the cant, I'm not sure anyone can understand you, Nicholas.' Now that was as big a lie as she'd ever told, but really, she was proud of herself. She'd almost become blasé by now.

'Ned, there.' He nodded over the sloping lawn, to where Mr Milford laughed with a group of Stephen's rowdy friends. 'A bang-up-to-the-mark sportsman. Good with his fists, rides like the wind, drives to an inch. I know he's only a younger son and not as important as some others see themselves.' He cut a look of disgust towards the next blanket, where Lord Peter was rummaging through a large hamper in search of Signore Napoli's special tarts.

'Ah ha!' Lord Peter cried. 'I thought I'd seen another in there.' Triumphant, he popped the pastry in his mouth and climbed to his feet. He crossed back over to them and wagged a finger at Annalise. 'Now do not dare move, Miss Fitzmanning, and do not eat another bite, for I have a special surprise planned for you. I shall fetch it and return shortly.'

Nicholas turned away as Lord Peter set off towards the house. 'Ned's a good man—and he don't mess around in the *demi-monde*, either.' He tossed back a long pull of lemonade and shot her a half-smile. 'Just thought you'd like to know.'

He was right—she did like to know. She hungered for information about Ned Milford nearly as much as she longed for him to kiss her again. But she could barely admit such a thing to herself. Never could she let Nicholas see a hint of it. She rolled her eyes at him instead. 'Unfortunately, the lot of you seem to be operating under a misunderstanding. Mr Milford is your friend, as I recall. Whether or not he queues up in the petticoat line is surely no concern of mine.'

Nicholas swallowed the last sandwich. 'Not the first to tease you about it, am I?' He shrugged. 'Don't take it the wrong way, m'dear. You know we all wish nothing more than to see you happy.' He tweaked her chin. 'We're just thrilled to see so much of you these last days.'

'It's not as if I'm a hermit,' she protested.

'Very nearly.' He grinned to take the sting away. 'Truly, has it been so bad?' he asked with sympathy. 'Have they all been after you?'

She gave it up and let her shoulders slump. 'Everyone but Stephen.' She looked out over the grounds. 'A hermit,' she mused. 'Peace. Quiet. Nature. I could have my own little cottage somewhere in the grounds, and pop out occasionally to scare the visitors.'

Nicholas laughed. 'Just what this family needs, another eccentric.' He craned his neck, searching among the people grouped on similar blankets and gathered down near the river. 'Speaking of eccentrics, where is Stephen? For all that he's the guest of honour, he's certainly been playing least in sight.'

'He's been spending a great deal of time with his friend, Captain Monroe. I heard Justine telling some ladies that the Captain is selling his commission.'

'Yes, I've seen Leo closeted up with them as well. He's been nattering about his horses, of course, and Stephan has been talking of nothing but racing courses. No doubt they've cooked up some misbegotten scheme between the three of them.'

'One that Brenner doesn't like the sound of, I'd say.' She'd caught sight of Captain Monroe staring fixedly beyond her. She followed his line of sight and pointed up the slope behind them to where Stephen and Brenner stood before a clump of shrubbery, huddled close and speaking low. As they watched, Brenner reared back in surprise. 'Race course?' she heard him say, incredulous.

'Oh, you're right. Neither of them looks happy.'

Justine, sweeping by their blanket, paused. 'Who doesn't look happy?' she demanded. 'And why not? It's a beautiful day, the company is genial and Signore Napoli's *pasticciotti* were divine.'

'The sandwiches weren't bad either,' Nicholas re-assured her. 'But we were referring to those two.' He hitched his thumb in their direction.

'Oh.' Justine's face fell. 'Well, it's true enough that Brenner is upset.'

'Why?' Annalise patted the blanket in front of her invitingly.

Justine sat. She leaned in close. 'This information stays in the family,' she warned.

Annalise duly nodded, her eyes widening. She supposed it would be wicked to hope that something had happened that would take the family's focus off her and her growing infatuation with Ned Milford.

'Brenner found Stephen kissing Mae Halford in the library last night,' Justine whispered.

'What?' Annalise and Nicholas let out matching gasps.

'My God,' Nicholas continued in a horrified whisper. 'Brenner will have the engagement announced in *The Times* by tomorrow and the banns read before the week is out.'

'No, he won't,' Justine said flatly. 'For Miss Halford has refused to allow it. She says that *she* kissed *him*, and she won't have him punished for it.'

'Stephen kissed an innocent girl and allowed her to take responsibility for it?' Now Nicholas sounded even more disgusted.

'There's more,' Justine said. She reached in her pocket and drew out a thick sheet of paper. 'This came in today's post.'

Annalise took it from her. It was a broadsheet, and quite well done, if one eyed it objectively. 'Oh, at least it's by that Prattle person. His are always a little more…gentle.'

This might be the one to prove her wrong, however. Amusing? Yes. Gentle? Perhaps not. It showed a hugely smiling Stephen strolling down Bond Street—stark naked. Luckily his important bits were covered by the money sack he carried. An appalled nurse covered her charge's eyes while the boy asked, 'Where's that man's clothes, Nanny?' In an elongated balloon, Stephen answered, 'I won the shirt off Harding's back, but I couldn't put it on, for fear of ruining my lucky streak!'

'Oh, Lord,' Nicholas whispered. He'd covered his eyes after the first glimpse. 'I'm not in there anywhere, am I?'

'No, just Stephen,' Annalise answered. 'Lord Peter told me he'd encountered Stephen on Bond Street with his linen askew and his coat on backwards. This is a gross exaggeration, of course, but how many people do you think might have seen him? Or do you suppose Stephen has gone about like that more than once?'

'What are you all whispering about?'

Annalise's heartbeat ratcheted as Ned Milford plopped next to her on the blanket. He'd got his emerald stickpin, back, she noticed. It served as a re-markable counterpoint for the lovely green of his eyes.

He smiled at her. 'Did you not hear Miss Char-lotte? Lord Bassington has been teasing her unmer-cifully about the failed scavenger hunt. She's lost her patience and challenged him to a race. Everyone's headed out to the summerhouse, as it's to be the finish line.' Gesturing towards the large group gath-ering on the riverside path, he asked, 'Will you walk with me?' He peeked at the sheet she held in her hands and abruptly the smile faded and his face went pale.

'It's not as bad as all that,' Annalise reassured him.

'It's bad enough,' Nicholas corrected her. 'People will be talking about this one all over town. And you know how Brenner has been harping at us all to toe the line.'

'Well, I admit I'm beginning to share Brenner's

frustration. Have they nothing more important on which to focus the acid of their pens?' Justine was all indignation. 'All this uproar over radicals, the unrest in Manchester and the north and still they must attack us? What could this Prattle mean, in portraying Stephen so?'

'It's just business, Justine,' said Nicholas. 'Caricaturists, engravers, printers—they produce these things to make money. Radicals sell prints, but the Fitzmanning Miscellany sells more. The only thing Prattle meant to do was to fatten his wallet.'

'Surely not,' Mr Milford protested. 'It's social commentary, no? Perhaps he meant to chide Stephen? Just enough to make him pause, perhaps, to think about his gambling? Or perhaps he meant to deter others from following that path.' He sighed. 'Or maybe you're right and he's just a selfish fool.'

'Perhaps he portrays the boys because he can show them a little sympathy without fear of arrest,' Annalise said with irony. 'That's not the case with radicals or unfortunate mill workers.'

'You're likely right,' Nicholas answered. He'd taken the sheet from her and examined it more thoroughly. 'But Prattle is not always so mild. He did that particularly scathing image of Miss Westby dancing on the table last year, do you recall? And Sir Thomas Jordan has scarce been seen in town since Prattle immortalised his unfortunate, uh, habits. We can only be thankful that he was feeling generous. He might portray us all as slightly ridiculous—and I admit we do at times make it easy for him—but he's not as vicious as the other caricaturists can be, portraying us as the spoiled, worthless products of debauched parents.'

'I don't believe Stephen will mind this one at all,' Annalise predicted. She tilted her head. 'Although he might wish the money bag had been depicted a little larger.'

'Annalise!' Justine scolded. She glanced over towards the river where a few stragglers still lingered before her worried gaze returned to her husband and brother.

'Stephen!' Brenner's voice rang out, suddenly loud.

'No, Brenner,' Stephen shot back over his shoulder. His angry response rang out as he stalked their way. 'This family's respectability is a heavy burden—and I won't let you lay it all on my shoulders. Or Nicky's or Leo's either.' He gestured back towards the villa. 'Not when Prinny spent so much time here dangling us on his knee and dallying with his latest mistress, not when Mama and Papa's antics made us all a subject of gossip and ridicule from the cradle.'

'Stephen, please.' They were all on their feet now and Justine was moving towards him.

Stephen looked up and realised that their argument had become public. It didn't slow him down. He gestured. 'Nicky and I may be legitimate Mannings, but we are painted with the same brush.

We are part and parcel of the Fitzmanning Miscellany.' He looked back again at Brenner. 'And that is no bad thing. Society is just going to have to accept us as we are.'

Brenner closed his eyes. 'A few months' quiet. Is it too much to ask? Long enough for your sisters to become established. Then you can open your damned race course or get up to any other half-cocked scheme you care to.'

Stephen let loose an ugly laugh. 'A few months? Not likely! Do you think that's all it will take to erase a lifetime of scandal? It's going to take a damned sight more than that!' He shook his head. 'Why are you worrying about this now, Brenner? Charlotte is too young to do more than giggle at a man. And Annalise?'

She flinched at the wealth of scorn in his voice.

'She's got more brains *and* courage than that fool you've selected for her. She's not likely to take him, Brenner. And then what? Will you thrust her headlong into the *ton*?'

Brenner had drawn closer. He looked over Stephen's shoulder and met her stricken gaze. 'Why not?' He spoke to her now. 'Shall I let her hide away here and waste her life?'

'Leave her be! Do you think to dress her in white and make a débutante of her? You'd just as soon shove a naked babe into a pit of vipers. She lives in her head, man! And in her fingers and her oil pots. She'll be cut, mocked, laughed at. Hell, she can barely manage life here at Welbourne. They'll break her. They'll shred her to ribbons and then she'll go to ground in her studio and never poke her nose out again.'

Annalise could not move. Each word pierced her, each an arrow destroying her newly expanding feelings of happiness and promise and security. Bad enough that they were shot by her brothers, the ones who intimately knew all the vulnerable spots of her soul, but they'd done it in front of Ned Milford, too. She let out a long, shuddering breath. Is this how her family viewed her? Did they all think her helpless? Defenceless? A coward?

Stephen must have heard her. Or perhaps he reacted to the stunned, uncomfortable silence of the people around him. He glanced back, saw her and flinched.

'Oh, Lord, Annalise. I'm sorry,' he whispered.

'Annalise,' Justine said softly. She reached for her.

Annalise stepped back, away. They all stared at her. She gasped for breath, reached for something to steady her. But there was nothing. It was her worst nightmare. All of them, they saw her now. Her every flaw and fault stood on open display.

'I have returned!' Lord Peter came from the direction of the house, a covered tray in his hands. 'And I've the surprise I mentioned, right here.'

No one answered him. They all stood frozen, as if in some hideous tableau. *The Mortification of a Girl*, it might be called.

Lord Peter didn't appear to notice. 'I know that you believe you do not like kippers, Miss Fitzmanning, but *I* believe it is only because you have not had them properly prepared. I've talked with Signore Napoli and shared one of my own cook's receipts. These have been stuffed with a delicious mix of chopped eggs and herbs.' He swept the lid from the tray. 'Just take a look at that!'

A horrible stench arose from the tray. 'No, thank you, Lord Peter.' She managed to choke the words out around the hard fist of despair and anger solidifying in her stomach.

'But I insist you try it!' He found a fork on the tray and, using it to spear a kipper, he waved the horrid thing under her nose. 'I am convinced that in this matter I know better than you. Come, then. Give it a chance,' he urged.

The anger pulsed. It moved, suffusing her with rage and indignation, exploding out of her in a flurry of movement. 'I don't want your kippers, Lord Peter!' She smacked his hand away from her face and felt a surge of satisfaction at his shocked expression. 'Nor do I want your advice, your instruction or your attentions.'

His mouth opened. It closed, and then opened again. 'Why, you ill-mannered little shrew!' he wheezed. 'I warn you to take care, Miss Fitzmanning! You put your very future at risk.'

Annalise pushed roughly past him and his foul tray. He reached for her and lost hold of the thing.

It rocked, he swayed and it was gone. Kippers flew in every direction and slithered down the front of him. White egg smeared his waistcoat and green herbed sauce dripped from his coat sleeves, even as the platter crashed at his feet. He burst out in indignation, but she did not stay to listen to him bluster.

She pointed a finger at Stephen, watching in awe like the rest of them. 'And I do not want your apologies, either.'

Turning her back on them all, she stalked off.

Chapter Five

Ned breathed deeply and reached for calm. How quickly a peaceful afternoon had become a muddied, mortifying tangle of emotion. He took a step, intending to go after Annalise Fitzmanning, but something, likely the anger he felt on her behalf, gave him pause.

'It seems we addressed many injustices here today,' he said aloud to the stunned group. He glanced towards the still-sputtering Lord Peter. 'And witnessed at least one well-deserved set-down. But aside from my own faults, the worst I've seen is your collective blindness regarding your sister. If any of you had paid half as careful attention to her as she does to all of you, you'd see how insightful and caring she is. Reserved and quiet, yes, but also wise. And vulnerable.' He looked at Stephen. 'I would ask that you consider celebrating those qualities instead of disparaging them.'

He turned on his heel and left them behind.

He went to her studio. His first thought was that she would retreat to its safety. But though he knocked loud and long, there came no answer. He attracted the attention of a maid, eventually, who informed him Miss Annalise was still outside with the party.

He considered the matter. He thought it highly likely that she was inside, ignoring him. But if she was not, then where would she be?

He had not even finished the mental question before his boots were pounding down the stairs.

He found her there, at the pond. He paused at the tree line to watch her. Agitated, she paced, from the bank to the maple they had rested against—and kissed beneath—then back again.

She turned, and caught sight of him. 'Please, go back.' She rubbed her brow. 'It was kind of you to follow. And a little unnerving that you found me so quickly.' Grimacing, she begged, 'But truly. I need to be alone. I have to *think*.'

Ned didn't want to leave. Pale and shaken, she'd wrapped her arms about herself. But her jaw was set and her chin thrust high. He longed to stay. He wanted to be there when she plumbed her own depths and found her strength. He wanted to observe the moment that she discovered herself—and rejoice in it.

He forced himself to turn and go.

'Wait!' she called. 'Tell me—did you look for me at my studio first?'

'Yes,' he admitted, though he knew what it said about them both.

'I started to go there first. It was instinctive.' She turned pleading eyes on him. 'It's my sanctuary, you see.' Her intriguing features hardened. 'But Stephen is right about one thing. I can't hide away there for ever.'

She fell silent and he turned to go.

'I just want someone to know—' She stopped herself and breathed deeply. 'No. I want *you* to know—I'm not afraid of life.' Her teeth gnawed at her lower lip. 'Well, perhaps I once was.' Her tone turned savage. 'But I had already set out to conquer it *before* Stephen insulted me in front of everyone.'

Ned's breath hitched. She was full of spit and fire and newly minted courage. He found it every bit as beautiful as her rare smile.

'I know you won't believe me,' she said. 'Especially after all that I told you when we were here last.'

He summoned his own courage and crossed over to her. He gathered her hands in his. 'I believe you.'

Distraught, she gazed up at him. 'Why?'

Reaching up, he ran a knuckle along the soft curve of her cheek. 'I see the truth in your eyes, in the determined set of your jaw,' he whispered. 'I feel it in the clench of your hand.'

She didn't look convinced. He searched for something to assure her. 'I wanted to open an art gallery, once.' It was out before he knew he meant to say it.

'What?' She looked confused.

'I told you, it was hard when I realised that, despite how much I loved art, I didn't have the natural talent to create it. Do you recall?'

She nodded.

'Well, when the Dulwich Picture Gallery opened, I was struck by the beauty of the idea: a gallery for the public. A small space in which anyone could feel comfortable enough to come and appreciate art. I thought surely I could do something similar, perhaps I could host temporary displays of different mediums: engravings, pottery, furniture, along with the work of artists that the Royal Academy wouldn't consider.'

'Why didn't you do it?' she breathed. 'Open your gallery?'

'I was young at the time, just out of Oxford. I had inherited a house in town that I thought to use as the gallery space.' He sighed. 'But my father wouldn't hear of it. He didn't want the family name dirtied by something that smacked so much of trade. When he couldn't dissuade me, he used his influence to block the permits that I needed to convert the space.'

'What did you do?'

'I sold the house. I suppose I could have used the money to buy another, smaller space, and proceeded on my own, but it would have meant being cut off completely from my family and the world I grew up in.' *So I set about showing my father how ridiculous the world he valued so much could be.* He lifted a shoulder. 'I didn't want to be alone in the world. So you see, everyone is afraid of something in life.'

Her eyes narrowed. She drew a deep breath, exhaled heavily. He could almost see the gears turning in her mind. What scheme was she hatching now?

He nearly recoiled in shock when she swiftly stepped forward. Her hands slid from his, encircled his waist, and crept up his back. He opened his mouth. To protest? It didn't matter, for she pressed hers home.

Thank God she had. She tasted of salty tears and sweet lemonade, of eager innocence and fierce desire. He wrapped an arm about her, steadied her and pulled her in close. The other hand cradled that wondrously pointed chin.

She remembered. Her lips opened willingly. Restless hands fluttered over his back as their tongues entwined. Gently, he tutored her. Quickly, she learned the dance, stirring his desire with her seductive artlessness.

Taffeta rustled as their breath quickened. Ned's hand slid from her jaw, nestled at the curve of her neck and shoulder. Her pulse beat beneath his fingers. His own kept time with hers, and with the faint throb of his cock.

He trailed his fingertips along her collarbone, and then down. His hand curved about the sweet abundance of her breast—and he realised what he was doing.

He pulled his hand and lips away. Panting, he rested his forehead on hers. 'We have to stop,' he said thickly.

'Someone might come,' she agreed. She stepped back and clasped his hands once more, clutching them close to the quick rise and fall of her bosom. 'Mr Milford.' She laughed suddenly. 'I think perhaps I could call you Ned?'

He smiled. 'Of course.'

Her laughter faded. 'I promised you a lesson in oils, did I not?'

'You did. But time runs short. I won't hold you to it.'

'Tomorrow is the last full day of the house party.' She hesitated. 'Might you extend your stay a little?'

Lord, but he wanted to say yes. But what he wanted and what was best for this remarkable girl were worlds apart. He recalled the sickening ache in his stomach when he'd found her holding that damned broadsheet. 'I regret not.'

Her jaw hardened. 'Then it will be tomorrow,' she said with determination. 'Will you come to my studio in the afternoon?'

He swallowed. 'I should not.'

'But you wish to?' she asked in a whisper.

He nodded.

'Then come. I'll expect you early in the afternoon. While the light is still good.'

It took Annalise all morning to prepare. She asked a maid in to scrub the studio until it shone. She spent a great deal of time mixing just the right shade of burnt umber. And then she went to see Brenner.

She found him at his desk in the bookroom, working his way through a pile of correspondence. She paused on the threshold. So many times she'd come here in the last year, seeking solace, advice or just company. In her mind, this room had become the centre of the house, just as Brenner and Justine's happy marriage had become the heart of their family. She squared her shoulders and took the seat across from him.

'Are you going to renege on your offer of a private showing,' she asked without preamble, 'now that I've run Lord Peter off?' Leo had reported the details of her erstwhile suitor's departure with relish.

Brenner sighed. 'Of course not.'

'Good. Because though he couched it in loathsome terms, Stephen was right. I'm no simpering miss. I never will be. If society is to accept me, they must take me as I am.'

'And if they will not?' he asked quietly.

She shrugged. 'I've discovered that there is more of Mother in me than I had believed. I'm ready to take what I want, and society be damned.'

Brenner set down his quill. 'We'll try it your way.' His focus shifted to his fingers, fiddling with a chunk of sealing wax. 'Nicholas has agreed to let us use Manning House. We will make it a select affair. The invitations can go out as soon as you are ready.'

Annalise stood. 'I'll start choosing pieces today.'

'Annalise,' he called as she turned to go, 'I'm sorry it turned out this way, but I'm not sorry we tried.'

'Neither am I.' She paused, crossed behind the desk and pressed a kiss to his cheek. He leaned into it and she gave him a crooked smile. 'I'm ready to stop hiding in the studio, Brenner, but I'm going after the life that *I* want. And I'm still not coming down to the last dinner tonight.'

She left him, her determination growing with each step. Damn Stephen, anyway. She was going to prove to him, and to herself, that she was done with hiding and fear. She was going to reach for life with both hands, and the first thing she planned to grab was Ned Milford.

It felt odd, welcoming Ned into her studio. Maids aside, only Brenner had been here in the last six months or more—and that encroachment had led indirectly to today's. Annalise had to clamp down on her growing excitement, for she was determined that this incursion would lead to even greater things.

'It's no wonder you spend so much time here,' he said, reverent.

She gazed in satisfaction about her lair, awash in light and colour, smelling of turpentine and soap, filled with all of her favourite things. 'I knew you would understand,' she answered.

She walked him through, showing him everything. They happily debated which London shop offered the best supplies and what might be achieved using watercolour techniques with oils. At last they reached the centre of the room, and the two waiting empty canvases. Ned's ease visibly faded.

'Every artist begins at the same place,' she said simply.

'You must prepare yourself to be disappointed.' He peeled off his coat and reached for the smock she'd left out for him.

Annalise crossed over to the door, standing correctly open. Deliberately she closed it and turned the lock. Pressing her back against the wood, she met his gaze. 'I promise I will not be disappointed, if you will not.'

His expression tightened. A long, drawn-out moment passed as he met her direct stare.

Never had she felt so resolute—or so vulnerable. She stood stock still, allowing him full view of every yearning, every ounce of determination coursing through her.

His eyes softened, then blazed hot. He did see— and he accepted. Tension built between them as he approached her.

Heart pounding, she waited. But Ned merely took her hand, brushed the lightest caress across it and brought it to his mouth. All the tiny hairs on her arms and the back of her neck raised in salute to his skill.

'Let's have that lesson first, shall we?' he asked, low.

She heaved a sigh, and agreed.

'Now,' she began, all business again as she donned her old, stained smock, 'a real teacher would insist that you begin with something still, something simple. But this is meant to be fun. Do a few sketches first, but draw what you like.'

His fingers flew over a sketch pad. 'I'd paint you, if I could do you justice,' he said wistfully. 'As I cannot...' He turned the pad and showed her a remarkable likeness of Oliver, a rope of diamonds in his mouth, looping and dragging between his legs. 'They never found them?' he asked softly.

She shook her head. 'No. Everything else was found, including your stickpin, I noticed. Miss Halford trounced everyone and won the contest—we suspect in an effort to get Stephen alone. But the necklace is still missing. And it is just as well,' she said dismissively. 'Now, do you have any other ideas?'

She talked and demonstrated and he listened carefully and understood quickly. 'You have the oddest set of skills and weakness,' she said some time later. 'You continually use the shallowest perspective, but your lines are so bold and fluid.' She held up the sketch of Oliver. 'I can nearly see him trotting away.' She picked up another, an image of Stephen and Miss Halford playing at battledore. 'Here, the swish of the racket is almost audible.' She peered closely. 'But you've oddly exaggerated their fingers and limbs.'

A sudden, loud knock upon the door kept him

from answering. Annalise's breath caught. 'Did you tell anyone you were spending the afternoon in here?' she whispered.

He shook his head. 'I told Cardle I was riding in to Richmond.'

'Annalise, I've brought you a tea tray.'

Justine. Annalise kept her eyes locked with Ned's and called, 'Thank you, dear.' She made her voice trail absently. 'Could you leave it? The door is bolted, I'm right in the middle of something and I don't wish to stop.' All true enough.

'Please, dear. You cannot stay cooped up in there all day. Brenner says you won't be at dinner—at least come down for tea.'

'I'm sorry.' Impatience this time. 'I cannot lose the light right now. And I'm spending the evening choosing pieces for the showing.'

Her half-sister's sigh sounded loud even through the door. 'Don't neglect to eat, at least. I'll leave the tray. I promise there's nary a kipper on it.'

Annalise laughed. 'Thank you.'

Ned made a move towards the door, but she held up a finger. Several moments passed before footsteps sounded, moving away. She grinned, and putting a finger to her lips, went to fetch the tray.

He put down his brush and stretched as she returned with it. 'Shall we have it while it's hot?' she asked brightly

'That depends.'

She arched a brow in question.

His eyes were roaming over the stacks of paintings turned against the wall. 'On how long you plan to torture me.'

She bit back a grin. 'A little longer, I thought.'

He turned a pleading look in her direction. 'You are going to let me see them, are you not?' He narrowed his gaze. 'Or are you afraid?'

She glowered at him.

'Please, Annalise?' He cocked his head. 'But start with something early and flawed before you work up to your best. I don't think my pride will bear it, otherwise.'

She didn't do as he asked. Instead she left the tray and hovered, undecided, until finally she brought him a piece that filled her with pride and trepidation all at once.

He didn't say a word. He stared and stared and eventually he reached for it, pausing to ask silent permission before taking it from her and moving to the window. He absorbed it in silence for some time and then he turned to her.

'Can I see the others?'

Her heart in her throat, she waved permission.

There followed the most nerve-racking hour of her life. In absolute silence he examined one painting after another. Annalise rather thought he'd forgotten she was there. She paced a bit and bit her nails. Finally she clasped her hands and slid down the far wall, settling in a nervous heap to wait.

Only when he'd seen every one did he turn to her.

For a moment he spun about, searching for her. She couldn't call out, couldn't move, could barely breathe as she waited for his reaction.

He spied her at last. 'You've never shown these to Stephen.' It was not a question.

That was it? Her heart fell to her feet and she shook her head.

'No one who has seen these,' he said fervently, 'could ever think for a moment that you are afraid of life.'

A thread of hope began to unravel. 'They aren't… grand.'

He'd spun back around to look at the lot of them. 'Not in subject matter, perhaps. Although I shudder to think what you could do with a history or an allegory…' He trailed off, but shook himself back into the present. He crossed the room, took her hands and pulled her to her feet. 'Annalise. My dear. These are indeed grand—not only in execution but in your incredible ability to make the viewer *feel* right along with the subject.' He rolled his eyes. 'Afraid of life?' he scoffed.

'Come.' He dragged her over to the easel, where he'd removed his own attempt and placed the first work she'd shown him. It was a simple scene, but one that had touched her—a moment she'd observed in the kitchen gardens between a maid and a footman.

'They are secret lovers, yes?'

She nodded. 'I'm afraid our butler doesn't condone relationships amongst the staff.'

'How did I know that?' he demanded. 'Because you've made it possible for me to experience everything right along with them. Good heavens, the protectiveness of his arm, the coy slant of her body. I look at it and *I* am in an illicit affair. All of it, the tenderness and desire, the trepidation, mixed with excitement at the possibility at being caught out—they all pour right off the canvas and into me.'

He shook his head. 'Afraid of life? I can't stop laughing at the irony. You had to open your heart and live and breathe every emotion you've depicted here. I don't see how you could have portrayed the moment so accurately without examining it, picking it apart, *living* it, even as you captured it on the canvas.' He gestured to the rows of paintings beside them. 'And you've done it again and again. It's all here. Hate and rage, laughter and joy, and everything in between. All the moments that make up a lifetime of emotion.' He reached up and cupped her face in his hands. 'You're the bravest person I've ever met.'

Incredible pleasure, intense relief, a great swell of gratitude—they mixed inside her so intensely it felt like pain. She opened her mouth, but only a choked sob came out.

He pulled her tight, holding her close against his solid, reassuring warmth. 'Don't you dare cry.'

'I can't help it,' she sputtered. 'No one has ever understood, not the way you do.' She struggled for control and raised her face to his. 'I'm so happy it hurts. I don't know how else to let it out.'

He pulled back. Compassion lived in his eyes, but the rest of his face had gone suddenly stark with the slow, coiling burn of want. 'I'll show you how,' he rasped.

There was no gentleness, no coaxing about him this time. Thank God. So many feelings boiled inside her, many long repressed, some startlingly new. She had to find a release or go mad with it. And Ned led the way. He bruised her mouth with wild heat and blazing passion. Willingly, Annalise followed. She moaned, drank in his desire, returned it in kind and asked for more.

Bold hands roamed over her. Fierce joy lit her up. *Whole.* This was exactly what she needed. Everywhere he touched, he smoothed a ragged edge, filled a missing piece—and made her complete.

'The window.' His voice had gone rough with desire. 'Move away before we're seen.' He trailed a hand down her arm and pulled her deeper into the room.

Annalise had planned for this. Earlier she'd stacked the old couch in the corner with several rolls of paper and a few small boxes. Nothing conspicuous, but all easily swept aside in a moment of passion. She grasped his hand and drew him towards it.

Except that Ned wasn't going to make this easy. 'God, Annalise,' he groaned. 'You've turned me inside out with wanting you.'

'Good,' she said, pressing herself close.

'But we both know what we're about.' He closed his eyes as she ran her hands over his shoulders and across his back. 'You are…incredible. I admire every damned thing about you.' She'd reached his buttocks and began to explore. He groaned and tilted his pelvis forward. The thoroughly satisfying evidence of his desire pressed into her belly. 'I never thought to consider marriage…' He groaned. 'But I can't give you what you want—what we both want—until you're considering it too.'

Her fingers pulled lightly now at the folds of his cravat. 'I'm considering the marriage bed.'

He choked out a laugh. 'Close enough.'

He bent down and kissed her hotly once more. His touch transformed her, making her a stranger in her own skin, and she celebrated it. Suddenly *she* was the canvas, stretched tight and ready to be painted by his hand.

His fingers took their cue from hers and attacked the buttons at the back of her gown. Annalise reached behind her to sweep the supplies off the couch and stepped back, hitching one leg upon it. In moments he had her bodice open and her stays undone. With his feverish help she wriggled quickly out of the rest of her clothes.

Enraptured, Ned laid her back. He stared at her, spread out before him like a Michaelmas feast. 'I didn't think anything could be more beautiful than your work,' he whispered.

She smiled, but he caught the shine of tears

welling in those enormous, dark eyes. 'No crying,' he admonished. He sat down beside her and began to struggle out of his boots. 'Had I known we were going to do more than paint, I would have told Cardle I was planning on swimming in the pond.'

The last boot popped off and he turned to her, marvelling. This house party could not have strayed farther from his expectations. It had changed the course of his life. Perhaps later he would be nervous about it, but right now he felt nothing but elation. He reached out and trailed a finger down the soft skin of her side. 'I have something important I must address in town,' he told her hoarsely. 'And when it's done I'll be back to talk to Brenner. Make no mistake,' he warned, 'this is a pledge we make to each other today.'

She reached for him. 'Too much talking.' She wound his shirt in her fists and pulled him down to her. He went willingly. She was all lips and tongue and smooth, creamy flesh, and he was the luckiest man in the world.

At last he touched her, exploring her lavish curves, teasing the soft, pink tips of her breasts. She gasped when he closed his mouth over one taut peak, and he played her like an instrument, coaxing soft sighs and sharp cries with his biting lips and wandering fingers.

He was hers. He knew it more thoroughly each time she moved and tightened under his hand. And she was his, hot and wet and ready when he tested the lovely mound of curls between her legs.

She gave him no chance for subtlety. Nothing was left between them but burning need. Her urgent hands encouraging him, he pressed himself home— and met the first sign of uncertainty from her.

'Oh, Lord,' he said. 'I'll stop.' *Somehow.*

'No. Don't.' She gripped him tight, inside and out. He felt her body shifting, accommodating, and she wiggled underneath him. 'Now,' she urged. 'Please.'

Yes. Please. He was awash with pleasure, lost in sensation. He began to rock, leisurely at first, until she responded, rising up to meet him stroke for stroke. He quickened the pace. Her eyes were closed, her face shone, a mask of concentration. Ned reached between them, found the hard little centre of her desire and made its pleasurable acquaintance.

He felt the approach of her climax before she did. She trembled, tightened and her eyes flew open, lustrous with surprise and uninhibited joy. She breathed his name with reverence.

He couldn't answer. She'd pulled him in even deeper than before. He arched his back, lifted her high and surrendered to her. And it was a surrender. He exploded, knowing it was a pledge of all that he was, all that he would be, and wishing at the same time that she could know how happy the giving of it had made him.

He had just enough awareness to shift his weight off her before his brain lost function. When he returned to himself, her fingers were moving softly across his chest and her gaze was fastened on him with an ominously familiar look.

'Oh, no,' he exclaimed. 'You are not to consider painting any of this.'

She frowned. 'A pencil sketch?'

'No!'

She pouted. 'I want to remember, always, how wonderful this was.'

'I'll remind you.' He placed a kiss on her chin. 'Any time you wish.'

Chapter Six

Ned set down his tools and stretched his cramped back. The close work of etching deeper texture and lettering into copperplate was always gruelling.

Carefully he spread the plate with printer's ink and pulled a trial proof. He examined it closely—the last of Prattle's caricatures.

Dubbock would not be happy, but Ned felt nothing but relief at leaving Prattle behind—and more than a little pride at this last print. It served as his apology to the Fitzmanning Miscellany, and as thanks for showing him the other side of this work. The largest print he'd ever attempted and richly detailed, it was a study of light and dark, truth and fiction. On one side he'd depicted the world's image of the jumbled Fitzmanning clan: dissolute parties, raucous manners, scandalous behaviour. On the other he'd shown the reality: an unruly family, boisterous and fun. He'd also done his best to portray how caring they were with each other, how loving, supportive and deeply attached they were. It was nothing like Dubbock had been looking for, but it was the truth, and the least that Ned owed them.

Stowing the proof carefully with the plate, Ned rang for Cardle and composed himself to wait. Dubbock was expected any minute and the visit was not likely to go well. And though his mind was focused on the coming confrontation, his fingers were otherwise occupied. It was some time before he looked down and discovered that he'd done it again.

That interesting oval face and pointed chin graced every pad of paper he owned. Large, dark eyes twinkled mischief at him from the backs of correspondence. His pencil had wanted to draw nothing but Annalise Fitzmanning since he'd returned from Welbourne, and he'd filled more than one sketchbook with images of her in every situation, mood and light he'd seen her in, and some that he had only imagined. Seven days until her showing and no good excuse for seeing her before then. But in the meantime, he had people to see, arrangements to make and his life to change.

He tucked the drawing into a sketchbook as Cardle backed in the door, a tray in his hands.

'I've finished it, Cardle, and I'm damned proud of it.' He held the print out for his manservant to see. 'What do you think?'

'Very nice, sir.' The Voice of Doom was back.

'But it's what Dubbock thinks that matters, and I don't think he's interested in the truth.' He sighed. 'And I think we'll be hungry enough to eat our scruples in a few weeks.'

'Don't fret, man…' Ned paused as a heavy step sounded on the stairwell outside. In a moment the door thundered under a vigorous pounding.

Cardle answered and Ned's publisher blustered into the room. Dubbock was a broad, bluff man, infamous within the sound of the Bow Bells for his bald pate and his legendary temper. The frayed edges of his bad humour were in full evidence as he huffed to recover his breath. 'What's this about, Milford? You know I don't fetch and carry for myself. What's so important about this print that I have to come to you?'

'There's brandy on the tray, sir,' Cardle interrupted. 'I'll just go and fetch some hot tea.'

'Don't bother, just shut the door behind you,' Dubbock growled.

'Come, have a seat,' Ned invited. He poured the man a drink and watched as, still standing, Dubbock tossed it back. He handed his glass back for another and removed the large, empty messenger's bag he carried across his chest.

'I thought you'd have something for me before this,' he grumbled. 'Hope this is worth the wait.'

'I'm happy with it.' Solemnly, Ned handed over the proof.

Dubbock glanced at it and thrust it away. 'That's not what I asked for.'

Ned shrugged. 'It's what you'll get. It's the *last* you'll get.'

The man breathed deeply. Ned could see him reaching for patience. 'Think I will sit down, at that.' He took the seat Ned indicated and frowned. 'Somebody offering you a better rate?'

'No, I'm afraid Prattle is retiring.'

'Don't be a fool,' Dubbock spat. 'You've only just made a name for yourself. People will know your name all over England if you keep going at this rate. Together we can far outshine Humphrey's and Gillray's partnership.'

'I'm sorry to disappoint you,' Ned said quietly.

The publisher merely watched him passively for a few moments. 'I'll give you a cut instead of a flat fee,' Dubbock offered. 'That's damned generous and you know it.'

He shook his head.

'I see.' Dubbock steepled his fingers. 'I suppose I could threaten to expose you.'

'You could,' Ned agreed. 'And I could take a notion to do a series about a certain publisher's sister, who secretly supplements her widow's pension with discreet visits to gentlemen's lodgings. I could do one print for each gentleman—can you imagine the excitement that would stir?' He fixed Dubbock's reddening face with an even stare. 'I might even consider a series about a publisher's wife who is dragging her husband into dun territory with her fondness for shopping. Maybe one print for each extravagant purchase?'

Dubbock's face had been growing redder the longer Ned talked, but unexpectedly, he laughed. 'All right, you win, boy.' He shook his head and his colour retreated. 'Damn, but I never knew anyone so good at nosing out a body's secrets.'

'We do what we can with what we're given,' Ned said with a smile.

'God's teeth, but I hate to lose you.' Dubbock ran an assessing eye over the desk, the pile of sketch books and the shelves lining the wall of Ned's make-shift studio. He leaned closer. But his attention did not truly appear to be focused on the collection of tools, prints, busts and artist's fragments. 'Don't suppose you still have that book of illustrations I loaned you? Doubt if I'll see you again to get it back.'

'Of course, I'd forgotten.' Ned stood. 'It's in my dressing room. If you'll excuse me a moment?'

Dubbock waved him on. 'I'll just have another go at your brandy.'

Ned fetched the book. When he returned, Dubbock was carefully manoeuvring the oversized copperplate into his already stuffed bag. 'Don't suppose you'll reconsider?' he asked hopefully.

Ned shook his head.

'Well, then.' He shook Ned's hand and gave him a hard look. 'Just remember, sir, that you aren't the only one able to spy out a secret or two.'

'Goodbye, sir.' Ned watched the publisher leave without regret, then turned as Cardle approached from the back rooms.

'I'll put the brandy away,' the manservant said morosely. 'It might be the last we see in a while.'

Ned eyed him thoughtfully. 'Cardle, do you recall last year when I did that broadsheet of Miss Westby, and later Lord Dayle came around, questioning me so closely about my activities?'

'Remember?' Cardle shuddered. 'I thought he'd found us out for sure.'

'He told me then that he could always use a man with his ear to the ground. Fetch my coat for me, please. I'm for Westminster. I think I'll pay the Viscount a visit.'

Nearly a week went by before the results of that visit arrived by post.

'Cardle!' Ned took the stairs in twos, waving the heavy parchment in excitement. He flung open the door to his rooms. 'I've need of that excellent nose of yours yet, old man!' He opened doors until he found the manservant in his dressing room. 'I've got an offer of a position with the Home Office! Instead of social commentary, we'll be using our skills in more concrete ways.' He looked down at the Viscount's letter once more, scarce able to believe his good fortune.

'Sir?' Cardle asked.

'He asked me how I thought I could be of use, and I told him I was good at finding nuggets of information and piecing them together. I told him how Pettigrew's youngest son had filled my ear with drunken radical ramblings at the Pageant just before skipping town without paying his gaming debts. Together with the rumours that Pettigrew is trying to repair his fortunes with heavy investment in the mills, I thought it worth noticing. What with all the unrest, Dayle agreed. He sent a few men north to investigate.'

'Sir…'

'Cardle, they found the boy! He'd stirred up his father's workers into a frenzy, but the air went out of them when Dayle's men dragged the pup out of a planning meeting. We've likely prevented a riot, Cardle!' He whooped out loud. 'The pay is decent and I'll still have plenty of time to look about for a spot for the gallery.'

Ned looked up, and finally noticed the state his man was in. 'Cardle?' The older man was slumped in a chair, white as a sheet, a sheaf of papers in one hand and a glass of spirits in the other. 'Sir, I think you'd better look at these.'

Puzzled, Ned took them. He glanced at the top one and his heart promptly dropped to the level of his shoes. 'No!' he gasped. He flipped through the rest in increasing panic.

'Sir.' The Voice of Doom had never sounded so low. 'I know you must be thinking that I—'

'No.' Ned said, grim. His mind was racing back. He remembered Dubbock standing at his studio table, stuffing the copperplate into his already full bag. 'No, I know exactly who is responsible for this.'

He sank into chair. 'The bag! Dubbock's bag was empty when he arrived, but it was nearly full when I came back into the room.'

Relief flooded visibly through Cardle. 'What will we do? When your lady sees—'

'Oh, Lord,' Ned groaned. He stood. 'I have to mend this. I have to explain.'

'Justine!' Annalise entered the drawing room at a clip. 'The boys sent a note from town. Manning House is ready for the showing and Brenner says that nearly everyone invited has accepted!'

'Wonderful, darling!' The note of false cheer in Justine's voice caught Annalise's attention. She looked up to find Justine and Charlotte huddled together on a sofa, each of their faces a carefully blank mask. Charlotte was surreptitiously trying to thrust a paper beneath her skirts.

'What is it?'

'Have you packed away the last of the paintings for the trip?' Justine tried to soldier through the awkward moment, but the truth struck Annalise forcefully.

'There's been another one, hasn't there?' she asked. She clutched the chair next to her and slid into it. Her excitement drained away. 'That's why they are all coming, isn't it?' Her hand crushed the note she held. 'They wish to see the notorious Fitzmanning chit. None of them care to see my work.'

'I don't care if that *is* why they will come,' Justine

said staunchly. She came over and took Annalise's hand. 'Once they are there, they will see your paintings and be struck with wonder. Then your skills will be the only talk of the town and none of the rest of it will matter.'

Summoning a wan smile, Annalise squeezed her hand in thanks. But no one in society was likely to forget that she was the latest Fitzmanning to capture the attention of the printers and publishers of Paternoster Row. Even as she'd been absorbed in a flurry of framing and packing, all of London had been delighting in vivid caricatures of her erratic behaviour.

The first had been relatively mild: an image of her with pointed ears and elfin features, smirking with mischief as she stood on a stool to paint devil's horns and tails on the portraits in Lady Blackthorne's infamous gallery. It had been titled *Troublemaker*. Though it had been disconcerting to be singled out, Annalise had merely laughed. 'I likely deserve it,' she told Brenner. 'I did get up to just that mischief and I suppose Lord Peter deserves a little revenge.'

The second incident had been more disturbing, although she nearly did not recognize it as pertaining to her at all. It had shown a dark-haired girl holding the strings of marionette puppets, setting them to dance. She might not have known it was supposed to be her were it not for the first print, and the fact that Stephen and Nicholas were obviously recognisable. *'Puppet Master?'* she'd asked upon seeing the title of the piece. 'What is that supposed to mean?' No one had had an answer, but Brenner had quietly packed up and left for London.

The third had been truly upsetting. *Husband-Chaser* portrayed her pursuing an assortment of men across well-tended lawns, Welbourne Manor vivid in the background. Her skirts were raised, her hand outstretched and an expression of determination writ clearly on her face. Lord Peter had been instantly identifiable. And so had Ned Milford. Annalise's face burned and mortification ate away at her insides. She could barely endure the thought that he must bear society's snickering because of her.

She had to know. Resolute, she went to stand before Charlotte. She held out her hand.

Slowly, Charlotte pulled the paper from beneath her skirts. Annalise breathed deep and unfolded it.

'I should think that this proves that it is Lord Peter behind these vile things,' Charlotte said acidly.

Fishwife, the label said in loud, glaring letters. It was a vibrant rendition of the final, embarrassing scene she'd had with Lord Peter. Except that in this depiction there was no platter of tiny kippers flying every which way. Instead there was a huge whole fish, and her unmistakable parody had hefted it from its bed of greenery and smacked a clearly astonished Lord Peter across the face with it. Beyond stood her family, in various stages of delight and despair.

Groaning, she sank down on to the sofa beside Charlotte.

'Really, this has gone far enough,' Justine raged. 'Oh, I hope Brenner and the boys find the cad behind this and teach him a thing or two about trifling with us. It's time he turned his odious attention elsewhere.'

'I don't understand why he doesn't turn his talent to something more constructive. Really, you cannot deny that some of these are well done,' Charlotte said critically. 'Look at the fluidity of the lines. So much motion is implied, I can clearly imagine Lord Peter's head snapping back from the blow.' She smirked. 'It almost makes me wish it had happened this way— and that I had been there to see it.'

Something in what Charlotte said struck a chord with Annalise. 'What did you say?' she asked.

'It's true. If only he had not stretched your chin out so far and lengthened your fingers to such a claw-like degree, I might have actually enjoyed this portrait of you.'

Clearly Charlotte was trying to raise her spirits, but Annalise's breath had stuck in her throat. 'Surely not,' she choked.

Wild-eyed, she stared at her sisters. 'The others! Fetch the others—I must see them.' She stood and rushed from the room.

'Annalise?' The cry followed her as she raced through the hall.

'Get them!' she cried. 'I'll be right back!' She stormed up the stairs to her studio, searching out the sketches that Ned had drawn at their lesson. 'No, no, no,' she chanted under her breath.

Downstairs again, she laid them all out. She snatched up the *Puppet Master* print and compared it to one of Ned's sketches. No. No tell-tale similarities. She breathed a sigh of relief.

'Look, you've discovered something,' Charlotte exclaimed. She held *Husband-Chaser* up next to the sketch Ned had done of Stephen and Miss Halford at battledore. 'Look at the swing of the skirts, the outstretched hands—they are nearly identical!'

The truth lodged in her mind, a wound just behind her eyes that ripped its way down to her heart. Her face flushed hot, but her extremities had gone to ice.

He'd watched her so closely and constantly. And she had believed it had been because they had so much in common, shared so many similarities. He'd been the first to look beyond the serene surface she showed the world—the first to glimpse the passion she hid beneath. But his motive had been to expose her, not to know her. And she cringed to think that she had felt guilty about dragging his name into a scandal.

'But what does it mean?' Justine asked. 'Annalise, where are you going?'

'To my studio,' she answered in a voice she barely recognised as hers. 'I have a new centrepiece in mind for the showing.'

Chapter Seven

Cool evening air retreated, replaced with swirling banks of dirty fog. It stunk with all the miasma of the river itself, but Ned could appreciate the cover it lent as he lurked outside Dubbock's shop. When the bustle inside had ceased, and everyone gone but the old devil himself, he entered and propped himself casually in the doorframe to the office.

Puttering about, Dubbock cast him a sour glance. 'Get out, Milford. I've nothing more to say to you.'

'Curious, when you had so much to say just a few days ago,' Ned remarked. 'Now, I knew you didn't mean a word when you apologised for stealing *my* sketches and parcelling them out to a bunch of hacks, but I thought you understood me when I said there would be no more of these attacks on Annalise Fitzmanning and her family.'

His erstwhile publisher hefted up his bag and grabbed a sturdy umbrella. 'Couldn't be helped,' he said pragmatically. 'These things sell like a clap cure in a bawdy house.' He scowled belligerently. 'You should understand. My wife, my debts…'

'Yes, your debts.' Ned straightened. 'They are mine now.'

'What?'

'I've bought them up. Took nearly all my savings, but they are mine.' He smiled. 'I believe that leaves you at my mercy.'

'Like hell it does.' Dubbock reddened furiously. 'Who do you think you are?' he asked in a snarl. Ned watched as the veneer of a gentleman dropped away, and the street thug that Dubbock used to be tried to emerge. Stiff-legged he approached the doorway, the umbrella swinging in a threatening manner.

Ned shook his head. 'Too many years of good meals and soft beds, Dubbock.' He wrenched the umbrella away. 'And it's not who I think I am. I *know* I'm the man in control of your destiny, and I say there will be no more broadsheets about Annalise Fitz-manning, her family or anyone connected with her.' He sighed and handed the umbrella back. 'Stick to politics, old man, or set someone on Prinny for a few days. He's always good for a farce.'

'And if I don't?' Dubbock didn't know when he was beaten.

Ned moved away from the doorway. 'Then I shall introduce you to my friend.' Dubbock paled as Ned stepped aside to allow a man into the office. 'Mr Skellot is a bailiff. I am fully prepared to engage his services to recoup my money. He will escort you directly to his sponging house, where he will explore all means possible to extract every last penny possible. After that, it will likely be the Fleet, or Marshalsea.'

Ned cocked his head. 'I might even record your downfall in a series of prints. A prosperous bully like you in debtors' prison? I think the populace would be quite interested. I might even reclaim a bit of money that way.'

'You are a cold-hearted devil,' Dubbock whispered.

'You are free to think so, as long as we understand each other?'

The publisher nodded.

'Good, then if you will excuse me, I have an engagement this evening.'

Ned pushed his way through the crush milling about Manning House. It appeared everyone in London had shown up to see Annalise Fitzmanning's work—or to see if she dared show her face.

He caught a glimpse of her ahead, amongst the crowd, and breathed a sigh of relief. Of course she'd come. The Fitzmanning clan had no room for cowards.

He could only hope they would make room for an impostor. Panic pushed its way into his throat again, a bitter taste that he'd become accustomed to over the last days. Cardle had tried to comfort him, assuring him that Annalise could not know that his drawings had contributed to her disgrace, but Ned knew he was going to have to confess—to all. He hoped the whole family might find forgiveness for him. He prayed that Annalise saw inside him as clearly as she saw the world around her, for surely she would see his sorrow, his contrition and his love.

Impatience and anxiety had him pushing aggressively through the throng, trying to press close to her. Manning House's ground floor had been designed for this, with the grand hall—complete with a dais and a hanging, draped painting—opening to a grander drawing room, and on to a parlour, music room, dining room and back again. It made a distinguished parade through which the crowd flowed like a lazy river.

The currents, however, appeared to be conspiring against him. Annalise's work adorned the walls all along the circuit and groups of admirers clogged the flow as they admired her skill. Annalise drifted ever ahead of him, mobbed by well-wishers and curiosity-seekers, protectively flanked by her family. He began to suspect that conspiracy had been the right thought, for though he caught Annalise's eye, someone always whisked her onwards when he drew close, or kept a moving barrier of guests between them.

After several attempts, he finally got near enough to speak to her—only to be abruptly blocked by Stephen.

'Milford! Leave Annalise alone. She has enough to deal with, without adding you into the mix.'

'Please, Stephen, you don't understand.' Ned allowed his exasperation to show. 'I have to talk to her.'

'Oh, I understand,' Stephen answered coldly. 'And so does she.'

The waking nightmares that had plagued him suddenly took on horrid life. 'She knows?' He could not force his voice above a whisper. 'Out of my way, Stephen! You must let me talk to her, I need to explain!'

Stephen pushed back, his brow thundered and his fists clenched. But Ned sighed in relief as Annalise stepped forward and laid a hand on his arm.

'Explain what, Mr Milford?' Her dark eyes held all the warmth of an iced-over lake. 'Shall you explain how your sketches have made their way into every corner of England? Will you tell me why you lied to me and abused my trust? Or perhaps you'd care to explain how you befriended my brothers under false pretences and used their friendship to line your pockets?'

He reached for her, grasped her arm in alarm. 'Annalise, no! It might have begun like that, but everything has changed!' She shook him off and his panic increased. 'You don't understand.'

'I'm afraid I do, but I fear you've forgotten who you are trifling with.' Her gaze remained level, but he'd never heard such implacable ice in her voice.

'You helped place me firmly beyond the boundaries of good society. Now I am no longer constrained to play by their rules.'

'Come, Annalise,' Stephen urged. 'People are beginning to stare.'

'Let them.' She paused. 'No, I've had enough. Let's end this.'

Stricken, Ned watched her walk away. He was helpless not to follow as she and all her brothers and sisters fought their way back to the dais in the central hall. They gathered in a loose group around the draped painting. Looking at it, dread began to roil in Ned's gut.

Nicholas, every inch the Duke of Manning, called his guests to attention. Once everyone had settled into a curious silence, he spoke. 'My family and I thank you for attending tonight. On behalf of my sister, I thank you for your many compliments to her amazing talent.' Soberly he raked his gaze over the crowd. 'I hope none of you ever realise how easy and terrible it is to become a target of public mockery, but we want to make it clear that, no matter what false and unkind rumours might be spread, *we* are all constantly aware of the treasure we have in our midst.'

A little flushed, Annalise stepped forward to a smattering of applause. 'Thank you all for your fervent interest in me and my work.' Irony laced her words. 'Thank you to those of you who kept your muttering about female painters at a whispered level tonight. And a special thank you for those of you who spoke so kindly about my paintings—and meant it.'

There was a wave of uncertain laughter.

'Perhaps some of you might understand what this showing has meant to me. An artist in any medium creates for an audience, and when normal avenues are closed, it can be disheartening. That is why I am so grateful for the opportunity to share my passion with you.'

Silence reigned as she moved to the centre of the dais and the covered frame. 'Some of you might also be aware of the difficulties I've lately faced.'

More than one person in the crowd around Ned shifted uncomfortably.

Steely determination crept into Annalise's tone. 'Like any good artist, I've put my inner turmoil to use, and now I'd like to share the result. Inspired by all the events of the last weeks, I give you…' She pulled the curtain from the painting in a sweeping, dramatic gesture. '*Mischief Maker: That Shrewd and Devilish Sprite*, or, its more succinct title: *Prattle Revealed.*'

There was a moment of utter silence as the audience stared. Ned's gut clenched in agony.

It was a gorgeously rendered portrait—of him. She'd painted him as a slyly grinning Shakespeare's Puck, complete with hooves, horns and a pen dripping red with blood. He stood before a large rendition of the last print that had featured her, and the others lay scattered on the floor. Behind him hung several of Prattle's more infamous prints, including the one of Miss Westby.

All about him, the rumblings began. 'Milford,' they whispered. Prattle's name echoed throughout the room. People moved away from him in disdain. Others drew nearer in anger. The tumult rose, but Ned ignored them all. He stared over the crowd at Annalise. Her chin high, her fiery gaze heavy with scorn and retribution, she turned and swept away, abandoning him to the firestorm.

Chapter Eight

Annalise stared at her canvas and willed her fingers to obey. But she couldn't find the connection with the brush today, or perhaps she was just too exhausted to paint. Her old self—the Annalise of reserved behaviour and repressed emotion, the one who could lose herself in the mix of light and shadow—felt far from her reach. It seemed Ned Milford had opened a Pandora's box of emotions, and try as she might, she could not get it to close again.

She'd run the gamut since she'd discovered his betrayal. Her initial, righteous anger had flamed high, then boiled down to crushing regret as she'd mourned the loss of the life she hadn't known she'd wanted, and nearly won. She'd swung back to anger at the realisation that those dreams had been built on lies, and settled into grim determination to see Ned Milford reap the same sort of notoriety and pain that he had served so well to so many others.

Now, in the aftermath of her showing and its shocking revelation, she felt only…empty. It was unclear how an empty heart could also feel so heavy in her chest, but there it was. She recalled the look of shock on Ned's face and waited for grief to return to bolster her. She read the few notes and letters of praise of her talent and support for her bravery and waited for pride and satisfaction to ease her. But none of it came. She had nothing to put back in the box, so she supposed it didn't matter if it stood open.

Ah, but perhaps she'd been wrong. A flicker of annoyance did spring up as loud voices rose in the hall outside. Her brothers again. And then Charlotte's voice joined the din and the feverish yapping of the pugs as well. Heaving a sigh, Annalise set down her brush and threw open the door.

'Will you all please stop?' she called, exasperated as she peered down into the open stairwell. 'It is hard enough to paint—'

She stopped as she grasped the reason for the commotion. Ned Milford stood halfway up the first set of stairs. Side by side, Stephen and Leo stood, resolutely blocking his way. At the bottom, Charlotte talked very fast while her dogs milled at her feet.

It was eerily like the first time she had seen him. He raised his head. She froze—and it all came rushing back. Everything that she'd felt since that first glimpse of him hit her like a carriage run amok. Every fluttering interest, pang of hope, stir of gratitude and rush of desire—they all crashed together and mixed with a weighty sense of loss and the deep pain of betrayal. She grasped the banister before her for support.

'Let me come up.' He said it quietly and directly to her. 'At least give me that much.'

'Don't you recall, Milford?' Stephen snarled. 'It's bad luck to pass someone on the stairs.' Roughly, he pushed Ned's shoulder, making him stumble back a step.

Annalise gasped, but Ned held up a hand. 'I've wronged you, Stephen, and I apologise. Not adequate, I realise, but right now your sister is my first concern.' He looked up at her again. 'She needs to hear what I have to say.'

She reached inwards and gathered strength. 'Let him by,' she said to her brothers.

A long moment passed before Stephen turned aside to let him pass. Ned nodded his thanks, but as he reached her brothers' level, Leo put out a hand.

'Wait,' he said. Faster than Annalise had ever seen him move, he reached back and landed a cracking blow to Ned's jaw.

Charlotte screamed. Annalise gripped the banister again, prepared to bolt down the stairs. But Ned merely straightened up, his eyes wide and his hand cradling his face.

'There,' Leo said. 'Now I can forgive you.'

Shaking her head, Annalise turned and retreated back into her studio.

She was standing by the window when he entered

and closed the door behind him. Her gaze remained focused on the gardens outside, but she knew when he stopped at the canvas.

'It's empty,' he said.

She nodded.

'Why?'

'Because I'm empty.' She sighed. 'I've discovered it's impossible to paint when your heart is a hollow shell.'

He came up close behind her and placed heavy, warm hands on her shoulders. 'I'm not empty.'

She sniffed. 'I'd rather be empty than full of hate.'

'Is that what you think? That I hate you?'

She kept silent.

He slid his hands softly down her arms and pulled her close. Part of her wished to lean back into the soothing heat of him. The other part wished to hit him just as Leo had.

'You couldn't be more wrong,' he whispered.

A little of the tightness eased inside her.

'Will you listen to my story? Will you let me explain?'

She spun around. 'I will. But I'll do it for my sake, not for yours.'

He took her hand in his and led her over to the old couch. He saw her settled comfortably and retreated to the window. 'This is my last chance. I want you to listen without distractions,' he said ruefully. He turned away and, for likely the last time, she fixed her gaze on the shifting glory of his hair in the sun.

'The first painting I fell in love with hung in a corridor of my family's home. It was called *Beginning* and portrayed a family boarding a ship. The family had two boys. One had run ahead on to the gangplank and was impatiently beckoning the rest of them to follow. The other hung back, clearly taken by the bustle on the docks.'

Annalise watched him. He gazed out of the window, but it was clear it was the painting he saw once more in his mind's eye. 'Lord, how I loved that picture. Where were they going? Why? How long would they travel? You would not believe the adventures I imagined for that family: shipwrecks, pirates, kidnappings. They were merchants, kings and indentured servants. I would lie in the hall in a patch of sunshine and dream for hours.'

He gave a sheepish little laugh. 'It took a couple of weeks before I thought of *drawing* their new adventures. I borrowed tuppence from my brother, bought a pad of sketching paper—and I was hooked like a fish. I drew everything. Anything. I begged my father for drawing lessons. He consented, but baulked later when I asked for a painting instructor. It took some fancy talk, but I manfully made my case and convinced him I deserved the chance to become the next great portrait artist.'

Fascinated, Annalise nodded. How well she could empathise with his story.

He sighed. 'Unfortunately, my instructor informed my father that I did not have the natural talent for such a fate. I was not allowed to apply to the Royal Academy schools. I was sent instead off to Eton and Oxford, like all the other Milfords.'

She shuddered. It would have been so easy for her own parents to have discouraged her. She closed her eyes and passionately thanked them for indulging her.

'Something died in me that day. It only grew worse later, when my father foiled my plan for the gallery. But I remembered how I had taken solace in my lampoons at school, and how popular they had been. All my father could see in my future was marriage to an heiress and a life lived out under the strictures of society. I thought instead that I would have a hand in showing him the hypocrisy of his world.'

'And Prattle was born,' she said softly.

He turned to face her. 'I enjoyed it at first,' he admitted. 'I liked the challenge of searching out the ridiculous and bizarre secrets of the *beau monde*. But it changed me, and not for the better. I grew bored and more than a little cynical. I was still dead inside. Until I met you.'

Annalise closed her eyes, but Ned had not finished.

'There you were, watching people as closely as I did, but you saw beauty instead of corruption. And your family—you all so obviously care for and about each other—I'd never seen anything like that before.'

He approached her and she watched him warily.

'I kissed you out there by that pond and I began to feel alive again. You showed me how to see the wonder about me again, you made me feel again.'

'And you betrayed me,' she said. 'Mocked me before all the world.' She could barely push the words past the lump of grief in her throat.

'No!' he denied sharply. He pulled a paper from his waistcoat. 'This is the print I made when I left here—the *only* print I turned in to my publisher.'

She took it, and softened when she saw what he had drawn. But she hardened her heart and her gaze again as she looked at him. 'But those prints of me—some of them were your work. I know they were.'

'When I went home, I was a lost cause.' He smiled. 'I only wanted to draw you. And I did. A hundred sketches that brought back every astonishing feeling you inspired in me.' His gaze narrowed. 'I turned that plate…' he indicated the print she held '…over to my publisher and told him that Prattle was retiring. When he couldn't dissuade me, he stole the sketches of you from my home, passed them on to other artists and commissioned the set of broadsheets mocking you.' He breathed deep. 'I didn't do it, Annalise. I would never hurt you.'

She believed him. Ned could see it in the way her shoulders settled and her ribcage expanded, as if she'd just taken her first deep breath for days. He saw the second that she realised what she'd done, too, for all the colour leached from her face.

'It wasn't you! And I—oh, Ned, I am so sorry! I

revealed your secret, and you had not even—' She couldn't continue. He sat next to her and she hid her face in his shoulder.

He ran a hand over her hair. 'I'd already given Prattle up. It makes no difference.' He tried for a light note. 'Except now I won't receive nearly so many invitations.'

She moaned into his coat and he pushed her away so that he could look into her dark eyes. 'I don't regret the loss, Annalise. And I could never be sorry that we met or that I fell in love with you.' He sighed and took her hand. 'And none of that negates what I did to your brothers, or countless other people. I'll do my best to make up for it…' he ducked his head to look into her eyes '…but do you think that you can trust me again?'

She took the question in earnest. His heart flopped when she met his gaze and did not answer straight away.

'I've got a new position,' he told her. She listened seriously while he explained about Lord Dayle. 'And I'll need your help,' he cajoled. 'I'm determined to have that gallery I've dreamed of—and I'd hoped for a whole new collection from you to open it.'

She laughed. 'You do know how to tempt me.'

'I promise, I'll do my best never to hurt you again, Annalise.' He squeezed her hands. 'I've only had your well-being in mind. And if you like, I can prove it to you.'

'What do you mean?'

'Shall I show you?' He raised a brow in challenge.

'How?' She pulled away and raised a brow back at him.

'Come with me.' He took her hand, pulled her off the couch and headed for the door.

He swung it open to find the entire Fitzmanning Miscellany standing outside, waiting in various stages of agitation. Ned laughed at the sight of them all, but only Justine had the grace to blush along with Annalise.

'Ned didn't do it,' she told them with relief. 'He's explained and I believe him.'

He stepped forward. 'I drew some of those sketches of Annalise,' he admitted. 'But they were stolen from me. I didn't make those prints attacking her.' He grew more solemn. 'But I have committed wrongs against some of you. I'd like the chance to make it up to you. But first, I'm taking Annalise outside. I have something to prove to her.' He smiled at them all. 'You might as well come along.'

Stephen scowled. Charlotte stepped forward, but Brenner gently drew her back. 'Go on,' he said to Annalise. 'We'll be waiting for you.'

Brenner nodded to Ned and he returned the gesture. Tucking Annalise's hand firmly under his arm, he led her outside, over the sun-kissed lawns, through the shade of the wood, to the little pond.

He stopped and Annalise pulled away, staring up at him in amazement. 'Surely not?' she asked.

He only smiled and crossed to the bank. It took a minute of pacing to find the right spot. Squatting down, he reached into the chilly water. He came up with a dripping loop of stones, half-covered in muck, the other half-sparkling in the sun.

He turned to her in triumph. She smiled at him in wonder and he strode back and placed the thing in her hand.

'I know you didn't want this found, but I was hoping you'd change your mind, since it comes with an offer of marriage.'

Tears stood out in her eyes. 'How did you know?'

'I saw it that first day we met here at the pond. But you were so adamant about not wanting it found, not wanting to have to see it and think that you had failed your parent's expectations.' His mouth twisted. 'I gave up billiards and endured poetry for you, Annalise. I'd say that demonstrates a significant level of devotion.'

She laughed and he pressed his advantage, gathering her close. 'You taught me to see below the surface, to the beauty that lies beneath. But the most beautiful thing I found was you, hiding your passion under a veneer of reserve and only letting it out through your work. I was hoping in turn you could see beyond how things look and see the longing and the desire and the love I have for you.'

She clutched the necklace and nodded. A sob escaped her.

'I want to remind you every afternoon to wash the

colour from beneath your nails before you pour the tea. I want to wake up every morning and watch your smile transform your face. I can think of nothing I'd like better than to spend a lifetime coaxing all that beauty out into the open for all the world to see.'

She reached out and placed wet fingers on his lips. 'Too much talking,' she said. 'And my answer is yes, to all of that.' She threw herself into his arms and Ned stopped laughing long enough to kiss her back.

* * * * *

Charlotte and
the Wicked Lord
by
Amanda McCabe

Dear Reader,

I was so excited to be asked to be a part of this collection! And what better way to celebrate romance than with diamonds? The Diamonds of Welbourne Manor, that is – three sisters of beauty, intelligence, and spirit, who find love with three equally wonderful (and handsome and rakish) heroes!

I was even more excited to do this project with two of my best writing friends, Diane Gaston and Deb Marlowe. Living far apart, we rarely get to see each other, but we managed to meet for a few summer days in Williamsburg, Virginia to plot out these stories (and have a little fun touring and shopping, too!). We were inspired by famous women like Georgiana, Duchess of Devonshire, and her sister the Countess of Bessborough, whose families were, er, blended. And tumultuous, quarrelsome, wild, teasing, unconventional, and very affectionate.

We've so much enjoyed spending time with the Fitzmannings, and hope to revisit them in the future! They feel like a part of our own families now, and we hope you enjoy them, too.

Amanda

Prologue

1818

By Jove! Was he naked?

Charlotte Fitzmanning balanced precariously on
a thick tree branch, one hand wrapped tightly around
its rough bark and the other holding the spyglass to
her eye. The glass, so very useful in keeping up with
all the interesting doings at Welbourne Manor, was
trained at that moment on the ornamental pond.

More precisely, on the man who swam in its
murky blue-green waters. Andrew Bassington. Her
true love. Not that he knew he was, of course. And
he never *would* know, not if Charlotte could help it.
But the one thing she couldn't seem to help, the one
thing she seemed horribly compelled to do, was to
follow him out here after she had overheard his plans
for a swim.

Charlotte frowned, lowering the glass so that Drew

was only a distant blur. She was a great fool to trail about after him like a puppy, she knew that well. And, what was more, at sixteen she was too old to do so. Drew only saw her as the little sister of his friends, her half-brothers Nicholas and Stephen. He teased her and laughed at her, but he was kind, too, putting up with her when she was bored and tagged along behind him.

Until now. Something, something vital and mysterious, had changed on this visit. Their conversation, so easy and joking before, had a strained quality. He no longer teased her, or tugged at the unruly, heavy dark hair she still insisted on wearing down, despite her sister Justine's gentle fashion advice and gifts of pretty combs and ribbons. And then, last night, over dinner, she had caught Drew watching her solemnly. His beautiful blue eyes were dark and opaque in the candlelight, hiding his thoughts from her.

Then he had smiled, his usual merry grin, and had winked at her, making her laugh into her soup. Yet that strange, serious look—and the uneasy feelings it stirred within her—had remained. She lay awake all night, fretting about what it all meant.

Perhaps, she worried, it meant she was becoming just like her mother, willing to make a great fool of herself for passion. Perhaps she was fascinated by Drew Bassington, with no hope at all he would be fascinated by her in turn. She might be as foolish as her mother, but she was not, alas, a great beauty like her. No man would be infatuated by a female as short, thin and dark as she.

When she had finally got out of bed that morning, she had a new resolution—to rid herself of this new obsession with Drew, and his sky-blue eyes and broad shoulders. With his smile, and his deep, infectious laughter. How she was quite to do that, she had no idea, and she had no one's advice to ask. Annalise was always wrapped up in her paintings, and Justine would just worry.

There was nothing else for it. She would have to start by following him to the pond.

And that was how she had ended up in this tree. Feeling even more foolish than ever.

She should climb down and go home before she got caught. Not that anyone would care one jot she was climbing trees, even in her new white muslin dress that Justine had bought for her. Nobody at Welbourne really cared what anyone else did, as long as it was amusing. But if it was her brothers who saw her, and if they realised she was spying on Drew—well, she might as well tumble from the branch and break her neck right now. The humiliation would be dreadful.

But her curiosity proved stronger than any threat of merciless teasing. She had to *see*! To know once and for all if she was indeed a Woman of Loose Morals.

And to know if Drew looked as fine outside his clothes as he did in them.

Charlotte again raised the glass to her eye. She was just in time, too, as Drew was headed towards shore. His long, sure strokes cut the waters of the pond like a knife, his slick, dark hair emerging from the surface. He was like a merman, she thought whimsically, a strong, mysterious creature of the deepest waves, of a different, hidden world. Perhaps she would write a play about the doomed love of a mortal woman for a sinfully handsome merman!

Or the doomed love of a silly girl from a scandalous family, who cherished a hopeless *tendre* for the gorgeous son of a respectable earl...

Drew emerged from the water, and she saw to her vast disappointment that he was not indeed naked. But he was very nearly so, clad in thin drawers that clung damply to his muscled thighs. He reached up to wring the water from his hair, his lean, bare chest gleaming golden in the sun.

Charlotte couldn't breathe. Her lungs felt so tight, aching with a sharp longing she could scarcely understand. She wanted to run to him, to throw her arms around him and feel his body pressed to hers. To taste those diamond droplets on his skin, and hear him moan with a longing that echoed her own.

Blast! So, she had her answer now. She *was* foolish like her mother. Only scandal and ruin could lie ahead—even more scandal and ruin, that was. But, she mused as she watched Drew dry himself with his shirt, the path to ruin might be quite fun.

She clutched tighter to the branch, watching

avidly as he slid into his breeches. Her moment would soon be over. He would dress and go back to the house, never knowing of her great longing for him. And she would have to tuck this precious memory away, like so many others, and bring it out to cherish on cold nights ahead. Or when she needed new fodder for her writing, of course.

She heard a soft, snuffling sound, and glanced down. For an instant, she still held the glass to her eye, and the green blanket of leaves and dirt swung dizzily before her. She quickly lowered it to find Oliver, the pug puppy Nicholas had just brought her from London to be a friend to her other dog Octavia, sniffing around the base of the tree. Looking for food, no doubt, as he always did seem to be hungry! But his presence would surely give her away.

"Oliver!" she cried softly. "Go home right now. Get Signore Napoli to give you scraps from the kitchen."

Oliver peered up with his large, near-sighted black eyes, his squashed nose trembling. For a moment, he seemed not to see her, his tail uncurled in uncertainty. Then it trembled in happiness, and he planted his front paws on the tree trunk. He gave a little whine, and Charlotte feared she knew what was coming—a full-throated pug scream.

She glanced frantically towards the pond. Drew had pulled on his boots, and covered his bare chest with his coat. Any moment now he would start down the path to the house, within sight of her tree. A cold dread washed over Charlotte, and she waved wildly to Oliver.

"Oliver! Go home!" she muttered.

Oliver twirled in a circle, overjoyed at this strange new game. Charlotte shoved the glass into her blue silk sash, clutching at the branch with both hands. She had to run, to hide, but she was trapped! Caught up a tree like a fox.

No, wait—could foxes climb trees? She had no idea.

She knew pugs couldn't climb, but they could assuredly bark. And shriek. Oliver let out a joyous, and very loud, yelp, and to Charlotte's horror Drew looked their way. She glanced up, hoping to find a leafier hiding place, but there was nothing. No going backwards or forwards.

Oliver's barks were now a cacophony, and Drew hurried towards the puppy. "What's the matter, boy?" he said. "Are you lost?"

Oliver whined and pawed at Drew's polished boot, leaving dusty prints before leaping again at the tree. This was the moment Charlotte had dreaded. The moment Drew spotted her.

He grinned, leaning his hand casually against the trunk. "Well, well," he said. "So you're not lost, Oliver. Just playing hide and seek with your mistress."

Charlotte clutched at the branch, trying to look cool and haughty. As haughty as one *could* look, while stuck up a tree. Her cheeks burned. "I was merely trying to find a cool breeze."

"Quite wise on such a warm day." He peered up at her. "Have you been there long?"

"Not at all."

"Hmm. No doubt you get a good view of the surrounding landscape up there, as well as a fine breeze." He gestured towards her spyglass.

Charlotte pushed it deeper under her sash. "It pays to know where my brothers are at all times. Especially if one is not in the mood to find a frog down one's back."

Drew laughed, and she was reminded that he was often a co-conspirator with Nicholas and Stephen in their pranks. In fact, Nicholas often said Drew was the only one who could out-prank them. "I think they are in the billiards room, so you are quite safe. Will you come down, Charlotte? It's nearly time for tea, and Oliver tells me he is quite famished."

Oliver yelped in agreement, staring up at Drew with adoring eyes. That little puggy traitor. "I am quite well up here, thank you."

"Indeed? Well, when you are ready to descend, I would suggest a bit of a swim. It's most refreshing."

He turned away, chuckling, and Charlotte felt her cheeks flame even hotter. He had seen her spying on him. He was laughing at her! In her flare of anger, her fingers loosened on the branch and she started to lose her balance. As her half-boots slipped on the bark, cold, clammy fear overtook hot temper, and she cried out.

In an instant, Drew spun around, his arms out to catch her as she tumbled from her perch. Her spyglass fell from her sash, rolling away as Oliver barked frantically. The sky twirled over her head, but all she felt, all she knew, were Drew's arms around her, holding her safe. Her cheek rested on his smooth, damp bare chest, and she could hear the pounding of his heart echoing her own. She wrapped her arms tightly around his neck, holding on as if she would never, ever let go.

"Are you all right?" he asked roughly.

Charlotte nodded, her throat so tight she could not speak. She could hardly even breathe.

She *was* like her mother. Overcome by passion.

Useless passion, she thought sadly as Drew set her on her feet with only a brotherly peck on the cheek. She stared up at him, at his gentle smile and those oh-so-blue eyes, searching for any sign of an answering attraction. She saw only amusement.

He surely still saw her as a child, and probably would even if she took off her gown and danced before him in her chemise. Not that she would—she did have *some* pride.

Not much, of course, after the tree and the spyglass. But enough that she could never let Drew Bassington see what she was truly feeling. What she really longed for.

She swooped up her spyglass with one hand and a wriggling Oliver with the other. He licked her chin ecstatically as she tucked him under her arm.

"Thank you for catching me," she said, with as much dignity as she could muster.

"You are most welcome," he answered.

Charlotte turned and strolled down the path towards the house, trying not to break into a childish run. *This* was certainly not going into one of her plays! It was all too confusing, too embarrassing.

Too—deep and hurtful.

Drew might not care for her. Not in the way she wanted him to. But she knew she would never forget the way his naked body looked, emerging from the water like some magical being. It would surely fuel her dreams for a long time to come…

Chapter One

Two years later

Haven't seen you in an age! You must come to Welbourne this time. It will be a great lark, and not the same at all if you aren't there. Remember how grand it used to be?

How grand it used to be. Drew Bassington crumpled the letter from his old friend Nicholas, now the Duke of Manning, and tossed it to the desk. Yes, it *had* been grand once, racketing around London with Nick and his brother Stephen. Racing their curricles, losing money at cards, meeting pretty women—being generally quite obnoxious. They had been very good at all that.

And Welbourne Manor was the grandest of all. A beautiful classical villa full of laughter, fun, and love. Drew rubbed at his brow, remembering the way the sunlight dappled the rambling gardens, turning the smooth waters of the pond to shimmering gold. The way musical ripples of merriment wound down the marble staircases and through the rooms, banishing any hint of gloom or misery. Long suppers full of jokes and teasing to go along with the fine wine, followed by raucous games of charades and blind man's buff.

Most of all, he remembered a girl with shining sherry-brown eyes. A girl who dashed around the house trailed by barking little pugs, so full of life and wild joy. So full of mystery, too, those eyes concealing too many secrets for someone so young. Charlotte Fitzmanning was the very essence of Welbourne, the epitome of freedom and passion.

Of course he was tempted to go back there. To recapture what it had all once meant to him.

But it was gone. That dream was over like those lazy summer days, and only the cold present moment was real.

Drew pushed himself away from the desk and strode to the library window. As if to suit his mood, the sky was grey, overhung with clouds that shrouded the trees and hedges with fog, clinging like bits of old tulle.

His sister-in-law, Mary, the Countess of Derrington, sat on one of the stone benches along the gravel path, her black taffeta skirts spread around her, an unread book open on her lap. Her small son, called little Will, toddled along the path under her careful gaze. The new Earl of Derrington, still in leading strings.

They were Drew's world now, his reality. Mary, little Will, and Drew's own mother, still incoherent with grief and ill health. Drew's brother William had been gone now for almost a year, and still they were a shadowed house of mourning.

William had never approved of Drew. A model of respectability himself, he had endlessly lectured Drew on his "rackety" companions, his bad habits. He'd urged Drew to marry, perhaps to take up politics. To find a purpose, a direction.

Now Drew did have a purpose. To take care of William's family. To make sure little Will's inheritance was safe. To become the responsible one.

Sunny, carefree Welbourne had never seemed so far away. And neither had Charlotte Fitzmanning. The wild, dark-eyed sprite.

Drew turned away from the window, retrieving the letter from the desk. At the bottom of the missive was a postscript he had missed.

Stephen and I hear you have the thought of getting married, of trying out politics. We can scarcely credit it, of course, but if it is sadly true you might be interested to know that Lady Emily Carroll is to be among the guests. She has quite the spotless reputation, and is pretty, too. And her brother is in Parliament. Surely you would like to make her acquaintance!

Drew arched his brow at that unexpected message. "Spotless reputation"—and at Welbourne, too! Things had certainly changed since Brenner had appeared there two years ago.

And it was true he had recently considered doing the unthinkable and marrying, if a suitable lady would have him. A quiet, responsible and, yes, respectable female who would help him with his family, his future. Who would be a proper hostess and chatelaine. He had heard tell of this Lady Emily, the third daughter of the Earl and Countess of Moreby. Blonde, accomplished, shy. Suitable.

Perhaps he *should* go to Welbourne, just to see what might happen. He wasn't going to meet anyone here at Derrington Hall, in the silent halls of mourning, and he had no taste for town at present. If Lady Emily suited, it could be a good thing.

And yet, somehow, all he could see in his mind was Charlotte Fitzmanning, laughing down at him from her perch high in a tree, the sunlight shining on her dark hair.

Chapter Two

Charlotte shifted on her chair, a tottering old bit of wood and shredded upholstery discarded in the depths of Welbourne's cavernous attics. She could easily bring a new, good chair up with her, but this one suited her, as did the old crate she used as a desk. They had a shabby sense of history about them, a character that new, shining furniture quite lacked. They brought her creative good fortune, an inspiration that came to her whenever she climbed up to the attic and sat down here.

Usually. Today, though, the words simply would not come. Maybe it was just too quiet, without Annalise painting on the other side of the wall in her bright studio.

Charlotte stared down at the blank page, clutching her pencil tightly in her fingers. Her mind was quite frustratingly blank. Her play, *The Witch's Curse, or Love Denied*, was at a standstill, and at a most vital moment. The hero and heroine, Count Darian and Lady Lavinia, were finally about to declare their undying love, a Love That Could Not Be, because of that witch's curse—and their own stubborn natures.

And they were mute. They could say nothing at all.

Charlotte tapped her pencil against the edge of the crate, listening to her pugs, Oliver and Octavia, snoring in their little beds. It was raining outside, the steely, cold drops pattering on the roof overhead. It was perfect writing weather.

But she knew what was wrong. A letter that had come yesterday from her friend Mae in London, with news of Drew Bassington.

Drew Bassington. How very irritating it was that, after all this time, that name gave her such a thrill. Made her stomach flutter, her hands go cold and shaky.

It was ridiculous! She was no longer the silly, smitten girl who had followed Drew about Welbourne, longing for just a word, a smile, from him. Who climbed up trees to spy on him. She was a lady of eighteen now. She needed to think of other things. Useful things, such as her own future.

She hadn't even seen Drew in many months. In the excited flurry of weddings, first Brenner and Justine, and then Annalise and Ned, Welbourne had been crowded and noisy, even more than usual. There had hardly been a moment to think.

But now it was quiet again. Too quiet. With the happy couples off on their honeymoon in Italy like Annalise, or taking care of business on their own estate like Brenner and Justine, and with Nicholas at his ducal estate and Stephen and Leo off racketing about on adventures, Welbourne was Charlotte's own domain. And it all left her too much time to think. To remember—and regret.

Hence the play. She had always loved scribbling, writing poetry and little stories, but she had never attempted anything like a play before. It was a great distraction, a way to exorcise the alluring memory of Drew Bassington.

Until now.

Charlotte drew Mae's letter from beneath the manuscript. It was a chatty missive, full of gossip, of tales from all the last soirées before the Season ended. Of new fashions, which interested Charlotte not at all, and new plays and concerts, which interested her greatly.

It was only at the end of the letter that Mae brought up Drew at all, in a most disquieting way.

You do, of course, remember Lord Drew Bassington! He has not been seen in Town at all since his brother died. So very sad. But now we hear the most astonishing thing! He has decided to reform. He has remembered what he owes to his family, and is seeking a wife. Someone quiet and respectable, accomplished, dedicated to "good works". They say he thinks now of going into politics! Every family in town with marriageable daughters is all a-twitter, as you can imagine. Such a handsome, wealthy young man, with only an infant between him and an earldom—though of course I do not think such things! I am sure my parents would insist I set my cap at him, if I did not have other ideas.

Really, Charlotte, can you credit this is the same gentleman we knew at Welbourne?

I am looking forward to your house party there immensely! It has been too long since I saw you. Much love, Mae.

Someone quiet and respectable. Dedicated to good works. No, Charlotte could *not* quite credit it. But Mae was always most truthful in her reports, and if she had heard such a thing there must be something in it. For the first time, Charlotte wondered if she had made a mistake in refusing Brenner when he offered her a Season.

People did change, as Charlotte knew all too well. Even Drew Bassington had to marry eventually. But why, oh, why, did he have to seek a lady who was the very opposite of herself!

Life was such a puzzle at times. Not like in a play at all, where everything had a neat arc of three acts before being tied up in some satisfactory manner.

She slumped back in her chair. Her brothers would be arriving soon, for the latest of Welbourne's famous house parties. They had been chums with Drew since school—surely they would know what was really going on, *if* she could find a way to get them to tell her, without giving away her own secret. She would perish with embarrassment if they knew of her old *tendre* for Drew, and they would tease her to fits.

It was quite obvious she would get no writing done today. She tucked the pages away in the crate, carefully covering them up with an old tablecloth. They were only safe from prying eyes up here, in her secret space.

Oliver and Octavia roused themselves from their nap, snuffling and yawning as they watched her through their big, dark eyes. She gave them a quick ear scratching before she went to the window. It was the only portal in her writing space, a small pane of glass tucked up near the eaves, and she had to climb on a stool to reach it.

She peered out at the gardens, at the gleaming white summerhouse and the curving pathways and drive beyond. The swathe of grey gravel that led away from the haven of Welbourne to the wide world beyond. The world so full of endless possibilities, ones Charlotte had never known. If she went out there, what would happen? Would she soar free, find herself at last? Conquer stages and literary salons?

Or would she sink under the weight of her name? Shattered, scattered—like her parents.

She thought again of Drew. *He* was out there somewhere in that world. She studied herself in the wavy old glass, examined her long, loose brown hair, the scattering of freckles across her nose that were the product of wandering free outdoors her whole life. What would he think of her now, after all those fine, pretty, *respectable* ladies of London?

"It does not matter," she told herself fiercely. "Drew Bassington was a childish infatuation, that is all. Who cares what he thinks of you?"

Who cared what anyone thought? That should be the Fitzmanning motto, she reflected. Her parents, her siblings—they all lived life to please themselves. Charlotte did, too. She was even allowed to play hostess for this house party, when no young lady of another family would be, and no one thought it odd of them.

Outside, the rain had ceased, but the sky was still that lowering grey. Not a fine start to their house party at all, not when activities included swimming and riding and pall mall.

As she watched the summerhouse, a carriage turned in through the gates beyond, dashing along clumsily like a big, dark dog in the gloom. Something happening at last!

Charlotte strained up on her tiptoes, trying to see who the arrival might be. At last the vehicle drew closer, and she glimpsed the arms of the Duke of Manning on the door.

"Nicholas!" she cried, jumping off the stool. She was brought up short by the terrible sound of ripping cloth.

"Oh, blast," she muttered, looking down to find that her hem had caught on a nail, tearing the white muslin. Another frock to be mended. Her maid would not be happy, and neither would Justine, if she could see. She was always sending Charlotte new gowns and pelisses in an effort to make her presentable.

But there was no help for it now. Her brothers were arriving at last! She ran out of the attic and down the narrow staircase, Oliver and Octavia right behind her, barking and snorting in excitement. She pushed through the old servants' door and into the grand marble entrance hall, just as Nicholas and Stephen bounded into the house.

They were merrily arguing about something, shoving and tripping each other as if they were still school lads and not grand dukes and lords. As always, light and colour burst through the house along with them, and the grey day was utterly forgotten.

"Nicholas!" Charlotte cried. "Stephen! I thought you weren't arriving until tomorrow."

"We missed you far too much, Charlotte old gel," Nicholas answered, catching her in his arms and twirling her around and around until she laughed dizzily.

"And Nick bet Lord Whittingfield he could make the journey in only two hours in that new carriage of his," Stephen said, grabbing her away from Nicholas and kissing her cheek.

"Did you, then?" she said, trying to shush the dogs as they twirled in a paroxysm of joy.

"Of course, what d'you think?" Nicholas said. "I totally fooled that silly Whittingfield, he said the carriage looked far too lumbering to go so fast. I told him appearances are always deceiving. I'm positively famished, is there anything to eat?"

"You are always famished," Charlotte said, laughing. "I'll ring for tea and sandwiches, but anything more substantial will have to wait for dinner. Signore Napoli is in a fit again, and everyone is busy getting ready for the party."

"Oh, yes, the party!" Stephen said. "It's going to be an absolute corker, sis. It's a dashed good thing Brenner won't be here to see it!"

Charlotte laughed, scooping Oliver up under her arm to stop him snuffling on Stephen's polished Hessians. "Come now, you two, it can't be *that* bad. Even we wild Fitzmannings have settled down over the years. Unless you plan a repeat of the infamous frog prank? Or that 'cursed' Indian statue?"

Stephen shuddered. "Don't even joke about that, Charlotte! It *was* cursed, I vow."

Nicholas grabbed her hand, pulling her with them into the drawing room. "We never repeat ourselves, you know that," he said indignantly.

"Yes, I do know that." Charlotte rang the bell for refreshments and sat down on a chinoiserie-style *chaise* by the window, studying her brothers warily. Oliver settled down on her lap, snoring softly as Octavia climbed under the *chaise*. "So, I must be on my guard for new and surprising pranks?"

"Of course you must," Stephen said. "We may be older and wiser, and some of us may be high-and-mighty dukes, but we still like a bit of fun."

"And speaking of older and wiser," said Nicholas, "you'll never guess who has agreed to come to the party."

"The king!" Charlotte said. "Oh, no. You said 'wiser'. That can't be, even if Prinny is monarch now. And I suppose it can't be anyone *too* wild, not with that prissy Lady Emily Carroll and her parents coming. I was most surprised to see them on your list."

"She's quite pretty," Nicholas said, lounging back on his couch. "And not nearly as fusty as you think. Her parents were friends with our father, after all— how high in the instep could they be?"

"Ah, I see now," Charlotte teased. "Is love in the air at last, brother?"

The maids brought in the tea trays just then, arranging them on the enamelled table next to Charlotte. Only after they had departed did Nicholas say, "Of course I am not in love with Lady Emily. She is far too good for me."

"A truer word was never spoken," Charlotte said, pouring out the tea. "And you never told me who our mystery guest is."

"Actually, it all has to do with Lady Emily," Stephen said, munching on a cucumber sandwich.

"She cannot be the mystery," Charlotte said. "She's been on the guest list for weeks, and I would wager she never did a surprising thing in her life."

"Well, you see, sis," Stephen said, "Nick and I have decided to play matchmaker."

Charlotte nearly choked on her sip of tea. "You two? Matchmakers? Never say so!"

"We'll be quite as good at it as old Dowager Lady Prouther," Nicholas protested. "Her schemes never come off because she always tries to pair the most improbable people."

"Like the time she tried to match Stephen to that bookish Miss Pitt?" Charlotte said.

"Exactly so," Stephen said. "Whereas we have a Method. It can't fail."

"Very well," Charlotte answered, highly amused by the thought of her brothers playing at being Dowager Lady Prouther. "With whom are you matching Lady Emily?"

"With Drew Bassington, of course," Nicholas said triumphantly, stuffing a salmon sandwich into his mouth. "Now that we have finally lured him out of mourning to come to the party."

"Drew Bassington?" Charlotte whispered, all her amusement suddenly turned to cold ashes. She shivered. "He is coming here? To marry Lady Emily Carroll?" She set down her cup with a clatter, her fingers too numb to hold on to it.

"He doesn't *know* he's coming here to marry Lady Emily," Nicholas said. "But he has been so fusty since his brother died, all locked away at his family's estate."

"He has some idea that he must take care of them

all now," Stephen added. "Be the responsible one and all that. Imagine that! A friend of *ours* responsible."

"We heard that he wants to find some suitable lady to marry," said Nicholas. "So, we thought we would just help him out a bit."

"And who could be more suitable than Lady Emily?" Stephen said. "It's a brilliant plan, Charlotte, don't you agree?"

Charlotte thought the plan was absolute rubbish. Drew, married to beautiful, perfect Lady Emily Carroll? That terrible numbness spread, until she could not feel or think at all.

"I think your matchmaking skills rival those of Lady Prouther," she muttered. "And you have as much chance of success as she does."

"Well, even if it doesn't end in wedding bells, it will make this party vastly interesting," Nicholas said, unconcerned. "Shall we have a wager, then, sis?"

"Certainly not. I learned not to wager with you ages ago." Charlotte pushed herself off the *chaise* and hurried towards the door, her torn hem dragging. The pugs did not follow her, but stayed firmly where there was the possibility of food.

Traitors.

"And I think you two have also wagered quite enough for the time being," she said. "If you'll excuse me, I have to consult Signore Napoli about the menus for the party, if he has finished with his sulk."

Only once she was away from the drawing room, did she break into a run. If only she could run away from the truth so very easily, too.

Stephen crept to the drawing-room door, listening carefully as Charlotte's footsteps faded. Once all was silent—or as silent as it ever could be at Welbourne—he grinned back at his brother.

"Do you think she believed it?" he said.

"Undoubtedly," Nicholas answered, with a grin of his own. He fed the last of his sandwich to the dogs, watching happily as they twirled around in glee. "Did you see how big her eyes became when we said we intended to match Drew to Lady Emily? I'm sure it's done the trick. Now we have to start working on Drew. I tell you, brother, they will be like clay in our hands. We'll see them happy in no time. And Lady Emily and her family will have a fine time anyway, they're always happy to receive invitations here."

Stephen threw himself back in his chair with a satisfied sigh. "Another start to a delightful Welbourne house party…"

Chapter Three

"Will there be many people there, Drew?"

Drew glanced up from his papers, startled. Their journey had thus far been a silent one, his sister-in-law sitting across from him with a book in her hands as he went over estate business. Mary's words suddenly broke that quiet, and he found her watching him with wariness in her blue eyes.

He gave her a reassuring smile. It was the first time he had been able to lure her away from the sadness at Derrington Hall since William had died. He didn't want to scare her off now.

"It has been a while since I've been at Welbourne," he answered. "But their guest lists are never large, and not at all formal. It will only be some friends, enjoying each other's company."

Mary laughed, a soft chuckle that sounded rusty with disuse. Drew was surprised to think how long it had been since she *had* laughed. She had been so light and merry when she had first married William, the pretty, sweet Lady Mary Smythe with her blue eyes and auburn curls. But life with his solemn brother, and now as a too-young widow, had dimmed her glow. She *did* need Welbourne, more than he had realised, and he was even happier he had persuaded her to come with him.

She had also left off black, for a carriage dress and pelisse of deep violet. Hopefully that was a good sign.

"I hope they do not *enjoy* each other's company too much," she said teasingly. "When I was a girl, I heard such tales of the doings at Welbourne Manor! Pranks, cut-throat card games where fortunes were lost. Theatricals, swimming outdoors. My mother warned me not to even look at those brothers!"

Drew smiled. That was all too wonderfully true. "And now you are going there yourself. Shocking, Mary."

"Will I lose my jointure in a game of piquet, do you think?"

"Only if you play with Leo. He is a terrible sharp."

"Then I will be sure to avoid him." She closed her book, her smile fading. "Perhaps I did make a mistake in coming. I will be like the ghost at the banquet."

"Nonsense. I promise, Mary, things at Welbourne are much quieter since Brenner came along. It must be a good thing for you to make new friends."

"And you, Drew? Will you make new friends, too?"

He gave her a puzzled glance. "What do you mean?"

"I mean, surely there will be young ladies there. Perhaps you will find one that you particularly like."

"Why, Mary. Are you hinting it is time I wed?"

She laughed, staring down at the book in her gloved hands. "Oh, Drew. You do seem a bit lonely, and all your time of late has been taken up with looking after little Will and me. You deserve someone who can help you, be a companion to you."

Drew, of course, had been thinking of the same thing. Was Lady Emily Carroll not the reason he was going to Welbourne? But to hear it said aloud was somehow—disquieting.

"I am not lonely," he said. "How could I be?"

"Well, what about children, then? Little Will adores you. You would make a fine father."

"All in good time."

"Of course. It is just—I care about you, Drew. You are like my own brother now! I want you to be happy."

"I *am* happy. Very happy indeed that you have finally agreed to leave the house."

Mary wagged her finger at him. "I will not be put off so easily! I have been quite selfish enough since William died. Now I want to think about someone else."

"And I am to be the happy recipient of your new bounty?"

"Indeed, for you are the only one nearby. Now, tell me—what qualities are you looking for in a wife?"

Unbidden, an image of Charlotte Fitzmanning flashed in his mind, perched up in her tree, her beautiful dark hair loose down her back, her white skirts fluttering in the summer breeze. She was like a spirit of nature, glorious and free, unconquerable. Everything he longed for, and which could never be.

Charlotte could never fit into his life now, even if she was *not* his friends' sister and thus beyond his touch. He remembered Mary and her lost laughter, that spirit stifled by life as a Bassington. He couldn't do that to Charlotte. Nor to himself. Knowing that he, his family and their way of life, had extinguished another wild soul—no.

In his vision, Charlotte turned away from him, fading until he could not see her at all.

"Someone pretty, I'm sure," Mary said. "Golden curls? Or dark?"

"Mary," Drew protested, "that hardly matters."

"It doesn't matter if she's pretty?" Mary teased. "Well, then, that expands the candidate list considerably. But I know she would have to be clever. A dull-witted lady would bore you within a week. And kind. And accomplished."

"Do you know such a paragon? Wherever have you been hiding her?"

Mary shook her head. "Protest all you want, brother. I *will* find the right lady for you. Ah, look, I think we're here at last!"

Drew glanced out of the carriage window to see that they had indeed turned through the gates of Welbourne. They stood wide to welcome guests, and beyond was a beautiful vista of gardens just made for pleasure. For long lazy days filled with fun and laughter, the cares of the real world left far behind.

And, as he watched the pale sunlight gleam on the glassy pond, the white classical dome of the summerhouse, Drew felt some of the weight fall away from his own shoulders. The tension of life at Derrington Hall, of responsibility and position, eased away as Welbourne worked its spell on him against his will.

The carriage rolled past the tree where Charlotte had perched on that last day, just beyond the pond and the summerhouse. Yes, Charlotte belonged here. Once, long ago, Drew thought he might, too. But that was only a dream that was gone.

A dream that beckoned to him temptingly once again.

"How lovely it all is," Mary murmured. "Like a fairy-world."

Drew glanced at her to find that she, too, watched the passing landscape with a wistful wonder on her face. A longing for something that could never belong to the staid Bassingtons.

"I hope that you'll enjoy yourself here, Mary," he said. "Forget everything else for a while."

"How could I help it?" she said. "But will you do the same, Drew?"

Before he could answer, the carriage lurched to a halt at the front door. All seemed in confusion there, with luggage piled up and footmen carrying away trunks and band boxes. Two little pugs trotted at their heels, snorting and barking.

Which meant, of course, that Charlotte could not be far behind.

The carriage door opened, and one of those footmen helped Mary to alight. Drew followed, finding himself drawn again into the noise and chaos of Welbourne Manor.

And Charlotte herself stood on the front steps with the old butler, watching carefully as the baggage was moved and shifted. For an instant, Drew himself could not move at all. All the light and sound, it faded away until there was only *her*. The long months and years fell back, and he remembered only that last day.

Remembered all the passionate longing of his youthful self to take her into his arms and never, ever, let go of her.

That all seemed a century ago now, and he felt like a fossilised old man. But Charlotte had not changed at all. Her dark hair, which she had always worn long and loose, tangled in the wind as she ran and rode across the estate, was loosely coiled and pinned atop her head. She wore a stylish gown of pale blue muslin with a white satin sash, a frock that was not even torn or stained. She wasn't even as tanned as he remembered, with her freckles pale amber against her newly white skin.

Yet there was still that glow about her, that light of freedom and energy. That irrepressible exuberance that made her look as if she would take off running—or flying—at any moment.

She half-turned to consult with the butler about something, gesturing to a list in his hand, and she had not even seen Drew yet. He stood there, just drinking in the sight of her. He feared he gawked like a ridiculous schoolboy, yet he could not help it. Charlotte Fitzmanning was the most beautiful sight he had ever beheld, like a glimpse of pure, burning *life* to a man half-dead.

But then Mary touched his arm, and the shimmering spell was broken. All the rush of sound returned, and he was just himself again. Newly responsible, dull Drew Bassington.

He held out his arm for Mary to take. "That must be the youngest Miss Fitzmanning," she murmured. "How pretty she is."

"Yes," Drew answered. "Very pretty indeed."

"I must say, though, I am rather disappointed not to see anything scandalous going on," Mary said with a laugh. "It is just like any other house party!"

"It's early yet," Drew said.

At that moment, Charlotte glanced up and saw him there. Her eyes widened, a slow pink stain washing over her cheeks. Was she remembering, as he was, that golden day by the pond? Her falling into his arms. The feel of their bodies against each other in that one breathless, perfect moment.

She moved slowly towards him, her lips tight as if she held her breath. As if she feared what she might say.

Or perhaps he was just putting his own fears on to her. If he opened *his* mouth, what would he say? "How beautiful you are, Charlotte." How this whole carefree life beckoned him again, just at the sight of her.

How he couldn't understand why he had ever stayed away from her at all.

But then he glanced down at Mary, and remembered why Welbourne Manor was beyond him now. People depended on him, and he could not fail them. He could never go back to that old Drew at all.

He looked back to Charlotte, who was still coming towards him, a tentative smile on her lips. A sudden, sharp bark rent the air, hovering above all the chatter and clatter. Charlotte's two dogs dashed across the drive, one of them in triumphant possession of a bone while the other chased in fury.

Charlotte did not see them, and of course disaster ensued. She tripped over the racing dogs, and pitched towards the gravel with a cry.

Drew saw it all in horrifying slowness, a blur of blue and brown, of frightened eyes. He lunged forward, catching Charlotte in his arms as they both tumbled down.

He managed to twist and roll so that he landed on his back, Charlotte on top of him. All the air was crushed from his chest, gravel painfully digging into his shoulder, and yet all he knew was the lilac scent of Charlotte's hair. The soft press of her breasts against him, her hands clutching at his shoulders.

"Oh, Drew!" she cried, sitting up beside him. Her hair had tumbled from its pins, her sash torn and a streak of dust along her cheek.

That was the Charlotte he remembered.

"Drew, are you quite all right?" she said, her voice hoarse with concern. She patted at his arms and shoulders, as if to see if anything was broken. "Oh, I am so very sorry. I'm always doing this to you, aren't I? Naughty Oliver!"

He felt a cold touch on his wrist, and glanced down to find that one of the pugs had dropped the disputed bone and had come to sniff at him. Charlotte shooed the dog away.

"Now this is what I call a proper welcome to Welbourne," he said wryly.

"Drew! Are you hurt?" Mary said, kneeling beside him. "Whatever happened?"

"I fell, and he saved me," Charlotte said. "Much to the detriment of his coat, I'm afraid. And he has a bump on his head!"

The two of them cooed and clucked, sweeping aside his hair to examine the purported bump. Drew sat up, gesturing them back.

"I am hardly at death's door, ladies," he insisted, brushing at his sleeve. Sadly, Charlotte was correct—the coat was beyond redemption. "It was nothing. I'm just glad I happened to be nearby to save the fair damsel."

"Too bad you weren't wearing your shining armour," Charlotte muttered, plucking at the torn sleeve. "I could mend it for you."

"No, thank you. I remember all too well your skills with a needle. Remember when you tried to make Leo a handkerchief and somehow sewed your skirt to the chair instead?"

Charlotte's blush deepened, making her even prettier. "I have got better."

"I prefer not to take my chances, thank you." Drew pushed himself to his feet, reaching down to help the ladies rise. Mary gave him a questioning glance, and he suddenly recalled exactly where, and who, he was.

And the fact that everyone in the drive was staring at him.

He carefully straightened his cravat. "Charlotte, Miss Fitzmanning, may I present my sister-in-law, Lady Derrington?"

"Oh, I feel like you should introduce me as 'Mary'," Mary said quickly. "It seems silly to stand on ceremony after what we've just witnessed! And I do feel I know you already, Miss Fitzmanning. Drew speaks of your family so often."

"I am most pleased to meet you, Lady Derrington," Charlotte answered, giving a polite little curtsy. She tried tucking her hair back into its pins, but it just tumbled down again. "I was very sorry to hear of your husband."

"Thank you," Mary said. "But Drew assures me

I will find great distraction here at Welbourne. It was very kind of you to include me in the invitation."

"I'm so glad you could come," Charlotte said. "We need more ladies here. Let me show you to your room."

As if to prove her words, Nicholas and Stephen came dashing out of the house, shouting exuberant greetings.

"Drew, you old rogue!" Nicholas exclaimed, pumping Drew's hand as Stephen clapped him on his newly bruised shoulder. "Came back to get into trouble with us at last, eh? Remember that time—"

Before Nicholas could go any further with possibly embarassing remembrances, Drew brought Mary forward to introduce her. Just as he suspected, they were shocked into manners by his sister-in-law's prettiness, and Drew could study Charlotte surreptitiously.

She stood off to the side a bit, smoothing her rumpled skirts—and refusing to look at him. That quiet tension, that shimmering bond of old memories and new, alluring attraction, tightened between them. He wasn't sure what to say to her. What to do, when he couldn't take her in his arms.

"It is so lovely to meet all of you," Mary said, laughing as she extracted herself from Nicholas and Stephen. "But if you will excuse me, I am rather fatigued from the journey, and your sister offered to show me to my chamber."

With one more charming smile, Mary took Charlotte's arm and turned with her towards the house, their heads bent together as if they were long-lost bosom bows. They disappeared through the doors with the dogs trailing behind them.

"By Jove, Drew," Stephen said, "but you never told us what a diamond your sister-in-law is."

"That is because Mary is far too good for you," Drew answered affably. Blast it all, but it *was* good to see his old friends again! To hear their laughter, and remember how close they had been. More like brothers to him than William had been, in truth. The old truths of Welbourne still held—family was where one found it sometimes.

Yet what would his old friends say if they knew of Drew's lust for their sister?

"I'm quite sure she is," Stephen said. "And speaking of ladies who are too good for us..."

"Lady Emily Carroll arrives soon," said Nicholas. "I am sure you're very much looking forward to *that*."

Lady Emily Carroll. Of course. Was that not the whole reason for this visit? To find a suitable wife?

Drew had forgotten all about her.

"I'm sure she will be a fair addition to your party," he said neutrally.

"A fair addition, indeed," Nicholas said. "And surely dull enough for your new matrimonial requirements, Drew."

"I never said I wanted a dull lady," Drew protested.

"No, you said 'respectable'," said Nicholas. "Same thing. But even with Lady Emily and her worthy parents, we should have a merry party. The Mortons are coming, and Lord and Lady Appleby. And Charlotte's friend Mae and her parents. Stephen's looking forward to *their* arrival very much indeed."

"I certainly am not!" Stephen exclaimed. But a dull red flush spread along his neck.

"Oh, never mind all that now," said Nicholas, clapping Drew on the shoulder. "We're all together again, that is what matters. Come along, Drew, you must see this new carriage of mine. It's wonderfully fast…"

As he was led away, Drew glanced back at the house. For an instant, he imagined he glimpsed a flash of blue muslin at one of the windows. But then it was gone.

Chapter Four

"May I help you with that?" Charlotte heard Lady Derrington say. Charlotte stared with increasing dismay into her looking glass, lifting a tangled lock of hair from her shoulder.

"Thank you," she answered. "I think I need all the help I can find."

Lady Derrington laughed, and shut the chamber door behind her. She laid her bonnet and reticule on a table, pulling off her gloves as she hurried to the dressing table.

"It is not so bad as all that, Miss Fitzmanning," she said soothingly. "Very easily mended. I don't know anyone who could remain immaculate after such a tumble!"

Charlotte groaned, sitting down hard on her stool. "It was dreadful. And after I wanted so much to…"

Her words trailed away into silence. How could she tell Drew's sister-in-law that she longed for him to think her pretty? To see her as more than his friends' wild younger sister? Those hopes were quite gone now, anyway, after she had made such a fool of herself. Again.

Lady Derrington reached for Charlotte's engraved silver-backed hairbrush that had once been her mother's, and drew it soothingly through Charlotte's tangled hair. "So much to what?"

Somehow the gentle motion of the brush, the soft words and Lady Derrington's kindness calmed her. She reminded Charlotte somewhat of Justine, who had much the same air of elegant serenity and gentle understanding. It made *her* feel gentler, too.

"I thought perhaps Drew could see me as a lady now," she murmured. "A lady who can dress well and behave nicely. Not a wild creature who climbs trees and plays cricket. I am nearly nineteen, after all."

Lady Derrington laughed. "Oh, my dear, that is quite ancient indeed."

Charlotte had to laugh, too. "Very well, so it is not *that* old. But I am meant to be hostess of this party, and I want to do it well. I want Dre—everyone to respect me."

"I am sure you need not worry about that," Lady Derrington said. She reached for Charlotte's pin box, taking out a handful. "Drew adores your family, and this place. He has been so anxious to come to this party."

Charlotte's gaze met hers in the glass, a tiny, tentative hope blooming deep inside. "Really? He said so?"

Lady Derrington twisted up a lock of hair, skewering it with the pins. "He thinks he hides it so well, that we imagine him entirely content with us at Derrington Hall. But he speaks of Welbourne, of your family and the times he spent here, far more than he realises. And I pay more attention than he thinks I do."

Charlotte was most intrigued at this little glimpse of Drew and his new life. "Really? Whatever do you mean?"

"Would you hand me that ribbon, please? I suppose I mean that Drew has the kindest of hearts. He thinks that now my husband is gone, he must take care of me and my son, and his poor mother. He talks of going into politics, of making improvements on the estate so that when little Will comes of age it will be far more productive."

Lady Derrington paused to loop the ribbon through Charlotte's hair before continuing. "My husband was a good man, Miss Fitzmanning, but a solemn one. Drew was the one who always made us laugh, even William. But now he seems to think he must take William's place, solemnity and all."

It was hard for Charlotte to think of Drew as solemn. There were too many glorious memories of him laughing and joking with them here at Welbourne. But she remembered the way he had looked when she had first seen him here today. Those beautiful blue eyes were dark and shadowed. Surely Lady Derrington was right. He had changed.

Could there be a place for her, one of the Fitzman-ning Miscellany, in that new, serious world?

She had not made a good start of things. Any man who had ideas of going into politics, of being the head of his family, needed a lady who could walk across a lane without tripping!

"But I do have hopes he will enjoy himself here," Lady Derrington said, tying off the ribbon.

"And you, too, Lady Derrington," Charlotte said. "I hope you enjoy your stay, too."

"I think I already am. There, now, what do you think of your coiffure?"

Charlotte's thoughts had been too far away to concentrate on what was happening on top of her head, but at Lady Derrington's urging she glanced into the glass.

And was quite astonished. Her hair, that heavy, straight mass of dark brown that never wanted to stay tidy, was looped up in elegant, glossy coils. The pale blue ribbon held it in place in a neat Grecian bandeau.

"It is amazing." She sighed. "Wherever did you learn to do that?"

"I had three younger sisters growing up," Lady Derrington said with a satisfied smile. "We could not afford ladies' maids for all of us, but luckily I found I had a talent for hairdressing. You look very pretty, and I am quite sure Drew will think so as well."

That hope gave another little pang at her words. But before Charlotte could ask for more treasured titbits about Drew, there was a commotion below her window.

Forgetting her resolve to be a truly dignified lady, Charlotte hurried to the window, throwing it open to peer down at the driveway below.

Two young men on horseback had arrived in a silvery plume of gravel dust, shouting and laughing. One of the horses, a pretty sorrel, pranced around in an exuberant circle as the rider's hat fell off to reveal an over-long fall of shining brown hair.

"Leo!" Charlotte cried, waving. "You're here at last."

"Charlotte," he called back. He started to wave, but had to grab the reins again as the horse tried to rear back. "You are looking very pretty today indeed."

She laughed. "You needn't sound so surprised. Wait there, I'll be right down."

"Who is that?" Lady Derrington murmured, peering over Charlotte's shoulder.

"My brother Leo," Charlotte answered. "And that must be his friend, Viscount Amesby. They're both horse-mad, and have been going to dozens of auctions of late. Leo wants to start a racing stable here at Welbourne."

"Viscount Amesby," Lady Derrington said thoughtfully. She picked up a shawl from a chair, handing it to Charlotte so she could wrap it around her rumpled dress. "That name sounds quite familiar."

"So it should," Charlotte said cheerfully. "He nearly eloped with Lady Newcombe two Seasons ago. It was quite the scandal! But Leo says he's a bang-up rider, quite the sportsman. And reformed now, reportedly. Why don't you come down with me and meet them?"

Lady Derrington glanced hesitantly towards the window. "Oh—no, my dear. *You* are the hostess, and I find I am a bit tired after all. If you will just have one of the maids show me to my room. I will meet your brother and his friend at dinner."

"If you are quite sure," Charlotte said, suddenly rather reluctant to part from this kind lady who reminded her so of Justine. And who deserved a large share of the laughter of Welbourne. "I will send the housekeeper to you right away."

"Thank you."

Charlotte turned to leave, but then spun back around to give Lady Derrington a quick hug. Suddenly embarrassed by her exuberant Fitzmanning-ness, she dashed out of the room.

Lady Derrington was right. She *was* the hostess, and she had to show Drew that she could perform that task very well. That she could be a good, respectable political wife.

Even if it killed her.

Mary laughed aloud at Charlotte's swift embrace. She couldn't help it—suddenly she felt strangely warm inside. Welcome, and—yes, and hopeful in a way she had not in a very long time.

She had not been quite sure about this party. It was easy to stay at Derrington Hall, to look after little Will and her mother-in-law and stay wrapped up in mourning William. She did not have to converse with anyone, or pretend to be happy. "Happiness" was an emotion she had only vague memories of.

She had only come to Welbourne because she thought it would be good for Drew to get away from Derrington Hall, to see his old friends again, and he would only go if she, too, agreed to the outing. But now she was rather glad she had come. Charlotte Fitzmanning reminded her of her own three sisters, who she missed so very much. And it was good to see Drew smile again.

Altogether a pleasant way to make her slow passage back into the world. Until Viscount Amesby—Dominic—had arrived.

As Charlotte's footsteps faded down the stairs, Mary tiptoed to the window and peeked outside. Yes, indeed, it *was* him. Dominic Spence, Viscount Amesby, his hair gleaming like old gold in the sunshine. Handsome—and dangerous—as Apollo, just as he had been all those years ago.

She bit her lip. Why, oh why, did he have to come along now? Just when she was starting to have fun again…

Chapter Five

"Leo!" Charlotte cried, bursting out of the doors and running into her brother's arms. "You're here at last. I feared you would stay at one of your precious auctions and not appear at all."

"Of course not," Leo said, laughing. "I had to show off my new sweetheart, didn't I? Just look at her, C., isn't she a beauty?"

"Indeed she is," Charlotte answered, gently stroking the mare's velvety nose. The horse pawed the ground restlessly, but her large eyes were kind and intelligent. Spirited and good-hearted—surely just like Leo. "When can I ride her, then?"

He laughed harder. "I knew you would love her! But you can't ride her, not yet. She's still a bit green."

"*You* rode her," Charlotte protested.

"That's different—she knows me," Leo said. "She's going to be the star of my stable, you'll see. Now, come meet my friend, Viscount Amesby."

Charlotte turned to curtsy to Lord Amesby, who grinned and politely raised her hand to his lips. She saw that reports of his handsomeness—he was called "The Sun God" in some of the more florid London papers—were not exaggerated. The angles of his face could have been sculpted out of finest Italian marble, they were so perfectly symmetrical and classically elegant. His golden cap of hair gleamed like a new coin, and his eyes were the violet-blue of a perfect summer sky. Altogether perfection. He would be ideal as a character in *The Witch's Curse*.

And yet, as she gazed at him, she found herself quite unmoved. She simply could not move Drew out of her mind to make room for Sun Gods.

"How do you do, Lord Amesby?" she said, taking back her hand. "You are most welcome to Welbourne."

"And I'm delighted to be here," he answered. "Leo talks in such raptures of his home, I was sure it must be an imaginary enchanted land."

Charlotte laughed. "Oh, Lord Amesby, we are all much too real here, I assure you."

"Not at all." He glanced at the house, gleaming white in the sunlight, bustling with activity. "It is just as lovely as he said. I only wish he had told me how pretty his sister is, as well."

Charlotte laughed even more as Leo playfully cuffed his friend. "Come now, Dominic, if you are quite done flirting with my little sister, we should see to the horses."

"Dinner tonight, Leo," Charlotte said. "Don't be late."

"Certainly not, C.," he said, kissing her cheek. "I know my duty."

The men turned towards the stables, leaving Charlotte alone on the drive. She waved them off, and looked back to the house. The footmen were carrying in the last of the luggage, but for the moment there were no new arrivals. Everyone was—probably—where they should be, though at this house one never knew.

She thought of all she could be doing—checking on the guests' chambers one more time, looking over menus for final approval. All the things Justine had been so good at.

But Charlotte was suddenly tired, her head aching from all there was to remember. From the sheer dizzying force of seeing Drew Bassington again.

She turned away, hurrying along the pathway that led to the pond and the pretty summerhouse. The further she went, the quieter it all became, until all she could hear was the rush of the breeze through the trees. The pounding of her own heart.

The pond looked like a sheet of blue-green glass under the sun, its surface rippled in tiny white wavelets as it brushed against the grassy banks. Towering, shady trees rose up in beckoning groves, the perfect spots for lazy picnics—or for reading and writing. And there was the wooden pier where the rowboats were tied up—and where one could run to the end and take a flying leap into the water.

There was no throwing herself into the pond today, though, no matter how much she might wish it. She had that new resolve to be a fine lady, after all. So instead she just walked to the end of the pier, wrapping the shawl tighter around her shoulders.

How very odd it was, she thought, that just one brief meeting with Drew, after all this time, had so disquieted her. He lived as a dream in her mind, a character in her play, so that she was sure the reality of him could in no way live up to her old infatuation.

And yet he *was* as wonderful as she remembered—and more. There was a new depth to his blue eyes that hinted of hidden sadness, of shadows and secrets she wished he would share with her.

And his touch—his touch made her feel hot and cold all at the same time. All a-tremble with sheer alive-ness.

For the first time, she had some real idea of what had made her parents sacrifice all for the sake of love. Give up reputation, standing, family, because the thought of being apart was untenable.

"Ridiculous," Charlotte muttered, kicking at a wooden piling. To compare her parents' grand passion with one fleeting embrace, which had only come about because of her own blasted clumsiness, was silly indeed.

"What is ridiculous?" Drew asked.

Charlotte spun about, so startled by the sound of his voice she almost tumbled into the water.

He stood at the other end of the short pier, watching her closely. The breeze ruffled his glossy dark curls, tossing them poetically over his brow. In that moment, the new seriousness was gone, and he seemed the wonderfully fun young man who had ridden with her down Welbourne's bridle paths. Who had swum in that very pond, sleek and graceful as a water god.

Then he frowned, and those memories burst like an iridescent bubble. Those days were gone. The responsible Drew was with her now.

"Oh!" she said. "Ridiculous that I let Signore Napoli get so carried away with the courses for tonight's dinner. I am sure we have no need of so very many removes, not for an informal party like this, but he must practice his culinary art. I am not so good at managing him as Justine was."

"I am sure it will all be perfect," Drew said, walking slowly towards her, the wood creaking under his boots.

Charlotte's heart pounded as he came closer, and she found she could not quite look at him. Just the fact that he stood near her, that she could smell his clean scent of soap and wool and leather, feel his warmth, made her shiver.

She wrapped her arms around her waist and said, "I don't know about *perfect*, but I hope everyone will have a good time."

"Yes," he said. "That is what this place has always been about, yes? Enjoying life. I've missed that about Welbourne."

There was a strangely wistful tone to his voice, one that emboldened her to say, "We have missed you here, too, Drew. We haven't seen you at all since Annalise's wedding, and you haven't been to a house party since…" Since that day by this very pond.

A half-smile quirked the corner of his lips. "I have been a bit preoccupied."

"Yes. We were all very sorry to hear about your brother."

"Thank you, Charlotte."

"But your sister-in-law is very kind! I was so happy to meet her today."

That smile widened. "I'm glad you liked her. Mary is a brick—William was lucky indeed to win her. I fear she has much need of Welbourne's fun this week."

"She is not the only one though, is she?" Charlotte said.

They looked at each other, and there, deep in those dark blue eyes, she did see the old Drew. That Drew who was full of laughter and life. He was just hiding very, very well.

"What do you mean?" he said.

"I mean, Lady Derrington is not the only one still sad. Still worried." She reached out and gently touched his arm. Under the soft woollen sleeve, his lean muscles tensed for an instant. Then he relaxed under her touch, and gave her a smile. It made Charlotte smile, too, and she felt absurdly as if the sun had come out on a gloomy day.

"I fear you are quite right," he said, pressing his hand over hers. "I have become a dull old stick of late."

"If there is anything we Fitzmannings are good at, it is curing anyone of dry old stick-ness. Look what wonders happened to Brenner when he met us!" she said happily. She tugged at his arm, drawing him to the end of the pier. "Do you remember picnics here by the pond? That time Stephen threw Nicholas into the water when they had that silly quarrel?"

Drew laughed, a wonderful deep, rich, chocolatey sound that warmed Charlotte to her very toes. "How could I forget?"

"Or when you would row Annalise and me over to the summerhouse, so we could paint and write in peace?" She gestured to the pretty white building, so near and yet so far in all it meant.

"Of course. I had a most delightful afternoon lying under the trees doing nothing while you worked."

"And Annalise drew your portrait." Charlotte still had that sketch, tucked away in her locked treasure box, but she couldn't tell him *that*.

"Do you still go there often? To the summerhouse?"

She shook her head. "Not now. You are not the only one with new responsibilities, Drew."

He was quiet for a moment before asking, "Do you miss your sisters a great deal?"

"Of course. But I see them often, and they are so

very happy in their marriages." Charlotte smiled. "I am hoping for nieces and nephews very soon."

Drew laughed. "They are indeed a blessing."

"Oh, yes! *You* have a nephew, do you not? He must be a handful indeed, if he is related to you."

"Little Will is quite an imp of mischief, true. He gives his mother and grandmother fits of worry! And he grows so very fast he should not be called *little* Will much longer."

She smiled wistfully at the unmistakable affection and pride in Drew's voice as he spoke of his nephew. "He is most fortunate to have you."

Drew's smile flickered. "He would be more fortunate to have his own father, I fear. William was far more steady than I could ever be."

Charlotte shook her head. "I miss my own parents terribly, but my brothers and sisters have been my rocks. Family is what matters, isn't it? No matter where we find them."

"I suppose so."

She looked again to the summerhouse. "That was my mother's favourite place at Welbourne. She used to say it was her own little enchanted circle of peace and tranquillity. I always think of her there—at peace."

"And yet you seldom go there now?"

"No." She turned resolutely away from the house, from the pond and its beckoning laziness, and hurried back along the pier. "I told you—I don't have time. And we should get back to the house. The other guests will be arriving soon, and I am sure my brothers are far too busy to greet them properly."

And, she remembered with a pang, those "other guests" included Lady Emily Carroll and her parents. The pretty, perfect Lady Emily, who was meant for Drew in her brothers' new matchmaking scheme.

Charlotte shook her head, feeling foolish for forgetting that even for a moment.

Chapter Six

Dinner was going quite well, as far as Charlotte could see. Signore Napoli's creations were delicious, as usual, platters of meats and fish and rich sauces, bowls of white soup and fruit salads, great pyramids of pastries, all well paired with wines and cordials supplied by her brothers. Conversation flowed along the flower-laden table like a rich Burgundy, laughter growing higher and higher, as if to join the frolicking gods in the ceiling murals.

All in all, another successful start to a Welbourne party, and she had organised and presided over it all. She should be well pleased indeed.

If only Lady Emily Carroll was not sitting halfway along that bright table. Lady Emily, who was so elegant, so perfectly golden and white, like an angel in fashionable sea-green silk. Lady Emily, who spoke quietly and laughed prettily. And who sat right next to Drew.

Charlotte gestured to the footmen, guiding them along as they carried in yet more dishes. Her brothers all seemed to be having fun, joking and jostling as usual. Leo was talking merrily about his newest equine acquisitions, and Nicholas and Stephen were doubtless congratulating themselves on their matchmaking abilities.

Blast them.

Charlotte shook her head, reaching for her wineglass to take a sip. It was silly of her, really. She had always known Drew was not for her. It wasn't until she had seen him here that all her old dreams had come rushing back. It should not pain her now to see him with a woman like Lady Emily, who was everything Charlotte wanted to be and knew she was not—calm, cool, collected, respectable, beautiful. Everything Drew needed now.

But it *did* pain her. And she did still have those longings.

"Leo says you are quite a gifted writer, Miss Fitzmanning," Lord Amesby, who sat to Charlotte's left, said, interrupting her melancholy musings.

She turned to smile at him. A lady such as Lady Emily would never neglect her hostess duties, and neither could Charlotte. "I would not say *gifted*, Lord Amesby. I do enjoy scribbling now and again, though."

He smiled back at her, and it seemed to light up his golden, perfect face from within. He really was absurdly handsome, perfect for one of Annalise's paintings of gods. Why didn't she feel anything when he smiled so? "Poems or novels? Or perhaps both. My sister says she is attempting to write an historical novel based on Alexander the Great."

Charlotte laughed. "She is far more ambitious than I am, then. I have not written any novels at all, and only a few poems. My brothers used to have a tendency to steal them, and use them to embarrass me at parties."

"I trust that won't happen now!"

"One never knows at Welbourne, Lord Amesby. But I have given up poetry to write a play."

"Ah! And will we have a sample of your work when we try our amateur theatricals?"

"Not at all," Charlotte said. "My play is not yet finished, and it would be too dull. You would be much better off with Sheridan or Shakespeare, I think."

"What is the plot of your play, then, Miss Fitzmanning?"

Charlotte glanced along the table to Drew, who was listening to Lady Emily with that crooked half-smile on his lips. What could she be saying, to make him smile like that? "It is a story of a man, a count, who has lost his way, until he finds his true love. She brings him his true purpose in life."

"I venture a guess that true love does not run smoothly."

Charlotte forced herself to laugh merrily, turning away from Drew. "Of course not, or it would be a very short play indeed. There are dark curses, forces that tear apart the lovers and try to make them turn from the true path. Their own hearts test them, as well."

"And how does it all end?"

She shrugged. "I am not yet certain. Well for them, I think." But sometimes, *well* was even too much to ask for.

"It sounds perfect for our theatricals, Miss Fitzmanning."

"Maybe for the next party, then, when the play is finished. Would you want to play the count?"

Lord Amesby smiled at her. "If you would play the true love."

Charlotte laughed again. "I will find you a better leading lady. My talents are entirely behind the scenes." She looked again along the table, past Lady Emily and Drew, who now talked with their other dinner partners, to Lady Derrington, who chatted with Nicholas. She was smiling politely, nodding, looking beautiful in violet-coloured satin, yet Charlotte could see those shadows still in her eyes.

"What of Lady Derrington?" she said. "She seems exactly right for a tragic princess."

Lord Amesby, too, looked to Lady Derrington, his own brilliant smile flickering. "She is certainly lovely enough, Miss Fitzmanning. But I doubt she would agree to the part."

Puzzled, intrigued by this little mystery, Charlotte nodded. "Well, as I said, my play is not yet finished. Perhaps you could favour us with a scene from *Romeo and Juliet*?"

Before Lord Amesby could answer, Nicholas rose to his feet, his wineglass held high. "My friends!" he said jovially. "I propose a toast to another fine gathering here at Welbourne."

Everyone agreed in a most enthusiastic chorus, all the men springing up to join him. As Charlotte laughed, Drew turned towards her. For an instant, his smile was that of the old Drew, full of the promise of mischief and merriment. It made her long to run into his arms, to hold him close. To imagine that they could at last be together, as she had always wanted.

But then he raised his glass to his lips, and over its gilded edge his eyes darkened as if he remembered who he was. Where he was. And when he lowered the glass he was the solemn new Drew once more.

"I say, you are all far too quiet," Stephen announced in the drawing room after dinner, as everyone gathered for tea and chatter. "We should play a game."

"Charades?" said Lady Appleby.

"Backgammon?" Lord Moreby said.

"No, no, far too intellectual," Stephen protested. "I propose something far more fun. A fine way for everyone to get to know each other better."

Lady Emily bit her lip, glancing uncertainly at her

mother. "Get to know each other better?" she said quietly.

Charlotte laughed. As hostess, she thought she should probably discourage Stephen's mischief. But she was too curious to see what he would say next. "Stephen, please. You're going to frighten everyone away."

"Not at all," Leo said. "If they come to Welbourne, they know what to expect. What game do you suggest, Stephen?"

"I suggest…" Stephen paused to sweep them all with an arch glance. "I propose hide and seek."

Charlotte's bosom-bow, Mae, who sat next to her on the couch by the tea table, laughed. "Oh, honestly, Lord Stephen. We aren't in the nursery."

Stephen frowned at her. "One does not have to be an infant to appreciate hide and seek, Miss Halford. Welbourne has many secret corners—what better way to discover them?"

"I think it sounds amusing," Lord Amesby said. "Who shall hide and who shall seek?"

"I think Emily and I shall do neither," Lady Moreby said slowly, after exchanging glances with her husband. "It has been a long journey today, and it is time for us to retire."

For one instant, Charlotte thought Lady Emily might show a flash of spirit and protest. She opened her rosebud mouth, but then closed it again, glancing down. She left with her mother without saying anything more than "Good night."

Charlotte looked to Drew, trying to see if he was disappointed by her departure, but he was talking with Lady Derrington and seemed not to notice.

"I say the ladies should hide," Stephen said, "and the gentlemen seek."

"Which is always the way," said Nicholas.

"So, ladies," Stephen continued, "we shall count in here, while you find the best hiding places. Starting—now."

Laughing, Charlotte and Mae clasped hands and dashed out of the drawing room, dodging around the other ladies who scattered in the hall.

"Tell me quick, Charlotte," Mae gasped. "Where is the best place?"

"You go that way, to the secret panel in the library," Charlotte said. "I'll go to the attics."

She hurried up the stairs, until she reached the doors to her own little writing room and Annalise's studio. She couldn't go to her own space—her precious manuscripts were hidden there, and she remembered all too well what had happened the last time her brothers had found her writings. She ducked into Annalise's studio, closing the door behind her.

The large space was rather eerie at night, with the moonlight shining in chalky-yellow rays through the high windows. The shadows fell on canvases Annalise had left behind, draped in cloths and propped against the walls. A faint smell of turpentine still hung in the air, but without her sister it all seemed terribly lifeless.

The quiet was so deep it almost echoed, and after the crowd at dinner Charlotte found it a relief. A moment to be alone with her thoughts, even if they *were* confused ones.

She found a niche behind one of Annalise's easels and settled herself on the floor there, tucking the skirts of her white muslin gown around her. Anyone "seeking" would not be able to see her there, unless they looked very well indeed, and she could wait out Stephen's silly game.

Charlotte drew up her knees, resting her cheek against them as she thought of dinner. Her first time to play hostess alone at Welbourne, and it had gone rather well. Nothing disastrous had happened at all. Surely Drew could see that she could be responsible and respectable—just as much as Lady Emily.

He would just have to see that she, Charlotte, could indeed make a good wife.

Overcome by a ridiculous wave of optimism, she closed her eyes and smiled. No, surely all hope was *not* lost. She had the rest of the party to show him she had changed.

The soft click of the door made her open her eyes, startled. Holding her breath, she peeked around the easel.

At first she could see nothing but a man's tall silhouette against the light outside. Then whoever it was stepped inside, closing the door behind him.

"Hello. Is anyone there?" Drew called softly.

Charlotte gasped, and pressed her hand to her

mouth. It was a sign—it had to be. She slid down lower.

"I know someone is here," Drew said, his voice full of amusement. "You might as well come out, so we can declare this game at an end and have a cup of tea like sensible people."

Charlotte tried to stifle a laugh, but it escaped anyway. The next thing she knew, Drew had ducked around the easel and seized her hand, pulling her to her feet.

"Ah-ha," he said. "I knew it was you, Charlotte."

They were pressed together there in the shadows, and she was sure the rest of the world had quite disappeared. There was only Drew, the warmth of his body close to hers, the clean smell of him, his strength wrapped around her. She leaned into him, fitting her body into the angles of his, and her eyes closed as she inhaled him deeply.

She felt his chin nestle on top of her head, his arms close around her to draw her even closer.

"How did you find me?" she whispered.

"I just—knew," he answered. And then he kissed her.

Their lips touched, softly at first, gently, and it was just as she had always expected. The way he tasted, of wine and mint and Drew, the way his lips felt on hers, the way they fitted. It was just as she dreamed, alone at night when she thought of him. She sighed happily.

On that breath, Drew groaned and dragged her

closer, so very close she couldn't tell where she ended and he began. His mouth opened, his tongue seeking hers in an explosion of sheer *need*.

Charlotte met him with a desperate desire of her own, desire so long denied. She clasped her fingers in the cool, curling silk of his hair, going up on tiptoe to greedily take him in. Hold him to her so he couldn't escape. This was *Drew* who kissed her, the Drew she had loved for so long. And it was so much better than she could have imagined.

Through the haze of her desire, she felt his hand caress her throat, skim over her bare shoulder above her sleeve. Her skin burned wherever he touched, as if it had never truly been alive before. As if *she* had never been alive before, until he touched her—like a fairy story. The cursed princess.

She longed to touch him, too, to feel even more of him, but he eased away from her. His lips slid from hers, and he rested his forehead against hers, his breath ragged. She opened her eyes, suddenly so bereft. So lost without his kiss. His eyes were tightly closed, his brow creased as if he was in pain.

"Charlotte, Charlotte," he said hoarsely. "I am so sorry. I don't know what madness came over me."

Sorry? He was *sorry*, for what was the most wondrous moment of her life? Cold, as if a chilly rain had suddenly dropped on to her sunny day, she pulled away from him, wrapping her arms tightly around her waist.

"Oh, Drew," she said, trying so hard to smile at

him. To pretend she did not care. "There is no need to be sorry. It's just a silly game, yes?"

"Charlotte, no…" he began. But she felt too fragile to hear any more gentlemanly apologies, explanations. She spun around and dashed away, leaving him in the studio.

Her vision blurred by a rush of hot tears, she tripped at the bottom of the attic stairs. Her hem tore with a loud ripping sound, and for an instant she wondered if it was her heart.

She stared down at the ragged tear, not sure if she was crying or laughing.

"Oh, blast," she muttered. So much for showing Drew what a responsible lady she was now.

Drew inhaled his cigarillo, feeling the bite of the smoke deep inside his lungs before he exhaled it into the night. Even the silvery smoke, the solitude of the garden, could not erase Charlotte from his mind. From all his senses. He could still feel her slender body against his, fitting so perfectly in his arms. Still taste her.

His reformed ways were delicate indeed. Only one day back at Welbourne and they had vanished.

Drew laughed ruefully, examining the fierce red glow in the darkness. Truly he knew it was *not* Welbourne—it was Charlotte herself, and his own nature.

He had watched her during dinner, the way she smiled at the cursedly handsome Amesby, laughed with him at some shared joke. The man they called "Apollo" in town, all the ladies sighing over him despite his scandalous past. Charlotte, too, seemed to like him, despite her distinct lack of sighs.

It all made it quite difficult to concentrate on Lady Emily. Or on anything at all but Charlotte.

"You are a fool," he muttered. But such a happy fool, when he kissed Charlotte Fitzmanning.

From the open drawing-room windows behind him, he heard the joyful clamour of those who hid and those who sought being reunited. He couldn't quite bring himself to go in there, not until his rebellious body was back under control. Until he could see Charlotte without grabbing her again. Without throwing away all he had built in his life since William had died.

Drew ground out the cigarillo on the gravel walkway and strolled out into the dark gardens, the lights and voices fading behind him.

Yet he was not quite alone. From a small Grecian temple, between the pale marble columns, he heard a man talking. Low and urgent. A lady responded, her voice soft and sad. A lovers' quarrel?

Drew quickly reversed his steps, not wanting to intrude on their privacy. As he turned back towards the house, just out of sight from the temple, a woman in a dark gown hurried out between those columns and down the steps.

To his shock, as she dashed by, he saw it was Mary. Tears shimmered on her cheeks, sparkling like the jet embroidery on her violet gown. And on the temple steps, the moonlight glinted on the golden hair of Lord Amesby.

Well, well, Drew thought, stunned. Welbourne held many surprises indeed.

Chapter Seven

Lady Emily Carroll gazed out of her chamber window, watching the morning sun burn away the mist. She didn't see the classical statues, the winding paths twisting away to intriguing little nooks. She didn't think of what to wear to the day's picnic. She was too worried.

She nibbled at the ragged edge of her thumbnail. Her parents had long been friends with the late Duke of Manning and his mistress, then Duchess, drawn together by their mutual love of art and Italy. But they had always kept her away from that family—until now. And she knew why they had brought her here this week.

They wanted her to marry the new Duke. Nicholas.

Emily shook her head. He was very handsome, of course, wealthy, affable. But he was so very—lively. His whole family was, constantly tussling and teasing and laughing. And she was too slow, too shy. He would never look twice at her.

He had shown no interest in her since they had arrived. She was doomed to fail, just as she always did.

"Emily!" she heard her mother say. She glanced back to see her standing in the doorway, already dressed for their outing.

"You are not yet ready. You should wear your blue-striped muslin—it brings out your eyes," her mother clucked. "And do stop biting your nails, dearest. A lady's hands are so important."

Emily nodded. "Yes, Mama. Of course."

Mary paced the length of her chamber floor and back, her dressing gown trailing behind her.

Why was *he* here? She had thought never to see him again, thought she would never have to remember. When she had seen him yesterday, it was as if lightning had flashed all through her body, tingling and warm. It was like—life.

She had forgotten what *life* felt like. She wasn't entirely sure she liked it.

"I should go home," she muttered. Home to her son, her ailing mother-in-law, the memory of William—to the chilly duty that had been her only companion for so long. Forget Dominic—again.

Yet she could not run away. Not this time.

Mary resolutely rang the bell for her maid. It was time to dress, and face the day. Whatever it brought.

* * *

"It isn't working, is it?" Stephen said glumly. "Drew and Charlotte aren't any closer to being together."

Nicholas leaned against the window frame in the library, watching everyone gather on the drive to make their way to the picnic. Charlotte, her face hidden by the brim of her straw hat, was directing the servants as they packed the baskets of provisions on to the carts. Drew stood at the opposite side of the drive with his sister-in-law.

The two of them did not even look at each other.

"I fear you might be correct, brother," he said. "This matchmaking business is not quite as simple as we thought."

"If only they would just be sensible, and see how happy they would be together," Stephen said.

"They're fortunate they need only consult themselves on who best to marry," Nicholas muttered. "Not who would make a suitable duchess."

Stephen laughed. "*I* need not worry about that, either."

"No, you needn't." Nicholas watched as Charlotte laughed with her friend Mae and Lord Amesby. "Good thing, too, as you would botch it completely."

"Well, *you* are not doing such a fine job either," Stephen said, joining Nicholas at the window. "When will you find that duchess, Nick?"

"After Drew marries Charlotte. So we had best hurry them along."

"How should we do that, then? At least Drew doesn't appear to have fallen madly for Lady Emily."

Nicholas turned his attention to Drew. He and Lady Derrington were chatting politely with Lady Emily and her mother, but with no evidence of extraordinary interest or sparks. Luckily.

Yet the morning sun gleamed on Lady Emily's beautiful, bright curls, on her shy smile, making her look like the veriest angel. Strange—he had never noticed just how pretty she was before.

Too bad she was such an icicle.

"Perhaps that was not the best strategy after all," he said wryly.

"Then we need a new one. Any ideas?"

"Not at present. But I suspect the clue to potential success might lie in Charlotte's attic."

"No!" Stephen gasped. "She will ring a peal over us for going in there. She told me she planted curses around the room to keep anyone out."

"You and your curses," Nicholas said, exasperated. "It is true that Charlotte would not be happy if she found us in there. But desperate times call for very desperate measures."

Charlotte stretched her feet out before her on the picnic blanket, reaching them out of the shade so just the tips of her shoes were warmed by the sun. It felt delicious.

All this trying to be the perfect hostess, trying to show Drew how accomplished she was, was really quite exhausting. Now that all the cold chicken and ham, the cakes and wine, had been consumed and everyone was happy in the warm afternoon, she could relax a bit.

Oliver and Octavia snuggled close to her skirts, napping after finishing their crumbs. Their snores blended with the soft laughter, the breeze through the leaves, the splash of oars in the water. Stephen, who had arrived rather late along with Nicholas—which usually signalled some mischief—rowed Mae about the pond.

Nicholas sat with Lord and Lady Moreby, who had cornered him under a tree, while Lady Emily chatted with Lady Derrington. Drew and Leo were having an obviously very serious discussion about horses down by the edge of the water. Everyone was comfortably disposed of for the moment.

Charlotte leaned back on her elbows, lazily watching the way the light turned Drew's dark hair to reddish fire. He turned his face up to the sun, smiling as if greedy for its delicious warmth, and her heart pounded in her breast. How very beautiful he was.

How she longed for him. For all he was—his humour, his good heart. His handsome backside in those tight breeches. All of it.

Yes, surely *this* was what drove her mother. This overwhelming need. If only Drew returned her passion, too.

"I say, Charlotte," Nicholas said, having escaped

the Morebys. He knelt down beside her, tugging on her foot. She kicked out at him, but he persisted in disrupting her reverie. "You look far too lazy sitting there. Why don't you let Drew row you about the pond? He isn't doing anything useful."

Charlotte glanced at Drew, sure he would protest. Surely after their kiss last night, and his apologies and regrets, he wouldn't want to be alone with her in a little boat, just the two of them out on the water. But he just shrugged, and gave her that unreadable little smile of his.

"Of course, if Charlotte agrees," Drew said. "After planning such a fine repast, she deserves to be carried away."

"I don't…" Charlotte began. Despite herself, her gaze shot to the edge of the pond, to the tree where she had once spied on Drew as he swam. Surely such a scene would not be repeated with so many people about, but she could always hope. "Thank you, Lord Andrew, that would be most pleasant."

"What's got into you, C.?" Nicholas scoffed, tugging on her foot again. "Lord Andrew! Are we at Court suddenly?"

"Oh, go boil your head, your Grace," Charlotte said, standing up and shaking out her skirts. "I am going off for a boat ride."

She hurried towards the nearest empty rowboat, Oliver and Octavia scrambling behind her. As they climbed in, Drew untied the vessel from its moorings and pushed them off into the glasslike water.

The pugs planted their paws on the wooden edge, happily watching the crowd fall away as they set off on a new doggy adventure. Charlotte herself found she could not be quite so sanguine, not when Drew was so very near.

She leaned back against the cushions, trying to relax, to imagine that this was just an ordinary day. A quick picnic jaunt. Trying *not* to think about that kiss. But the more she tried, the more she remembered.

And the warmer the day became. She loosened her fichu, surreptitiously fanning her neck.

Drew, too, seemed not to know what to say. They were halfway along the pond, to the footbridge that led to the summerhouse, when he cleared his throat and said slowly, "Charlotte, I—well..."

Charlotte felt a sudden pang of disappointment, which was silly really. What did she expect? Declarations of undying love? Of eternal passion? Surely she knew better than that by now.

"You aren't going to apologise again, are you?" she said.

Drew smiled ruefully. "Honestly, Charlotte, I was not entirely sure *what* I was going to say. If you would like me to apologise again, I certainly can."

"There's no need at all. It was just the party atmosphere, my brother's silly game."

"No, that wasn't it."

She glanced at him sharply. "Then what was it?"

He shook his head, a lock of hair falling enticingly over his brow as he pulled harder at the oars. "I would never want you to think I hold you, or your family, in some disrespect."

She laughed. "You would be one of the only ones then, Drew."

"That is not true. And I, of all people, know the great harm of petty gossip." Talk over his own youthful antics had marred his relationship with his family for so long. "But last night…"

His words faltered, just as things were getting interesting. Charlotte sat straight up. "Last night— what?"

"Last night you were so damnably pretty," he said roughly. "Something just came over me, and I had to kiss you. That's all."

"Oh, Drew!" she cried. It was as if the sun had come out at last, as if a bright flower of hope suddenly bloomed. She was *damnably pretty*. It was sad that so few words could make her so hopeful, but there it was.

She wasn't sure how to tell him that she felt the same, that he was "damnably pretty" himself. So, she just lunged across the boat, throwing her arms around his neck.

Unfortunately, by doing so she unceremoniously dislodged the dogs, and they set up a great wail of pug shrieking and twirling. Just as Charlotte's lips touched Drew's, the boat tilted perilously to one side. Entwined, they lost their balance and toppled into the cold water.

The pond was not terribly deep, and they quickly resurfaced, Drew dragging her up by the waist as they gasped for breath. But her dignity was not so easily restored. Charlotte pushed back her sodden hair, staring disconsolately at the shocked onlookers ashore. Lady Emily still looked perfect, of course, all golden and prim.

This on-dit would surely be making the drawing-room rounds in no time at all.

"Are you quite all right, Charlotte?" Drew asked in concern, lifting her back into the boat.

Charlotte collapsed on to the bottom, wishing with all her might she could just vanish. She was an utter drowned rat-urchin now, a hoyden of the first order. And just when Drew had called her "pretty"!

She wasn't very pretty now, with her skirts soaked with pond water.

Oliver and Octavia stared down at her with their big eyes, completely unrepentant at the havoc they had wreaked.

"Oh, yes," she muttered. "Quite all right indeed." Except for her dignity, of course. And surely dignity was a quality Drew would want in a wife. Like Lady Emily, standing so still on shore.

Charlotte groaned, closing her eyes tightly. She was a scandalous Fitzmanning through and through, and she could surely never escape it!

Drew struggled to hold in his laughter as he rowed back to shore, his sodden boots squeaking at every movement. It was clear that Charlotte was in no mood for mirth, sitting opposite him with her hair dripping around her like a mermaid.

Yet it was blasted hard to keep from bursting out. Their situation was so ridiculous, so utterly Welbourne-esque. And Charlotte, damp and dismayed, with a clump of wet leaves caught in a lock of her hair, looked so very pretty again.

And she had been about to kiss him. He was sure of it!

He felt absurdly alive as he pulled towards shore. His life had been so void of laughter of late, so lacking in silliness and fun, that even this seemed wondrous. He longed to catch Charlotte in his arms, to haul her against him and kiss her as they both dripped water all over the place. Kiss her until she laughed, too, and everything else was completely forgotten.

He had the distinct sense she would not welcome kisses just at the moment. That she did not quite see the delicious humour of their situation, and her urge for kissing had passed. Well, he had become a patient man. He could wait.

For a while.

The boat bumped against the shore, and before he could help her Charlotte jumped out, stalking away towards the house. The dogs gambolled after her, unconcerned about what had happened, chasing each other's uncurled tails. Leo hurried to his sister's side, but she just shook her head at him and kept walking.

Drew leaned on the oars, laughing deeply now that Charlotte could not hear him. Once he started, he found he could not stop. He tilted his head back to the sky, howling.

Ah, yes. It was a good day indeed.

Chapter Eight

Charlotte glanced down at the note in her hand. *C.—come to the summerhouse as soon as you can. A party disaster looms, and your help is desperately needed. Nicholas.*

A party disaster? In the summerhouse? Charlotte shook her head in puzzled impatience. Her brothers were often prone to exaggeration, not to mention pranks. This was probably one of those, though she could not fathom how.

But then again, they *had* planned a luncheon outing to the summerhouse for the day after tomorrow, and there was a chance there was some real "disaster" connected to that. She had to see what was happening, or she would lie awake worrying all night.

She tugged her shawl closer around her shoulders, holding her lantern higher. It was quite late—most of the guests had already retired. She had just gone to her own chamber when the cryptic note had arrived, and she still wore her thin silk dinner gown.

"If this is a joke, Nicholas," she muttered, stepping over a loose board on the footbridge to the summerhouse, "I will make you very sorry indeed."

At last, the house came into view. Only one window was lit, and it seemed very quiet. Surely whatever "disaster" loomed it could not be a great one.

Charlotte let herself in by the side door, which led into the main salon. Two smaller rooms led off it, and it was from one of those that the light shone.

She put the lantern down on a gilt table and unwound her shawl. The rooms had the stuffy, warm feeling of an unused space, and yet she thought she smelled roses. Fresh white roses—her mother's old favourites.

"Nicholas?" Charlotte called. "Stephen? Are you here? What is the meaning of this?"

"Charlotte?" someone answered. But it was not one of her brothers—it was *Drew*'s voice, full of surprise to match her own.

He appeared in the doorway, the light behind him casting a soft golden glow around him in a corona. He had removed his coat and loosened his cravat, his hair falling over his brow in that rumpled, poetic way she so loved.

"Charlotte, what are you doing here?" he said.

She glanced back over her shoulder, as if some

answer lurked in the thick shadows of the salon. She thought she saw a movement, but it was just a breeze through the curtains.

This *was* some sort of prank, then! Some silly, unfathomable joke of her silly brothers'. Oh, she would *kill* them when she next saw them!

Charlotte wrapped her arms around her waist, turning back to Drew.

"You're cold," he said quickly, hurrying over to take her hand. "You shouldn't be out here in the middle of the night. Come in here, it's warmer."

She let him lead her into the smaller room, a cosy space her mother had once used as an intimate sitting room on summer days. The lightweight white-silk curtains were drawn over the windows, and a fire even crackled in the little pink-marble grate. The lamps cast a warm amber glow over the white silk and gilt chairs and couch.

Over the fireplace, her mother's portrait smiled down at her. Catherine's eyes shone as brightly as the painted diamonds around her neck, as if she, too, were in on the joke.

And set before the fire was a small table, set with wine glasses and a plate of cakes.

"What is all this?" Charlotte whispered.

Drew shrugged. "I received a note from Stephen and Nicholas, saying they needed my urgent help. I assumed they wanted some advice on some prank they're planning."

"I had a note from them, too," Charlotte said,

holding out the crumpled missive. "Oh, Drew. I think we *are* the prank."

Drew laughed ruefully as she tossed the note into the fire. "Why make us come out here, though? Even for your brothers it makes no sense."

"When did things have to make sense for them?" she muttered. Still, it *was* rather strange. Why wouldn't they lure Drew here with Lady Emily, if they were so intent on their matchmaking scheme? "I suppose they just wanted to cause a spot of inconvenience."

"Let me walk you back to the house, then," Drew said with a gentle smile.

At least someone is getting a bit of amusement out of all this, Charlotte thought. But after the embarrassment of her dunking that afternoon, she would much rather have stayed hidden in her room!

"Thank you," she said. "Tomorrow we must come up with a way to have our revenge on them for bringing us out here."

"Agreed," Drew said.

But as they turned to the door, it suddenly slammed shut. There was the unmistakable metallic "snick" of a lock shooting into place.

"Nicholas!" Charlotte screamed. "Stephen! What have you done?" She ran to the window, throwing back the curtains just in time to see her brothers' shadows dashing over the footbridge. Their lanterns bobbed off into the distance, like mocking little bubbles of laughter.

"Come back!" she called, rattling the window. But the ornamental little gilded bars held fast. They were trapped.

She was trapped, with Drew. In the darkness of the night. How could she trust herself not to behave like a fool again?

Drew laughed and Charlotte spun around to face him. He sat on the couch by the fire, one of the wine-glasses in his hand.

"Well, I am glad *you* are enjoying yourself," Charlotte said. "We're locked in here!"

"Oh, Charlotte," Drew said, giving her that alluring little half-smile. "Don't worry. I am sure your brothers won't gossip about you. You won't compromise me."

"Why would they do this, though?"

"No doubt for some mysterious reason of their own, which will be revealed to us tomorrow."

"They've probably been drinking to excess."

"Then so should we." Drew picked up the other glass, waving it at her enticingly. "It's quite good. French."

Charlotte glanced back out of the window, but she could see only the dark outlines of the trees. Whatever Nicholas and Stephen were up to, they weren't coming back any time soon.

"Oh, very well," she said, with a shrug. "It will pass the time." She went to take the wine from Drew, perching at the other end of the couch. Even from that distance, she was completely aware of him. Of his nearness, and the cosy intimacy of the scene.

Her mother still smiled down at her, as if encouraging her to naughtiness.

Charlotte took a deep gulp of the wine. It *was* good, though she hardly tasted it. She gulped it again and again, feeling its reassuring, numbing warmth spread to her toes.

Drew leaned back on the cushions, still smiling at her. The firelight turned his skin and hair to molten gold, like some ancient idol. "At least they left us well provisioned," he said.

"Very kind of them, I'm sure," Charlotte answered. She took another drink, draining her glass, starting to feel just a bit more relaxed. She, too, leaned back, kicking off her shoes under her skirt hem. "Your sister-in-law seems very kind. Not at all the sort of sibling to play a prank on you."

"She is very kind, yes. My brother never had a luckier day than when she married him."

"I hope she isn't too bored here."

Drew laughed ruefully. "I don't think *bored* is the word."

"And you?"

"Me? I am never bored at Welbourne."

"Things are a bit quieter than they used to be, before Brenner came along."

"I'm quieter myself." Drew reached for the bottle of wine, refilling their glasses.

"Do you miss your brother terribly?" Charlotte asked.

"Miss William?" Drew shook his head. "We

weren't very close, not like you and your siblings. Mostly he lectured me, and I rebelled against him and his strictness. I suppose I miss that sometimes."

"It's hard to rebel effectively, when there is no one to rebel against," Charlotte said.

"Exactly so. I must be the stern one now, once little Will is older."

"He is fortunate to have you. Complete freedom is never easy."

"What?" Drew said teasingly. "An endorsement of stern lectures from one of the Fitzmanning Miscellany?"

Charlotte laughed. The wine was doing its work, spreading warm lassitude all through her veins. "I know. Shocking. But it's probably nice to know someone cares what you do."

"And doesn't lock you up in a summerhouse?"

"That, too."

"But they left us wine. And cakes, too, I see." He reached for the plate, offering it to her with a flourish.

Charlotte took a lemon cake. "Delicious. All captivities should be like this."

"And with such lovely company."

She laughed happily. "Wouldn't you rather be here with Lady Emily?"

"Why would I want that?"

"She is so very pretty. And she would make a fine wife, especially for someone intent on being a stern lecturer in future."

Charlotte suddenly felt his touch, light and gentle, on her cheek, brushing back a stray lock of hair. Soft as it was, it sent a sizzling bolt of summer lightning all through her.

She turned to find him watching her intently, his blue eyes hooded and serious. His fingertips trailed over her cheek, along her neck to her bare shoulder, leaving a ribbon of fire in their wake.

"No one could be prettier than you, Charlotte," he said hoarsely. "I'm tired of being stern, of being the responsible one. I only want…"

Overcome with the emotion, the yearning, of years, Charlotte leaned over and kissed him. She kissed him with all of her might, all of her heart, and she felt him respond. His arms came around her tightly, pulling her close until there was nothing between them. No past or future—only their kiss.

His tongue lightly teased the seam of her lips, until she opened and let him in. She pushed aside his cravat and the edges of his shirt, touching at last the warmth of his bare skin. His heart pounded under her palm, strong and frantic, echoing her own.

He groaned deeply against her mouth, dragging her even closer until she lay on top of him. They toppled off the couch, landing on the carpet in a tangle of limbs and fabric, but Charlotte hardly noticed. All her senses were full of *Drew*, the taste, the smell, the wonderful feel of him.

He rolled her beneath him, his lips trailing from hers to kiss her jaw, her cheek. He caught her earlobe between his teeth, biting lightly until she moaned. Every nerve seemed alive with sensation, awareness. She had never felt so glorious, so vibrant! So perfectly where she should be.

His kiss slid down the arch of her throat as she threw her head back. He traced the tip of his tongue along her collarbone, the curve of her shoulder, easing the bodice of her gown lower.

Suddenly impatient, desperate to feel *more* of him, feel him closer, Charlotte pushed his shirt over his head, tossing it away. Her greedy touch swept over his naked chest, the lean muscles gilded in bronze satin skin, roughened with dark hair.

It was so strange, so foreign to touch him, and yet so very familiar. She had dreamed of it for so long, imagined it. But the reality far surpassed any fantasy.

He slid lower, kissing the upper edge of her breast above her chemise. Charlotte gasped as she felt the roughness of his tongue on her soft skin, raking her fingertips along the hollow of his spine. She clasped his hair, pressing him against her.

Drew groaned against her breast, capturing her nipple in his mouth. The wetness against the fabric of her chemise, the friction, made her frantic. She arched up into his body, her legs falling apart to cradle him against her.

Drew reached down to catch the hem of her gown, drawing it up over her legs and hips, dragging it against her stockings. She wrapped her thighs around him, fearful he might try to escape her. She couldn't lose this feeling, this wonderful sensation. Not ever.

Yes, *this* was indeed what her mother had sought when she had run away with her father. What her sisters found with their husbands. She understood now, for she, too, would give anything to keep it. To keep him.

She swept her caress to his backside, squeezing the firm curves as she pulled him closer into the warmth of her body. His erection, so carefully illustrated in the ancient manuscripts and etchings her parents had brought back from Italy, was iron-hard against her. She knew what *that* meant—he wanted her as much as she wanted him.

"Please, Drew," she whispered. "I want you now, please."

He glanced up at her sharply. His blue eyes were unfocused with desire, but in their depths she could see the first hateful glimmer of doubt. Of gentlemanly hesitation, as had happened in the attic.

"Charlotte," he muttered roughly. "I'm not sure— no, I *am* sure we shouldn't go on. The first time…"

"I know," she said hastily. "Remember my family? I know what happens. I'm ready. I—oh, Drew. I've wanted this for so very long. Haven't you?" She prayed he said "yes". He *had* to say yes!

"Yes," he said. "God help me, but I have."

And then he kissed her again. There was no art to their kiss, no careful technique. Just that desperate need, that blurry rush of heat and need.

Charlotte edged up so he could unbutton her gown, fumbling on the slippery little pearls. Those dispensed with, he drew it off along with her chemise, casting them aside with his shirt. They fell back to the floor amid more kisses, more desperate caresses.

At last, she felt the pressure of him at her entrance, the heavy press as he eased inside her, his body rigid with control. She had known it would hurt; Justine and Annalise had told her as much. Still, the burning of it surprised her after the fiery pleasure of their embraces. The slide of him inside of her expanded until at last there was a tearing sensation and he stopped.

She gasped and tensed, unable to hold it back.

"I'm sorry," he whispered against her hair. "I'm sorry, Charlotte. It will be better now, I promise. Just lie still for a moment."

"I know," she answered, smiling up at him. "I know."

And the pain *did* ebb away, leaving only the warmth of them together. Slowly, he eased back and then forwards again. As he moved, the ache was replaced by pleasure again, by delicious tingling that spread through her whole body.

Charlotte closed her eyes, arching her head back, moving with him as they found their rhythm together. That pleasure built and built inside her, until at last it burst free in a shower of fiery white sparks.

"Drew!" she cried out. "I feel—feel…"

"Charlotte," he gasped. "Charlotte, Charlotte."

And his body tensed above hers, taut as he shouted out her name. Then he collapsed to the floor beside her, his head on her shoulder.

Charlotte was suddenly deeply exhausted, more tired than ever before in her life. Yet there was also sheer exhilaration at what she had just felt. She closed her eyes, smiling as she turned her head to kiss his damp brow.

She longed to say something, anything to tell him what she was feeling. But words scattered in her mind, half-formed, and she could only whisper, "Thank you."

As she drifted off on a blissful cloud of sleep, she felt him draw the satin blanket from the couch over them and then pull her back into the curve of his body.

Charlotte snuggled closer, easing into soft, dreamless sleep.

Chapter Nine

Drew gazed at Charlotte as she slept so peacefully beside him, a tiny smile on her lips as if she dreamed sweet dreams. He smoothed her hair back from her forehead, easing the blanket closer around her bare shoulders.

The fire smouldered low in the grate, but he scarcely felt the new chill in the room. He felt at peace, truly at peace for the first time in all his life.

He had been trying so very hard to fight who he really was, to be someone he was not. Perhaps he was trying to be his brother, to replace him. That would never work, though, not for long. He would always return to himself—to who he was when he was with Charlotte.

His mother might not be entirely happy with a Fitzmanning daughter-in-law, but Mary and little Will would love her. All would be well for the four of them, he was sure of it.

Drew nearly laughed aloud. Sometimes, despite all his efforts to the contrary, things *did* turn out right in the end.

He gently kissed Charlotte's cheek, holding her close as she sighed and snuggled deeper under the blanket. He would have to give Nicholas and Stephen his most sincere thanks. If they ever came to let them out, that was.

Charlotte stirred, her eyes blinking open. For a moment she gazed at him, unfocused as if she was not sure where she was. As if she was still caught in dreams.

Then she sat straight up, clutching the blanket around her. "Oh!" she whispered.

Drew sat up beside her, not sure if he should put his arms around her. She looked a bit fragile, as if she might snap at the smallest touch. Was she sorry for what had happened, then? Regretting it?

But he *had* to touch her, had to connect to her again. He took her hand gently, lifting it to his lips for a kiss. "Good morning, Miss Fitzmanning. I trust you slept well?"

Her fingers curled around his for an instant, before she pulled away. "I thought perhaps it was a dream," she murmured.

Drew leaned back, smiling at her. "A good dream, I hope."

"I never—that is—yes, of course. It was—astonishing. But…"

"No 'but'. Let's just leave it at astonishing, shall

we?" Drew said. Charlotte looked so adorably confused he could not help himself. He took her in his arms and kissed her, tasting the wine on her lips. The memory of the night they had just passed.

And she responded, melting against him, her lips parting under his. But then she drew away, turning her back to hunt for her discarded clothes. As Drew watched, confused, she pulled her rumpled gown over her head and tossed him his shirt.

"I never, ever, wanted to ruin your life, Drew," she said, her voice heavy with tears.

"Ruin my life?" he said, even more confused. Women—who could understand them at all? He was almost always bemused by Charlotte, astonished by her. This time, though, he feared that whatever labyrinthine path her mind was taking was *not* to his advantage.

"I would imagine that this was more a case of *me* ruining *yours*," he said, pulling on his shirt and fastening his breeches. "But once we are married…"

"Married?" She spun around to face him, her eyes wide.

"Of course. Surely you don't think I'm cad enough not to marry you."

"I never thought you were a cad," she said thickly. "But how can you marry me? You wanted someone like Lady Emily. I can never be like that. I thought I could, that I could make you see, but I just can't."

"I don't want you to!" Drew cried, utterly exasperated. Here he was, trying to propose to a lady, and she just would not let him. "I don't want you to be anyone but Charlotte."

She shook her head, scrambling to her feet. "I couldn't live with myself, knowing I had taken you from what you really need."

She ran to the door, frantically rattling the handle of the door. Drew stood up slowly, expecting that it was still locked, that she would have to stay with him and listen to reason. If a Fitzmanning could *ever* listen to reason, that was.

To his surprise, the door swung open. They must have been quietly released while they slept. Before he could stop her, she ran out of the door, her footsteps fading as she fled the summerhouse.

Drew hurried to the window, raking his fingers through his hair in mingled frustration and amusement. It was nearly dawn, the light a hazy silver-grey, and he saw Charlotte disappearing over the bridge and into the gloom. Her pale gown was like a beacon, but then she was gone.

He was deeply tempted to chase after her, but he knew it would be futile. Charlotte needed time to calm down, to come to rational thought in her own way. Then she would surely see they belonged together.

And if she did not—well, then, he would just have to persuade her.

Charlotte hurried up the narrow stairs to her attic room. It was only instinct that led her there, a need for its quiet sanctuary before she had to face a house full of people needing to be amused.

Before she had to face herself, and what she had done.

She sat down at her crate-desk, burying her face in her hands. Making love with Drew had felt so very *right*. It had felt as if her whole life had led up to that one moment, and it was everything she wanted. It was perfect.

But then she had woken up, and came to cold re-alisation. Drew did not really want her, a wild Fitz-manning; he wanted Lady Emily Carroll, or someone very like her. If she, Charlotte, really loved him, she couldn't ruin his life by shackling him to her and her family for ever. She had to let him go.

If only doing the right thing, the loving thing, did not hurt so very much!

She wished Justine were here, to help her decipher things in her calm, sweet way. Or her mother. Yes, surely her mother would know just what to do.

But her mother was gone, and Justine was far away. Charlotte had to puzzle things out on her own.

So, she turned to the one thing that never let her down—writing. Pouring all her feelings out on to the page in the person of the Count and Lavinia and their cursed love.

She reached into the crate, searching for the manuscript. But it was not there.

* * *

"That doesn't appear to have gone quite as we hoped," Stephen said glumly. He and Nicholas watched from the shadows as Charlotte ran hell-for-leather up the stairs to the attics, her hair flying behind her.

"Not at all," Nicholas answered. "Don't you have some talisman or amulet to repair this?"

"I'm superstitious, perhaps, but not a miracle worker," Stephen said.

"Right. We'll just have to go to the next plan, then."

Stephen nodded glumly. "And hope Charlotte doesn't kill us for it."

Chapter Ten

Charlotte sat down in one of the gilt chairs lined up in the drawing room, glancing around as all the guests found their own seats. She smiled and folded her hands in her lap, outwardly calm. Inside, she was terribly nervous indeed. She couldn't stop going over and over her night with Drew, and the mysterious theft of her play. This house party was surely the strangest Welbourne had ever seen!

She had managed to get through the day without making a fool of herself, and without being alone with Drew. She had organised the luncheon on the terrace, followed by an outing to view some picturesque ruins. She had presided over dinner, and a tantrum from Signore Napoli, trying not to stare at Drew as he sat there beside Lady Emily.

But now her brothers had insisted on presenting some surprise, refusing to give her a hint of what was going on. They had not even let her into the drawing room until now.

She had had quite enough of their surprises, though, and was not at all sure she wanted to see this one.

Set up at the front of the room was a makeshift stage of some sort, hung about with muslin curtains. Every once in a while a strange clanking noise came from behind that curtain, but nothing to give her any clue. She just had to sit and wait, and she was *terrible* at sitting and waiting.

On the other hand, look what trouble she made jumping in with both feet. Maybe patience was the key after all.

Charlotte glanced surreptitiously at Lady Emily, looking so cool and serene as she sat with her parents. Her mother appeared to be speaking to her most intently about something, but Emily's smile never wavered. However did she do that?

Perhaps I should learn to be more like that after all, Charlotte thought wryly. But then, if she was more like Lady Emily she would not be in her current conundrum at all.

As she looked back to the stage, avoiding Drew's eye as he stood by the wall, Lord Amesby sat down on the chair beside hers. "So, Miss Fitzmanning," he said affably, "what amusements do your brothers have in store for us now?"

"I fear I could not say, Lord Amesby," she answered. "They have been most secretive. Should we be afraid, do you think?"

Amesby laughed. "Perhaps so. Who knows what will happen? I have heard such tales of Welbourne parties. Frogs released, sudden showers of confetti from above…"

"I hope not frogs. We don't want to give the ladies a fright."

"I think not all the ladies here would take fright," Amesby said, shooting a quick look at Lady Derrington. "Yourself, for instance."

Charlotte laughed, too. "Oh, no. I became immune to frogs long ago, growing up around so many practical jokers. Swooning gets a lady nowhere here."

"And Lady Derrington? Do you think *she* is of a delicate constitution?"

There was such a strangely wistful note in Lord Amesby's voice. Charlotte looked at him quizzically, then back to Mary, who chatted with the Mortons on the back row of chairs. Mary and Amesby did seem most careful *not* to pay attention to one another—much like herself and Drew.

Most interesting.

"I do not know her as well as I would like," Charlotte answered carefully. "But she certainly is not as delicate as she looks."

Amesby laughed, but they had no time to say anything further. The stage curtains parted, a new scene revealed.

Somehow, Nicholas and Stephen had managed to build a pasteboard castle, complete with little turrets and a drawbridge. False trees and topiaries dotted the walls, and a large silvery moon hung overhead. Everyone in the audience quietened, watching to see what could happen next.

Leo stepped onstage, having donned a dark, medievalesque robe and tall hat. "Ladies and gentlemen of our audience," he announced, obviously trying to be deeply serious, "welcome to Welbourne Theatre. We hope you enjoy the début of a new play tonight."

"It's quite rubbish so far," Amesby called.

"Silence, heathens!" Leo thundered, pointing at his heckling friend. "Pay heed to this tale, for it is a grave one."

Charlotte longed to laugh, for Leo did look so terribly ill at ease. Theatricals were never his strong suit, and this "grave tale" was surely more of a farce. A holiday pantomime. But she bit her lip, forcing herself to stay silent.

"We set our scene at a most mysterious and remote castle, the domain of the wicked Count Darian," Leo said, sweeping his long sleeves around. "It is the days of—well, of a very long time ago. And a young, innocent bride makes her way to this frightening place."

The castle of Count Darian? Charlotte sat straight up in her chair, remembering that missing manuscript.

Oh, surely they wouldn't! Her brothers were terrible pranksters, it was true, but they held to the Welbourne code that artistic pursuits were sacred.

They had never invaded her attic space before. They wouldn't.

But then again, if they could lock her up with Drew in the summerhouse for some silly lark, perhaps they would not scruple at theft. Maybe she really did not know them at all.

Charlotte felt her face burn as Stephen entered from stage left, clad in a toga-like gown and some silly blonde Viking wig. The fools! They could not even get the tale's time period right.

She wanted to sink into the floor, to hide under her chair, yet she feared she could not tear her horrified stare from that stage. Even Oliver and Octavia had run off somewhere, unable to bear it.

"Hark," Leo said. "Here approaches our heroine, the fair Lavinia. She beholds her fearsome new home for the first time."

"Alas!" Stephen cried, in some horrible falsetto. He pressed the back of one hand to his brow, holding out the other as if possessed by the spirit of Mrs Siddons. "That I, an innocent maiden, should be sold into marriage for my father's debts. And to a man of such black reputation! Whatever shall I do? Alack!"

And they could not even keep to her original lines, the wretches. She would *never* pen such drivel. If they were going to steal her story, the least they could do was present it properly. Charlotte slumped down in her seat, deeply fearful of what might be coming next.

"Here approaches the bridegroom," Leo said,

doing that sleeve-sweeping thing again. "The dark Darian, whose name is connected with so many black deeds, whose family is cursed by a witch. And with him are his fearsome hounds of hell."

Nicholas stomped onstage, dressed all in black with a pasteboard crown on his head and a false black moustache attached to his upper lip, which contrasted terribly with his fair hair. Crowding at his heels were Oliver and Octavia, spinning and snorting in excitement.

But when they saw Charlotte, the "fearsome hounds" leaped off the stage and clambered on to her lap. She hugged them close, burying her flushed face in their ruffs as events onstage steadily went from bad to worse.

"Fair maiden," Nicholas shouted, "I have won your hand in marriage, and you must live with me here in my haunted castle, full of old, dark memories and sadness, for evermore!"

"Alas!" Stephen cried, swooning.

And so it went. The marriage of the always swooning princess—who nearly fell off the stage more than once—and the Fearsome Dark Lord started most unpromisingly indeed. The ill-starred union of two incompatible souls who seemed to want very different things in life, caught together in a house of sadness.

Yet, as the story went on, Darian and Lavinia found more things in common, more shared bonds, more chances to laugh together. More ways they needed each other in order to be whole and complete, to be happy. And the hounds of hell fell asleep under the chairs.

In the end, True Love broke the curse of the sad castle and the lovers were united for ever, among howls of helpless laughter from the audience and much applause.

Charlotte hardly knew whether to laugh or cry, or what to think at all. Her brothers had stolen her play and made a mockery of it, and yet—yet it *was* quite amusing. And sweet, in its own way.

"And so you see, love conquers all—even curses," Nicholas said as they took their bows. "And for this tale tonight we must thank its creator, our sister Charlotte!"

Oh, that tore it. Charlotte could simply take no more. She jumped up from her chair and ran out of the drawing room. Even in the hall, the laughter and mayhem followed her, and she hurried out of the door and into the night.

The breeze was cool on her burning cheeks, and she headed blindly down the moonlit drive towards she knew not what. What game did her brothers play? She could not understand it. First they locked her up with Drew, as if they sought in their clumsy way to bring her together with him. Now they tried to make her look silly in front of him, to make her seem the authoress of drivel.

"Men," she muttered, kicking at the gravel. She did not understand their irrational ways at all.

"Charlotte!" she heard Drew shout. She glanced over her shoulder to find him hurrying down the steps towards her. "Charlotte, wait. Please."

For a moment, she was tempted to run away. But she knew she could not. The time had come for her to stand her ground, to decide what she wanted once and for all and then fight for it.

"That was not my play," she said.

Drew stood before her, his handsome face carved by the moonlight into something mysterious and beautiful. Her true knight, her real Darian. "I know that. I have read some of your poems, remember? You are a wonderful writer. Far better than that."

"I don't understand what my brothers are about," she said, exasperated and confused.

"I think that in their own clumsy way they are trying to help us."

"Help us?"

"Yes. Don't you agree? They seem to see what we could not."

Charlotte frowned up at him, still caught in that spell of confusion. Of wild hope. "And what is that?"

"Why, exactly what the play said. Love conquers all—even curses. Even blindness. Perhaps even stubborn people who don't listen to their own hearts. I—well, I love you, Charlotte. I think I always have. And I know now that I can never be happy, never be myself, if we are not together."

"I…" Charlotte choked on a sudden rush of tears, of the rising up of sheer, wondrous joy. "Oh, Drew."

"I know I am hardly the best catch. I'm a mere younger son, with a family to take care of," Drew said, reaching out to take her trembling hand tightly in his. "But I need you. I love you. And I vow I will spend the rest of my life making you as happy as you make me. If you are willing to take a chance on me—on us."

Charlotte shook her head, tears spilling helplessly from her eyes. She could not seem to stop them—this moment was all she had ever dreamed of, longed for. And it was so much sweeter than any imagining.

"Yes," she said at last, throwing her arms around Drew's neck. "Yes, I will marry you! I love you, too, Drew. So very much."

"Finally!" he shouted, lifting her off her feet and twirling her around and around until they both laughed giddily. "Oh, Charlotte, you won't regret it. I promise."

"*I* never shall, but *you* might." She gestured towards the house, where her brothers and all their guests gathered to watch them. It was almost as if she and Drew were an extension of the evening's play, but Charlotte did not care. Not when she was so unbearably happy. She wanted to throw her arms wide and embrace the whole world.

"You are not just marrying me, you know," she said, "but my whole family. My whole play-stealing, prank-causing family."

Drew grinned, leaning down to kiss her as everyone applauded. "Even better," he said. "I always did want to be a Fitzmanning."

Epilogue

"There now, Charlotte. You look absolutely beautiful," Justine said happily, fluffing the last lace ruffle of Charlotte's bridal attire.

Charlotte turned to face the mirror, which Justine, Annalise and Mary had kept away from her while they did their handiwork. And she was quite astonished at the sight that greeted her.

Clad in her mother's silver-satin and white-lace wedding gown, redone to fit her, with her hair curled and twined with pearls and white rosebuds, she looked like some creature of moonlight. A delicate, ethereal being.

If only she could maintain the illusion all the way to the altar!

"Oh," she sighed. "You are miracle workers."

Justine laughed, her cheeks glowing pink with happiness. Marriage and motherhood agreed with her, for she was always glowing now. And baby

Catherine, who cooed softly in her ruffled basket, was the most perfect infant ever seen. Except when she tried to reach out and pull the pugs' tails, which she did so often…

"Do be still for a moment longer, Charlotte," Annalise warned, her hand flying over her sketchbook. "I want to capture exactly the way you look at this very moment. You are a Bronzino princess in that gown."

"Oh, you think everyone is a Renaissance noble since you returned from Italy," Charlotte teased. But she was still absurdly pleased at the compliment.

Everything pleased her today, her glorious, long-awaited wedding day. Her family was together again at last, gathered in their home, and her bridegroom waited for her in the Welbourne drawing room. Love could create wonders indeed, and she would never doubt it again.

Charlotte glanced at Mary in the mirror. Her soon-to-be sister-in-law smiled at her, so pretty in her first post-mourning dress of buttercup-yellow silk, but Charlotte thought she saw something wistful lurking in her eyes. Surely she, who had been so kind and welcoming to Charlotte, should find love again, too.

Charlotte feared she would turn to matchmaking now, like her brothers.

"There!" Annalise said with satisfaction, giving her sketch one last stroke. "It is done. Once I finish the painted portrait, we'll hang it beside Mama's in the summerhouse. You're both wearing the same gown, after all."

"Mama," Charlotte said quietly. "Oh, I do wish she could be here now."

"Perhaps I can help with that a bit," Brenner said from the doorway.

"Brenner!" Justine scolded fondly. "You were to wait until we called you."

"I couldn't wait any longer to see Charlotte in her finery," Brenner said, kissing his wife on the cheek. "It isn't every day a man's baby sister marries."

"Well, then, what do you think of her?" Annalise said, closing her book and straightening her hat. "Does she not look like a Renaissance princess?"

"She looks—exactly as she should," Brenner said. "The most radiant of brides." He came to take Charlotte's hand, pressing a gentle kiss to her fingers.

Charlotte feared she might start crying, for possibly the tenth time that day. Her eyes prickled when he smiled at her, this dearest brother. She had not grown up with him, had not even known him until two years ago, but now she could never do without him.

"We will just go and see how the bridegroom fares," Justine said, lifting Catherine from her basket and cradling the baby on her shoulder.

"He was pacing enough to wear out the drawing-room carpet," Mary said with a laugh.

"I've never seen a man so impatient to be wed!" said Annalise.

"Except Ned, of course," Justine teased, bouncing the baby in her arms as Catherine cooed happily.

"Now, Charlotte dear, do be careful of your lace. And don't keep her too long, Brenner. You must escort her down the aisle before Drew storms up here to find you!"

"Of course, darling," Brenner said. "I am entirely aware of my duty today."

After Justine, Mary and Annalise departed, with Catherine starting to fuss at being parted from her beloved pugs, Brenner took Charlotte's hand again, giving her a smile.

"You do look most beautiful, sister," he said. "I have few memories of our mother, but I do remember how she looked when she was dressed for some grand gala. She would come to the nursery to kiss me before she left, and I would think she was an angel. A beautiful, celestial being."

Charlotte bit her lip, quite certain now that she *would* cry. "I remember times like that, too, Gerry— oops, sorry, Brenner! Mama was so lovely, I knew I could never be like her."

"But you *are* like her. In this moment you are her very image," Brenner said. "And I hope that you have found true love, as she did."

"I have." Charlotte nodded, as full of certainty as it was possible to be. "I love Drew with all my heart, I always have."

"I am very glad to know it. If he ever hurts you, though, he will have all of us to answer to."

Charlotte laughed, squeezing his hand. "I did warn him of that! Yet he still wanted to marry me."

"Then I am sure he is all our mother would have wished for you." Brenner reached inside his coat, drawing out a velvet jewel case.

Charlotte held her breath, watching as he opened the case to reveal a dazzling diamond necklace. Shaped like a delicate garland of spring flowers, it shimmered in the light, as alive and welcoming as her mother had been. Vibrant and warm.

"I was entrusted with this to give you on your wedding day," Brenner said, fastening it around her neck. "I hope a part of her is with you today, and always."

She gently touched the strand with her fingertips, feeling the gems warm under her caress. "I know she is here, with all of us. And she sent you to us, too. That is a gift beyond any diamonds."

Brenner kissed her cheek, holding her close for a long moment. Then he stepped back and offered her his arm.

"Shall we go down to the drawing room, then?" he said, smiling down at her. "Before your impatient bridegroom quite ruins the carpet."

Charlotte laughed, slipping her hand over his sleeve. "Oh, yes. I have nothing better to do than get married today."

They left the chamber, followed by Oliver and Octavia, who wore fresh garlands of flowers around their necks in honour of the day. The banisters were also decked in flowers, and as Charlotte and Brenner turned into the drawing room she felt sure the entire

Welbourne gardens were completely denuded. The mantel, the picture frames, even the chair backs and tables were covered in wreaths.

Nicholas, Stephen and Leo, all grinning like mad, showered her with rose petals as she entered the room. Every corner was filled with colour and sweet perfume, with memories and hopes.

Yet all she could see was Drew, waiting for her by the flower-bedecked fireplace. Her handsome knight, all curses broken and sadness dispelled, hers at last.

Welbourne had done its magic for all of them, and surely the future was every bit as dazzling as her mother's diamonds.

* * * * *

Rakes and rogues in the ballrooms — and the bedrooms — of Regency England!

6th March 2009
A Hasty Betrothal by Dorothy Elbury
A Scandalous Marriage by Mary Brendan

3rd April 2009
The Count's Charade by Elizabeth Bailey
The Rake and the Rebel by Mary Brendan

1st May 2009
Sparhawk's Lady by Miranda Jarrett
The Earl's Intended Wife by Louise Allen

5th June 2009
Lord Calthorpe's Promise by Sylvia Andrew
The Society Catch by Louise Allen

8 VOLUMES IN ALL TO COLLECT!

Regency

HIGH-SOCIETY AFFAIRS

Rakes and rogues in the ballrooms – and the bedrooms – of Regency England!

3rd July 2009
Beloved Virago by Anne Ashley
Lord Trenchard's Choice by Sylvia Andrew

7th August 2009
The Unruly Chaperon by Elizabeth Rolls
Colonel Ancroft's Love by Sylvia Andrew

4th September 2009
The Sparhawk Bride by Miranda Jarrett
The Rogue's Seduction by Georgina Devon

2nd October 2009
Sparhawk's Angel by Miranda Jarrett
The Proper Wife by Julia Justiss

8 VOLUMES IN ALL TO COLLECT!